CRUEL CHOICES

Recent Titles by Charles O'Brien in this Series

MUTE WITNESS
BLACK GOLD
NOBLE BLOOD *
LETHAL BEAUTY *
FATAL CARNIVAL *
CRUEL CHOICES*

* *available from Severn House*

CRUEL CHOICES

Charles O'Brien

severn
House

This first world edition published in Great Britain 2007 by
SEVERN HOUSE PUBLISHERS LTD of
9–15 High Street, Sutton, Surrey SM1 1DF.
This first world edition published in the USA 2007 by
SEVERN HOUSE PUBLISHERS INC of
595 Madison Avenue, New York, N.Y. 10022.

British Library Cataloguing in Publication Data

O'Brien, Charles, 1927-
    Cruel choices
    1.   Cartier, Anne (Fictitious character) - Fiction
    2.   Women teachers - France - Fiction
    3.   France - History - Louis XVI, 1744-1793 - Fiction
    4.   Detective and mystery stories
    I.   Title
    813.6 [F]

    ISBN-13: 978-0-7278-6463-5

All Severn House titles are printed on acid-free paper.

Typeset by Palimpsest Book Production Ltd.,
Grangemouth, Stirlingshire, Scotland.
Printed and bound in Great Britain by
MPG Books Ltd., Bodmin, Cornwall.

Acknowledgements

I wish to thank Gudveig Baarli again for her substantial assistance with the maps. I am grateful also to Andy Sheldon for various computer services. Fronia Simpson and Evan Marshall read drafts of the novel and contributed to its improvement. My wife Elvy carefully edited the text and enriched it with her suggestions. Finally the staff of Williams College's Sawyer Library and the Clark Art Institute Library, Williamstown, deserve special mention for their expert aid to the research for the Anne Cartier series.

Cast of Main Characters
In Order of First Appearance

Lucie Gigot: *young country woman, tenant of the Comtesse Marie de Beaumont*

Denis Grimaud: *Marquis de Bresse's valet*

Marquis de Bresse: *libertine nobleman, disciple of the Marquis de Sade*

Anne Cartier: *teacher of deaf children, former music hall entertainer, wife of Colonel Paul de Saint-Martin*

Colonel Paul de Saint-Martin: *Provost of the Royal Highway Patrol for the area surrounding Paris, husband of Anne Cartier*

Comtesse Marie de Beaumont: *Paul de Saint-Martin's aunt*

Micheline [Michou] du Saint-Esprit: *deaf artist*

Sylvie de Chanteclerc: *goddaughter of Baron Breteuil, distant cousin and childhood acquaintance of Saint-Martin*

Madame Tessier: *millinery shop owner, procuress*

Georges Charpentier: *Saint-Martin's adjutant*

Inspector Quidor: *Paris police crime investigator*

Renée Gros: *prostitute, Grimaud's companion*

Bernard Fontaine: *waiter at the Café de Foy*

Lieutenant General Thiroux DeCrosne: *chief of French police*

Berthe Dupont: *daughter of Jean Dupont*

Jean Dupont: *father of Berthe Dupont, blind old army comrade of Georges Charpentier*

Michel Fresnay: *deaf beggar*

Philippe Pinel: *medical doctor, expert on mental illness*

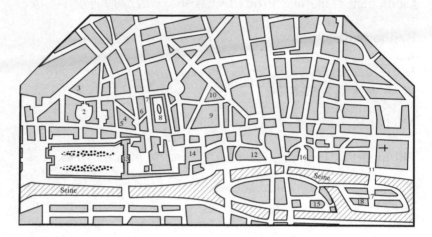

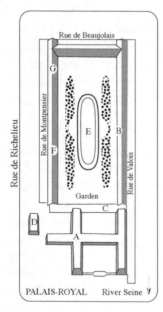

CENTRAL PARIS 1788

1. Residence/office of Paul de Saint-Martin & Anne Cartier,
   Rue Saint-Honoré
2. Place Vendôme
3. Bureau of Criminal Investigation, Hôtel de Police,
   Rue des Capuchines
4. Abbé de l'Épée's Institute for the Deaf, Rue des Moulins
5. Church of Saint-Roch, Rue Saint-Honoré
6. Comtesse Marie de Beaumont's townhouse,
   Rue Traversine
7. Rue de Richelieu
8. Palais-Royal
9. Central Markets (Les Halles)
10. Church of Saint-Eustache
11. Pont Marie
12. Châtelet
13. Palace and garden of the Tuileries
14. Louvre
15. Notre Dame
16. Place de Grève
17. Isle Saint-Louis
18. Town house of Marquis de Bresse

PALAIS-ROYAL 1788

A. The duke's palace
B. Valois Arcade
C. Camp of the Tatars
D. Comédie Française (under construction)
E. Circus
F. Café Odéon
G. Café de Foy

One

A Dangerous Experiment

Paris, 15 April, 1788

Lucie woke from a troubled sleep. In her dream the village priest had tormented her again, with threats more cruel than ever before. 'Satan holds you tightly in his claws,' he had said. His eyes, bright as burning coals, his grizzled face twisted into a dreadful scowl. He had raged, 'Before highnoon, you will be in Hell.'

She felt groggy, but managed to shake the priest out of her mind. Her eyes focused poorly. Sunlight was pouring into the room. Half the morning must be gone. She lay on her back, staring at shifting shadows on the ceiling, bringing up impressions of her visit. They were strange and exciting – and frightening.

Last night at supper she had drunk wine. Perhaps too much. She remembered feeling light-headed afterward when making love with Denis. She looked around. No sign of him. Must be downstairs, dressing his master. Prior to coming here last night, she had seen the Marquis de Bresse only from a distance, had admired his fashionable clothes, elegant manners, handsome features. But at supper, she had noticed his eyes, pale blue, cold as ice, even when he smiled and gave her compliments. He had studied her as if she were a choice cut of meat. She shuddered. How would it be to work as a maid for such a master?

He would teach her, he said. And last night at supper, he had dressed as a waiter in pink livery. Denis, playing the host, had on a splendid pink suit with silver embroidery. She was supposed to be a distinguished female guest, a courtesan, Denis had said. Whatever that meant. He had dressed her in a fashionable, low-cut silk gown, taught her how to sit at the table, and how to comment on food and eat it properly.

During the meal, she boldly asked the marquis how much he would pay for her services.

He gave her an odd look. 'As much as you're worth.'

She needed a more encouraging answer than that! Madame Tessier and Denis had loaned her money, much more than she could hope to repay. She had no job. They were losing patience with her, would turn her over to the police and she'd go to prison. Her only options were to work for the marquis or to sell her sexual favours at the Palais-Royal. She could never ask her father for money. He would mock her.

She recalled the day that she had left home for Paris. The priest had confronted her in the village street. 'You are a vain, obstinate, ungrateful girl,' he had shouted. 'You should obey your parents, stay at home and work hard like your mother and sisters.' He had shaken his finger at her. 'Paris will be the death of you. And you will surely end up in Hell.' At night, while she was asleep in her garret room, he would sneak into her dreams like a hideous monster, his piercing red eyes reproaching her shameful pleasures.

She heard steps outside the room. Her heart leaped. She clasped the cross hanging from her neck. At her confirmation the priest had said it would ward off evil demons. Denis didn't knock, just opened the door for the marquis. He walked in, still playing the waiter, carrying a breakfast tray. She pulled the thin woolen blanket up to her chin – she was naked. Unbeckoned, terror was setting in. What was going on? There was a sinister air about these men.

'Sit up,' Denis commanded and shoved a bolster behind her back. Meanwhile the marquis set the tray on a table, then came to her with a cup of coffee.

'Drink this,' he ordered. 'It will do you good. I made it myself and spooned in much sugar.'

The coffee was black, its aroma strong. She took the cup with trembling hands, nearly spilling its contents. The taste was curious, sweet and bitter at the same time. She drank half the cup and handed it back to the marquis.

He frowned, waved his hand. 'Finish it.' His gaze had become intense, as if his eyes could bore into her head.

'I can't drink any more. It's too strong.'

'Finish it, or I'll pour it down your throat. It's expensive. I'll not have you waste it.'

All the frustrations of these past few months in Paris without money or friends came crashing down upon her. She felt utterly defeated. Tears came to her eyes. But she took the cup, this time shaking it so much that drops spilled on her hands. When she finished the coffee, the marquis took the cup, then pulled away the blanket and leered at her.

She clutched her cross, tried to protest, but she couldn't speak. Then a powerful sensation of unease and fear raced through her body and seized her mind. Suddenly, she choked, couldn't breathe, ripped the cross from her neck, flailed her arms wildly. Her body jerked and twisted out of control. The marquis's leer turned into an angry frown. He lifted the cup, glared at it. Moments later, Lucie fell into a dark abyss.

Two

Château Beaumont

15 May

'Would I know the young woman who has gone missing?' Anne Cartier asked her husband, Colonel Paul de Saint-Martin. Under a dull grey sky, the air heavy with moisture, their coach was rumbling out of Paris toward Château Beaumont, a few miles south of the city. His aunt Marie, the Comtesse de Beaumont, had invited them to her chateau to discuss serious business matters. Her message had briefly mentioned the missing person.

'She's called Lucie,' Paul replied. 'I don't know who that might be. Marie's message was cryptic. If the girl were one of my aunt's domestic servants, I would have recognized her.'

'The name sounds familiar,' Anne remarked, searching

her memory. 'She might belong to a family of tenants working for the countess. Marie knows most of them personally and looks after them.'

The coach turned off the Orléans road in the direction of Villejuif. Several months had passed since Anne and Paul had seen his favourite aunt. For the sake of his health they had wintered in the warm, dry air of the Mediterranean coast in the county of Nice. Upon their return to the Paris region they found a scene of devastation.

'The crops appear beyond redemption,' remarked Anne, gazing out the window. A few stalks of wheat struggled to reach knee level. Most of the plants lay in a sodden mess in the fields.

'Yes, I've heard that hail and heavy rain have ruined them. This summer's harvest will be pitiful.'

'And last year's wasn't much better,' Anne added.

Paul agreed. 'The countess and I shall have to find a way to carry our tenants through the bad months ahead. Unfortunately, most landlords will be neither reasonable nor humane and will demand their dues. Their tenants will resist. My troopers will have a busy time keeping order in the countryside.'

The countess had invited him to share views on the present rural crisis. Ever since Paul left France a decade ago to fight on the side of the colonists in the American War, she had looked after his family estate a few miles away from hers. A rich banker leased the chateau for himself and his mistress. A competent steward managed the property under Marie's vigilant eye.

Among the issues she wanted to discuss was whether to raise rents and fees to make up for a steep decline in income due to failure of the crops and a rise in costs.

'What will you do, Paul?' Anne asked.

'The countess and I have works of art we could sell. And the banker can certainly afford to pay more rent for the chateau. But that's only a start. Peasants all over the region are desperate. Raising their rents and fees is unrealistic. If I were to evict my tenants, where would I find others who could pay me?' He leaned back, a troubled expression on his face. 'I seriously wonder if Marie's town house on Rue Traversine could be used to produce revenue?'

Anne quickly grew concerned. 'I would hope that Michou could remain in her studio on the second floor.' Michou was short for Micheline du Saint-Esprit, a petite deaf artist of Anne's age and one of her best friends.

'Michou should stay,' Paul assured her. 'And Marie could set aside a few rooms for the rare occasions when she visits Paris, then rent out the rest. Many of the fine furnishings could be sold.'

'How would the countess feel?'

Paul grimaced. 'Any change would be hard. Marie has fond memories of life in the house with her late husband. Nonetheless, we must include the house in our discussion.'

The coach swung into a graveled lane bordered with chestnut trees. Fragrance from their blossoms scented the air. The curved wings of the chateau soon welcomed them. This had been Paul's favourite place as a boy. While his father was away at war, his mother had sunk into a deep depression. His aunt Marie had taken him into her household and given him understanding and love. The coach rattled across the paved courtyard up to a porticoed entrance. A servant directed the coachman to the stables while another led the visitors to a parlour.

A few minutes passed, steps were heard in the hall. The countess entered briskly. On first impression, Marie hadn't changed in the several months since Anne last saw her. Tall, erect, she wore a lemon yellow muslin dress that flattered her slim figure. Her thick wavy, grey hair was lightly powdered. Her complexion was still clear, but she had put a touch of rouge on her cheeks. Her grey-blue eyes seemed as perceptive as ever and now they were also welcoming.

On closer inspection, however, she seemed rather uneasy – her gaze wasn't quite as cool and steady as Anne had remembered. The reason, Anne surmised, probably had to do with the business that Paul and Marie were about to discuss.

'I'm so glad to see both of you.' She embraced them, then stepped back and inspected her nephew. 'You look fit, Paul. The southern sun was just the medicine you needed.'

She turned to Anne. 'Does he cough and wheeze any more?'

'No,' she replied. 'He's hard at work in the office.' As

Provost of the Royal Highway Patrol for the region around Paris, he needed to be fit. The city and its countryside were seething with discontent. Parlement and the king were at odds, the government was bankrupt and paralyzed. Prices were rising, unemployment growing. And the worst was yet to come. Peasants would harvest very little grain in the coming months. Food shortages threatened. Paul would soon have to cope with violent protests.

They moved to the study where an afternoon tea was set with fine Sèvres porcelain. A servant in pale blue livery poured, another offered sweet biscuits. The countess inquired about their stay in Nice. They spoke of the lush orchards and gardens of the south, of the blue sky and sea, the mild, fresh air, their charming villa and its elevated, picturesque setting amidst vineyards and Roman ruins.

As she sipped tea, Anne surveyed the room. Its book-lined walls moved one to speak in hushed tones. Here Paul had cultivated the quiet, reflective side of his character. Aunt Marie had been his early mentor and spiritual guide, sharing her impressions of Voltaire and other enlightened authors whom she had met in the salons of Paris.

With tea served and the servants withdrawn, the conversation shifted to pressing, immediate problems. 'You wrote that a girl Lucie had disappeared. Who is she?' Paul asked.

The countess put down her cup. 'Lucie Gigot is a tenant's daughter, the youngest of three. She's sixteen years old, pretty and shapely, sparkles with vitality, loves to sing and dance. An intelligent girl, she can read and write simple French. But I'm sorry to say that she's flighty, rebellious, and rather vain, seeks the attention of men more than is good for her reputation. Her father couldn't persuade or force her to work in his fields or in the chateau's kitchen. Still, she enjoyed occasionally posing for Michou.'

As guest of the countess, Michou had lived and worked at Beaumont for months at a time and had become familiar with its people. Anne had watched her friend sketch Lucie. Her features began to come back to Anne's mind. She made a mental note to speak to Michou. Her sketches might prove useful to the inquiry.

The countess continued her story. 'In January, after a terrible row with her father, Lucie ran off to Paris to work in a millinery shop in the Palais-Royal. Despite her mother's entreaties, she refused to return home.'

'Do you have any reason to believe that she might have been ill-treated, kidnapped, or killed?' asked Anne with growing concern. The Palais-Royal was the Duc d'Orléans's notorious complex of buildings in the heart of the city.

'No, other than the fact that she's missing,' replied the countess, 'but I really don't know the girl or her story well enough. She usually avoided me, afraid that I might put her to work. At this point, I'm concerned chiefly with her mother. Lucie was her darling – a child she badly spoiled. She hasn't heard a word from the girl in over a month and has become anxious to the point of distraction.' The countess turned to her nephew. 'Paul, do you think that the police could look for her?'

Paul's expression was doubtful. 'This doesn't sound like a case for the Paris police – there must be hundreds like it. The inspectors are very hard-pressed these days. If you were to report Lucie, I doubt that they would do more than add her name to the long list of missing persons.'

Anne raised a hand. 'May I make a suggestion?'

'Of course,' the others replied in unison.

'While you two study account books and discuss business, I could speak to the anxious mother, find out more about her missing daughter, and promise to make inquiries in Paris. That might ease the mother's mind and give her hope. At least she would feel better for knowing that someone took her seriously.'

'My dear,' asked Paul in a mock-testy voice, 'are you thinking that my adjutant, Georges Charpentier, could be enlisted to help you? I sympathize with the mother. But I cannot in conscience devote any of the slender resources of my office to this case. There are far more serious matters to investigate, to begin with, the unrest in the countryside.'

Anne felt a bit ashamed that her intention was so easily found out. 'I confess that I had thought of approaching Georges. He knows the criminal world of Paris so well.'

'And you know that you can twist him around your little finger,' Paul added with a smile.

'That's true,' Anne granted. 'But I'll let you have him this time.' She paused. 'Seriously, I would like to visit the

mother and her family, then spend a day or two searching
for her at the Palais-Royal. Michou and her friends virtually live there and can help me.'

Paul hesitated for a moment, then said, 'A quiet voice
inside me warns that this may be the entrance into a long,
dark tunnel.'

The Gigot family lived in a cottage in the village near
Château Beaumont. A brisk five-minute walk in a light rain
brought Anne to a rough wooden door. Lucie's father,
Monsieur Gigot, opened for her. He was short, muscular,
and broad-shouldered with dark flashing eyes, a square,
jutting jaw, and a thick neck. His face seemed set in a permanent scowl.

'It's the colonel's wife,' he shouted, and stepped back to
study her as she entered.

The cottage consisted of a single, large, low room, a
hearth at one end, sleeping alcoves along the sides. A long,
heavy wooden table stood in the middle. Oiled paper covered
the unglazed windows. The family appeared well-fed and
clothed, their quarters clean and dry.

Monsieur Gigot dragged a stool to the table for Anne.
The entire family was at home, since there was no work in
the fields. The women were sewing clothes, a tired, dejected
expression on their faces. They brightened when they recognized Anne as the countess's friend and a frequent visitor
to the estate. The man looked sullen; he scarcely spoke a
word.

With a shy smile, Madame Gigot brought Anne a cup of
cider. She had once been a handsome woman, from whom
Lucie inherited her good looks. But hard labour at home
and in the fields had taken its toll. Her hands were calloused,
her body thick at the waist. The sun had burned her face to
the texture of creased brown leather.

Anne commiserated with the family for the failed harvest
and gave assurances that the countess would do her best for
them. The husband picked up the scythe that he had been
sharpening, his face clouded with disbelief, his neck taut
with suppressed anger. But he held his tongue and resumed
work on the tool.

His wife brought the conversation around to her missing

daughter. 'I suppose the countess sent you here to talk about Lucie. Might you be able to find her?'

Anne wasn't aware of having been sent. After all, she had suggested the idea. Still, the countess's ways could be subtle. She had put the case in a light that attracted Anne's interest.

'What my friends and I can do,' Anne replied, 'is to look for Lucie at the Palais-Royal, the place where she is most likely to be. Now tell me about her.'

Madame Gigot drew a deep breath and began her story. 'Lucie left home almost five months ago, after a quarrel with her father.'

He looked up sourly at his wife. 'And good riddance. She's a lazy, ungrateful wench!'

His wife bit her lip, trying to ignore his outburst, and struggled on. 'Lucie's a good girl, just young and trusting. I believe she was enticed by an older woman from Paris who bought a small neighboring estate and appeared fashionable and prosperous. The woman promised Lucie a job in her millinery shop. A few weeks later, I visited Lucie there. She said she was happy and wouldn't return home. I waited several weeks and went back again. This time she wouldn't see me. I went back a few days later. Same answer. I insisted on meeting her or I'd call in the police. The lady grew frightened, admitted that Lucie had quit the shop and had run off with an older man. A few people have since claimed to have seen her, but not since the end of March. I'm worried sick. Something terrible has happened to her.'

Anne reassured the mother that she'd make a serious effort. 'Give me the address of the millinery shop and the name of the lady who runs it. I'll start there tomorrow.'

The mother's face brightened with renewed hope. 'She's Madame Tessier. Her shop is in the Palais-Royal's Valois arcade.'

Anne wrote down the information, then bid goodbye and left the cottage.

The rain had slackened to a drizzle. On the way back to the chateau, Anne conjured up a mental picture of Lucie Gigot, a penniless, naive, young country woman standing in the middle of the vast garden of the Palais-Royal. Mouth agape, she was staring at the bustling shopping arcades, the theatres, brothels, and restaurants that surrounded her. In Anne's mind they took on the lurid aspect of a jungle. Her stepfather and his mistress had met their violent deaths here, while working at one of the theatres. That was almost three years ago. She still shuddered at the horrid memory. All sorts of predatory men and women infested this place. How easily Lucie could be exploited! A sensation akin to dread stirred in the pit of Anne's stomach.

Back in the chateau, Anne stood for a moment between two slender pillars at the entrance to the picture gallery, observing Comtesse Marie and Paul. They were pointing to various paintings on the wall and discussing which ones to sell. A weak northern light struggled to illuminate the room. Anne thought it could not be easy to judge pictures here.

As she watched Marie and Paul, a disturbing, unwanted sense of exclusion flashed through her mind. They had encouraged *her* to visit Lucie's mother, while *they* dealt with issues of property and money. She was reminded how the law and social convention put a wife down, treated her as a child. How unfair! The injustice rankled deep in her mind. Before her marriage to Paul, she had managed her own affairs very well, if you please.

Theirs was a so-called morganatic marriage, one between a commoner and an aristocrat. She was barred from his noble title and privileges. Were he to die, his estate would pass to a distant male relative instead of to her. Moreover, as in any marriage, Paul gained control over all her assets as well as her person. She had entered into the marriage freely, for Paul had promised to treat her in all respects as an equal and an adult. And he had been true to his word. Yet, the sense of unfairness persisted, gnawed insidiously at her spirit, despite her best efforts to suppress it. She didn't want it to come between them.

So she put on her best smile and asked, 'Have you two selected the paintings to sell to the rich banker who leases Paul's estate?'

'Yes,' replied Marie. 'It was painful. But Paul and I need money to buy seed for next year's crop. Our financial reserves will soon be exhausted and we do not wish to raise rents or fees from our tenants. They can't afford to pay more. Evicting them could make them desperate. They might cut my throat.' She gave Anne a wry smile.

She drew Anne's eye to the somber picture of an oily sea beast. 'The banker once showed interest in that copy of Chardin's still life, *The Rayfish*, for the dining room.' She took Anne by the hand, led her to the painting of a beautiful recumbent nude woman, and commented with a smile, 'We shall also offer him Boucher's *Diana Bathing after the Hunt*. That would be suitable for his mistress's boudoir.'

The conversation turned to Anne's visit to the tenants' cottage. Marie asked, 'Suppose you were to find Lucie, could you persuade her to return home?'

Anne thought for a moment, then recalled the mother's fretful, cloying concern and the father's harsh words: 'good riddance, lazy, ungrateful wench!' Anne answered thoughtfully, 'No, I don't think she would want to return.' And she added mentally, Nor would I, if I were her.

Three
A Suspicious Disappearance

Paris, 16 May

The next day, Anne hastened to the countess's town house on Rue Traversine near the Palais-Royal. She would begin the investigation into Lucie's disappearance with a visit to Michou. Her sketch of Lucie could be useful. Those who didn't know her name might recognize her face. And if she wished to break entirely with her family, she might have chosen a different name.

Michou's studio was located in a large room on the second floor. In the studio with Michou was her friend and lover, Marc Latour. An academically trained and experienced artist, a hearing man who could sign, he often visited the studio to give Michou advice and instruction. She was mostly self-taught. If she were to become a fully professional painter, she'd have to learn how to portray the human body. As Anne entered the room, Marc was standing behind Michou, one hand caressing her shoulder, the other guiding her pencil.

Another friend, Sylvie de Chanteclerc, was posing nude as the goddess Diana after the hunt. The young woman came from a distinguished aristocratic family – Paul de Saint-Martin was a distant cousin and Baron de Breteuil was her godfather. But Sylvie rejected the parasitic pretensions and privileges of her class, as well as its frivolous pleasures. She now aspired to be natural, strong, and useful, and had chosen Anne as mentor. After learning to sign, she often served as Michou's model and managed her business affairs.

To become a financially successful artist, Michou needed this assistance, since she was not only deaf but also barely literate. The legal language of commerce baffled her. Still, she had an extraordinary painter's eye. Encouraged by friends, her talent had blossomed. She had recently sold several miniatures and children's portraits.

Anne waited in the room, watching from a distance, until Michou laid down her pencil and nodded to Sylvie, who left the studio to dress. Marc embraced Michou, saluted Anne, then returned to his own studio in the Louvre.

'Welcome, Anne!' signed Michou. 'Come see my Diana.'

The sketch was nearly finished. Seated on a rug-covered box, the goddess bent forward, removing a sandal from her foot. A quiver of arrows, Diana's symbol, lay at her side. The celebrated François Boucher's earlier, wistful painting of the scene had inspired Michou, but she gave it a darker, brooding tone.

Physically, Sylvie was a perfect Diana, blonde and slender, demure, ravishingly beautiful. Anne remarked, 'It's lovely, Michou. I look forward to enjoying it in oil.'

The two women discussed the sketch for a few minutes. Then Anne asked, 'Do you remember Lucie Gigot at Château Beaumont? You sketched her months ago. She has run away to Paris and has gone missing. I'm going to search for her.'

'Yes, I recall her fondly. Such a pretty girl.' Michou grew pensive. 'If she's missing in this place, I fear for her. What can I do to help?'

'Give me a picture of her that I can show to others.'

Michou nodded, went immediately to her sketchbooks, and found several studies of the young woman. Within an hour she made a fair copy of the most characteristic sketch.

Anne took it in her hands and recognized Lucie's oval face, large, widespread eyes, fine nose, beautifully sculpted chin, and full lips gathered in just the hint of a pout. Anne felt a stirring of affection for the young woman.

With the picture in her bag, Anne set out for the millinery shop where Lucie had worked, located in the Palais-Royal's eastern or Valois arcade. As Anne entered, the middle-aged woman at the counter looked up from the cloth she was cutting.

'Madame Tessier?' Anne asked.

'Yes.' The woman laid down her shears. 'How may I help you?'

She was a fashionably dressed, self-consciously elegant woman with a hard, cunning look in her eyes. Heavy doses of powder and rouge only partially concealed the ravages of the pox on her once lovely features. Her expectant smile vanished when Anne explained who she was and why she had come.

Anne held up Michou's sketch. 'I'm searching for this young woman, Mademoiselle Gigot, called Lucie, who used to work here. Have you seen her recently?'

'No, not for a long time,' replied the milliner, grimacing at the young woman's name. 'Weeks ago, her mother also came looking for her. When I said that Lucie had quit the shop, the mother cried profusely, loudly cursed me, threatened to call the police.'

'Tell me about Lucie. Was she a good worker?'

'At first she learned quickly, did a good day's work. But she grew bored and undependable, arrived late in the morning, daydreamed. I wasn't sorry when she left.'

'She went off with an older man, I understand. Do you know him?'

'I've seen him before but don't know his name.' Her reply was much too quick.

Out of the corner of her eye Anne noticed a flash of surprise on the face of a young assistant, sewing at a table off to one side. Anne thanked the milliner and departed.

She waited at a café with a view of the shop until the assistant came out on an errand. Anne followed her from the Palais-Royal on to Rue Saint-Honoré. Near the church of Saint-Roch, Anne fell in step with the woman, took her under the arm. 'Keep walking. Don't be alarmed,' Anne murmured. 'I work for the police and won't hurt you. Just tell me the older man's name and where he lives. Your mistress will never find out that you've told me.'

'I don't know what you mean.' The woman tried to pull away, a frightened expression on her face.

'Would you rather speak to Inspector Quidor?' That threat had a sobering effect on the woman. Quidor was an intimidating, gruff bear of a man, the police officer who investigated crime in the district of the Louvre and the Palais-Royal.

'The man you want is Denis, valet to the Marquis de Bresse. He lives with his master on the Isle Saint-Louis, but he's often seen in the Valois arcade.'

Anne released her, pressing a small coin into her hand. She hurried away.

As Anne returned to the Palais-Royal, the little salute cannon in the garden sounded the noon hour with a blast. Anne asked herself, Why would the milliner pretend not to know the valet? Could the reason be shameful or illegal? The next step in the search for Lucie was to make this man's acquaintance.

'Bonjour, Madame Cartier.' A familiar voice jarred Anne out of her reflections. Georges Charpentier came alongside her in the Montpensier arcade and fell in step. 'What brings you to the Palais-Royal?'

'My search for a missing young woman,' Anne replied, pleased to meet him. She took Georges's arm and they walked out into the garden to escape the bustling crowd. She described her quest for Lucie thus far. 'What can you tell me about the Marquis de Bresse and his valet?'

'I've heard that the marquis is a notorious libertine, a disciple of the Marquis de Sade, one of many in Paris.' Georges shrugged. 'I don't know Bresse's valet. A man to his master's taste, I would guess.'

Anne's face must have betrayed her ignorance of Sade and his following.

'I thought everyone in France knew the Marquis de Sade,' Georges remarked indulgently. 'He's a notorious rogue, comes from a wealthy aristocratic family. He claims that men should live by their basic instincts, especially the sexual. The rules of religion, law, conscience lead men astray, fill them with fear, regrets, and false shame.'

'He sounds like a harmless mad man,' Anne offered. 'Why would anyone pay attention to him?'

'Unfortunately, given the opportunity, he practices what he preaches. His brutal attacks on women have scandalized the public. The courts have condemned him. Ten years ago, his family persuaded the king to commit him to the royal fortress of Vincennes. Since 1784, he's been in the Bastille. Other libertines like Bresse share Sade's views but practice them cautiously and avoid our clutches.'

'I'd rather not meet the marquis, but I need to talk to his valet. How can I find him?'

'You can ask Inspector Quidor. Come with me. I'm on my way to meet him at the Café de Foy. He should be there by now.'

'I know the valet hardly at all,' said the inspector, seated at an outdoor table, where Anne and Georges had joined him. 'His name is Denis Grimaud. My colleagues say that he occasionally runs dubious errands for his master and for a few magistrates on Isle Saint-Louis, like picking up the occasional prostitute for an evening. Usually, he works in the Palais-Royal and out of our reach.' Quidor sipped his coffee thoughtfully for a moment, then asked Anne, 'Why are you interested in him?'

'As far as I know,' she replied, 'he was the last person seen with the missing Lucie Gigot. I'd like to talk to him.'

'The marquis frequents an elegant brothel on Rue Valois. His valet cannot be far away. Try the wine taverns nearby. If you do, you'd better dress in common clothes and take him along.' Quidor pointed to Georges. 'The company might be rude, or worse.'

Georges waved his hand in protest. 'The colonel has ordered me to stay out of this case.' He turned to Anne. 'You don't need me, at least not now. Go to Bresse's neighborhood wine tavern on the Isle Saint-Louis. His valet must shop there. Find out what he looks like. Then watch for an opportunity to catch him alone. If you sense danger, avoid it and let me know.'

After Anne finished speaking with Georges and Quidor, she walked across the garden and joined Sylvie and Michou at a bench near the millinery shop. She had asked them to keep an eye on its clientele. For a couple of hours, they had observed persons going in and out. Michou took note of a few whose features looked familiar. One was a middle-aged man whom she recognized as probably a pimp. He had come as if on business, spoken familiarly with Madame Tessier.

'Here he is.' Michou handed Anne a small, rough, three-quarter sketch of his face with its thick lips, bulging eyes, and receding chin. 'Later the pimp returned with a petite prostitute on his arm. I had seen her before and sketched her features.' She showed Anne another quick sketch, this time of a heart-shaped face, large eyes, high cheekbones, small, determined mouth.

Sylvie pointed to the sketches that Anne was studying. 'I made a few inquiries in the Valois arcade about the man and the woman. They are well known among prostitutes. The pimp is Denis Grimaud, his companion is Renée Gros. They frequently visit Madame Tessier and her shop.'

'You have been most helpful,' Anne said, putting the sketches in her bag. 'In my investigation I've already heard of Grimaud, valet to the Marquis de Bresse. Now I know his appearance and have a sense of his character. I intend to confront him. Please find out more about his companion Renée.'

During this conversation, the three women continued to observe Madame Tessier's shop. Very few genuine customers came for a milliner's products. Most were country girls, brothel madams, pimps, and prostitutes who left the shop without new bonnets or ribbons.

Anne concluded that Tessier's business seemed mainly to broker country girls into prostitution. Her shop was a kind of bourse or market. Its typical commodity was a girl like Lucie – young, naive, simple, pretty. The realization that Lucie might have fallen into prostitution caused Anne a sharp pang of sorrow. But at least her search now had a certain direction. The marquis's valet appeared to traffic in country girls, and might have pimped for Lucie. Or, he could have simply kept her for himself. It was hard to imagine that he had honourably befriended her.

Anne sat at a table in the Chat Noir, a wine tavern on the Isle Saint-Louis, hoping to meet Denis Grimaud. Servants, male and female, came for wine, chatted with each other, throwing side glances at Anne, a stranger, the only woman seated with a glass in her hand. Ill at ease and nervous, she hardly touched her wine.

For an hour, she had walked through the neighbourhood and closely studied the Marquis de Bresse's town house on Quai Dauphin. A modest portal opened into a small court-yard flanked by a carriage house and a stable. Opposite the portal was a simple, narrow stone building of three storeys and a mansard roof. A crooked alley from Rue Poulletier led to a rear entrance.

The tavern's barman replied freely to her questions. Yes, he said, he knew the marquis's valet, a daily customer. A strong, clever man, he knew how to mind his tongue, never spoke about the marquis's private affairs.

Anne learned that the marquis lived in the house with his valet and a cook. During the day, a porter and a few other servants came to work for him. Having expected a more ostentatious residence and greater luxury, Anne was put to wondering. Was he short of money? For what other reason might he prefer such simplicity?

While she was pondering these questions, a middle-aged man in pink livery walked into the tavern with a large jug. 'Here he comes,' said the barman to Anne. Then, turning to Grimaud, he said, 'This lady is inquiring about you.'

Grimaud placed the empty jug on the counter and stared at Anne, his brow creased with confusion. 'Do I know you?' he demanded.

Anne started, recalling from the sketch in her bag the features of the pimp who frequented Madame Tessier's shop. Grimaud's face was rather ugly. His thick lips, receding chin, and the bulging eyes made Anne think of a peeping Tom. Still, he appeared to have considerable reserves of animal energy and a low, cunning intelligence.

'We've never met,' Anne replied, 'but I'd like to speak to you privately.'

The valet hesitated for a moment, scanned Anne quickly, then left his jug on the counter and led her to a secluded table in the back of the room. 'We can talk here. Be brief. I'm busy.'

'My name is Madame Cartier. I'm attempting to trace a missing young woman, Lucie Gigot, on behalf of her mother. A few months ago Lucie quit the milliner's shop where she had been working and was last seen with you. Would you tell me what you know about her?'

'Who told you that I knew her?'

'A reliable witness. I shall not give out the name.'

Grimaud studied Anne intently, calculating his response. His expression was enigmatic, cold, distant.

'I showed her around the Palais-Royal a few times, treated her to a glass of wine or two. She was a pretty girl but empty-headed and found the life of a shopgirl not to her taste. The only position I could offer her was that of a kitchen servant in my master's house. She turned up her nose at that.'

'Did she actually visit the house?'

'No, she didn't,' he replied without blinking.

Anne murmured to herself, 'Grimaud, you're a practiced liar.'

The man went on without a pause, 'A month ago, we said goodbye at her door. I haven't seen her since.'

'Where did she live?'

'In a garret on Rue Saint-Roch, looking out over the church. Now I must go back to work.' He rose from the table. 'Good day, Madame Cartier.' He paid the barman, took his jug of wine from the counter, and strode out of the shop without looking back.

It was late in the afternoon by the time Anne found the house on Rue Saint-Roch. The concierge was an older woman, but still robust and alert. Like most of her tribe, she was suspicious of strangers and therefore reluctant to talk about Lucie. But when Anne identified herself as a police colonel's wife, the concierge began to speak freely.

'Fresh from the country, the young woman was as poor

as a church mouse. Lived alone in the garret for a few months. Still, she had a high opinion of herself.'

'Did she have any friends?'

'A fashionable older woman visited her from time to time in her room. Brought her a few decent gowns to wear.' She described the milliner Madame Tessier. 'A young woman about your age also used to visit her.' Anne showed Michou's sketch of the petite prostitute on Grimaud's arm at the millinery shop. 'That's her,' said the concierge, 'called herself Renée.'

Anne returned the sketch to her bag. 'Did Lucie have any male visitors?'

'A man sometimes came for her.'

'Did he have bulging eyes?' Anne showed her Michou's sketch of Grimaud.

'Yes. That's him. Denis was his name. I knew from the look in his eyes what he wanted. But I never let him in. I called her and she went out with him.

'Then one night she didn't come home. When I checked her room, it was empty. She had taken her things with her. I don't know how she slipped out on me like that. She owed some rent and the landlord took it out of my hide. I don't know where she went or what happened to her. When I didn't hear from her for several days, I called the police. They took down the information that I gave them, then glanced at her room.'

'Did they find anything of value, any letters or a journal?'

'I don't think so. A few days later, an inspector came around, asked about her, told me that her acquaintances couldn't give him any useful information.'

'Did the inspector search the room?'

'I took him up there. He looked around for a few minutes. I can't say that he really searched.'

Anne learned that the room was still empty, hadn't been rented since Lucie disappeared. The walls and ceiling were in poor condition. The owner intended to repair them, but hadn't gotten around to it yet.

'May I see the room?' Anne sensed the woman's reluctance, so she added, 'I'd be happy to pay you for the trouble.'

The concierge hesitated, looked Anne up and down, then gave her a key. 'I guess I can trust an officer's wife. I must watch the front door. I expect you back here with the key in fifteen minutes.'

Anne gave her a coin and climbed quickly up the stairs to the mansard. The room was a ruin. Plaster had fallen from the ceiling, the walls were badly cracked. The only furniture was a plain table, two chairs, and a chest of drawers, covered by cloths. Anne hurriedly searched the drawers. Nothing. She checked the floor for loose boards. None.

She was looking for a small diary. At Château Beaumont Michou had seen Lucie writing in one. Anne stood in the middle of the room, closed her eyes, and tried to imagine where the young woman might have hidden it. When Anne opened her eyes, she was looking at the room's only window. She opened it and looked out at the church across the street. As she closed the window, she felt the sill yield. It was loose. With careful manipulation, she removed it and found an empty space, Lucie's hiding place. Wrapped in a fine piece of cloth was the diary, along with a small bundle of papers.

There wasn't time to read, so Anne tucked the discovery into her bag. In the next moment she heard footsteps on the stairs and nearly panicked. She replaced the sill just before the concierge walked into the room.

'You were supposed to return the key to me downstairs in fifteen minutes.' The woman's eyes narrowed with suspicion. 'Did you find anything?'

'Lots of broken plaster. I can understand why the owner doesn't rent out the room. How could Lucie have lived here?' Anne gave back the key and walked out.

'It's better than the street,' the concierge replied, locking the door. 'I'm concerned. Something bad must have happened. Would you tell me if you find her?'

The woman obviously hoped to recover the rent that Lucie had failed to pay. Nonetheless, Anne made the promise with a mental reservation, then thanked her, pressed another coin into her hand, and left the house.

Back at home in her room, Anne studied Lucie's hidden diary. The spelling was poor, the choice of words limited, but the meaning was clear to Anne if not to Lucie. Madame Tessier was grooming her for work as a prostitute, improving her speech and dress to enhance her value. 'In Paris,' Tessier told her, 'you must present yourself well.'

Lucie's short comments reflected a slowly growing disillusion with life in a decrepit garret room. Work at the shop was poorly paid and had become boring. Also, Madame Tessier expected to be repaid at a high rate of interest for the clothes and the money she gave to Lucie.

The young woman found pleasure in the arcades of the Palais-Royal and listed men and women whom she met there. On April 1 she began to mention Denis Grimaud. She was soon enjoying his company. It was hard to judge from the diary whether their relationship had become intimate. He was her father's age and hardly attractive. She may have thought that he was merely befriending her, though for a price. On April 13 she wrote:

> Denis found a position for me in his master's household and will take me there tomorrow for an interview. Rumours about the man frighten me. But I must take the risk, so that I can repay Denis and Madame Tessier. If this doesn't work out, I should go home ... I'd rather die.

Among the loose, hidden papers were letters to her mother, asking for money. Copies? Anne wondered. No, they were the originals. Anne surmised that Lucie had never sent them, or her mother would have said so.

At this point, Anne sat back and reflected. Denis Grimaud had not mentioned taking Lucie to an interview, only that he offered her a menial position and she had rejected it. She might have initially misunderstood him.

Still, something was amiss. If Lucie slipped out of the house to avoid paying rent, or for whatever reason, why didn't she take her diary and papers? They were precious to her, especially the diary. She would not have left it behind. Someone else must have sneaked into the room and cleared out Lucie's things, intending to create the appearance that she had run away. Only two persons were familiar with the room but unaware of the diary: Madame Tessier and Renée Gros. Young and agile, the latter was the more likely culprit, abetted by Grimaud.

What then really happened to Lucie? Immediately, Anne suspected a crime, perhaps Lucie's abduction. That put the search for Lucie in a different, sinister light and raised the danger of violence. It was time to bring the matter to Paul and Georges.

Before supper, Anne joined them in the provost's office. She had asked for this meeting. The two men sat at the conference table, their expressions a mixture of curiosity and concern. They realized that she wouldn't have called them together without a serious reason.

'Gentlemen,' she began as she took her place at the table. 'I now have evidence of a crime. Lucie has been either abducted or killed.' She handed the young woman's diary to Paul, who skimmed through it, then gave it to Georges, who did the same.

'Are you sure this is Lucie's diary?' Paul asked.

'Yes, and its last entry indicates that she was going with Grimaud to Bresse's town house for an interview about a job.'

The two men sat up, their expressions of concern sharpened.

'What's even more significant,' Anne went on, 'is that the diary remained in its hiding place even after Lucie secretly moved out of the room and disappeared without paying back rent. The concierge noticed her absence a few days later, after her visit to Bresse's house.' Anne paused, glanced at Paul, then at Georges. 'Lucie would *not* have left her diary behind. Someone removed her things to create the appearance that she had sneaked out. I believe the culprit was Renée Gros, working for Denis Grimaud.'

Paul tapped the diary. 'The implications are quite clear, and serious. The valet and his master must be suspected of causing her disappearance.'

Georges nodded. 'Before confronting them, Madame Cartier and I should visit Inspector Quidor, early tomorrow morning, to check his list of missing young women. He and the other inspectors might also tell us more about our suspects.'

Four
A Country Girl's Roots

17 May

Quidor looked up crossly as Anne and Georges entered his office, as if displeased to have been interrupted. They had found him at the Hôtel de Police on Rue des Capuchines. A busy man with an abrasive manner, he meant no offense. Anne offered him a polite apology, then described her discovery of Lucie's diary. The inspector grew interested, laid down his pen, and soon gave her his full attention.

'We now suspect that she has met with foul play,' Georges added. 'Could we study your list of missing young women?'

'Of course, just ask my clerk.' He nodded toward the ante-room.

The clerk greeted them with a rueful smile. 'Unfortunately, our list of missing persons is incomplete and outdated, and includes men and women of all ages. What's more, young women come and go without telling us or anyone else. For what it's worth, here it is.' He placed a record book before them.

After a fruitless hour of skimming over hundreds of names, Anne and Georges went back to Quidor.

'We'll pay a visit to the morgue,' Georges said, 'to see if Lucie ended there.' He beckoned Anne to leave with him.

But she had a question for Quidor. 'Renée Gros, a young female prostitute working for Grimaud, is also involved in Lucie's disappearance. Can you tell us anything about her?'

Quidor stroked his chin, calling upon his vast, tenacious memory. 'The name is familiar. One of my colleagues has dealt with her. He's out of the office now. After you've checked the morgue, come back here. My colleague will join us.'

*   *   *

The morgue was located in the ground level of the Châtelet, the ancient stone building that also housed the city's courts and a prison. Anne regarded the building with a strong feeling of repugnance. The morgue's ghoulish task, the court's harsh judgments, the prison's brutal punishments – in a word, the business of the place – seemed to taint the spirit of all who worked there. To Anne's eyes, they appeared coarse, devoid of human feelings, even cruel. The building itself – drab, long and narrow – took on a forbidding aspect.

'Are you feeling well?' Georges asked as they walked through a portal on Rue Saint-Denis.

'I'm coping,' Anne replied. In truth, she wasn't sure she could go through with the ordeal. In her mind she already tasted as well as smelled the putrid odor of death and decay. Gruesome images of cadavers and body parts, mingled with sights she had recently seen in the nearby slaughterhouses on the river's bank. Her knees felt as if they would give way beneath her. Nonetheless, she managed to reach an ante-room to the morgue itself.

'You're as pale as chalk,' said Georges, taking her under the arm. 'We might not need to go inside and look at the corpses. Give me Michou's sketch. I'll ask the guard on duty to study Lucie's features and tell us if she's here.'

'I'll do what I must. But the morgue might be too much for me today. I can also hardly bear to see such a young, fresh, beautiful woman as a lifeless, stinking corpse.'

Fortunately, after a careful look at the sketch, and having heard Anne's physical description of Lucie, the guard shook his head. 'We don't have her.'

Once outside, Anne breathed deeply of the city's air, though it was far from fresh. She felt relieved and hopeful again that Lucie might be found alive, perhaps hidden in one of the city's many brothels.

An hour later, Quidor ushered Anne and Georges into a conference room at the Hôtel de Police. His fellow inspector was waiting for them. Introductions were made and brandy served.

'Madame,' the colleague began, 'so you want to know about the young prostitute Renée Gros. Let me warn you, she's half-crazed.' He explained that, several months ago, Renée came to the Hôtel de Police and complained that he had failed to find a missing young friend and cousin, Yvonne Bloch.

At the time of her friend's disappearance, Renée was imprisoned in the Châtelet under suspicion of shoplifting. A few weeks later, after the charges were dropped and Renée released, she looked in vain for her friend and reported her missing. She was last seen in the company of Denis Grimaud, valet to the Marquis de Bresse. Since Yvonne was a prostitute, poor and without connections, the police hadn't really searched for her. Or so Renée claimed.

The inspector's eyes opened wide in amazement. 'Renée screeched at me, demanded that I undertake a new investigation in earnest and interrogate Grimaud, who must have caused more than one young woman to disappear.

'An impossible task!' the inspector exclaimed, addressing the visitors. 'Hundreds of young women go missing every year. The police haven't the time or the resources to pursue them. The highway patrol had in fact called on the girl's father, who said that his daughter had run off with an unknown man. He didn't know where they were living. As far as he was concerned, his daughter was old enough to manage her own life.'

Georges and Anne nodded that they understood.

Encouraged, the inspector continued, 'I told Mademoiselle Gros "come back to me when you find evidence of a crime".'

The inspector drank deeply of his brandy, looked to his companions for sympathy. 'Well, she became angry, and abusive – called me *un cochon*, a pig. I threatened to lock her up for a year in the Châtelet. She calmed down and apologized, but said that she'd find out the truth herself and punish the villain who had hurt her friend. I haven't heard from Renée since.'

Anne asked, 'What do you make of the fact that she's become Grimaud's companion and is somehow involved in Lucie's disappearance? Isn't that odd?' Anne described the clearing of Lucie's room and the discovery of her diary. 'Renée was almost certainly working on Grimaud's behalf. As his companion, she might also know what happened to Lucie. Couldn't she see the similarity to Yvonne's fate? Had she allied herself with the enemy to discover his secrets?'

'That would be a dangerous game,' the inspector replied.

'I had the impression that she strongly suspected, even hated, Grimaud, but I also believe that she's not entirely right in the head. Her eyes have a wild look. Her mind is a jumble of disconnected ideas. And her moods change like the sky in summer, calm one minute, thunder and lightning the next.'

'Where did Renée's missing friend come from?' asked Georges. 'I'll go there, learn as much as I can about her and perhaps find a clue to Lucie's disappearance. It might fit into a pattern of crime that would lead us to the perpetrator.'

'Yvonne Bloch was from the hamlet of Barbizon near Chailly, a three or four hour ride south from here – my clerk would know precisely. Yvonne had not been long in the city.' He lifted his arm and saluted Georges. 'Good luck.'

'Thanks. I'll speak to your clerk, examine your records, then visit Barbizon and talk to her father.' He turned to Anne. 'While I'm gone, you could learn more about Grimaud and his master. This case is becoming a tangled web.'

In the criminal investigation records Georges found a file on Yvonne Bloch that identified her parents and the location of their cottage in Barbizon. He had never been there, but he recalled reports of poachers and bandits infesting the adjacent royal forest of Fontainebleau. It might be wise to bring along as a companion one of the troopers who had previously visited the place and had spoken to Yvonne's father.

Late in the afternoon, their coats soaked by a spring shower, they reached the church in Chailly, a few miles from the Bloch cottage. The priest, a vigorous, wiry man with thick, pepper-grey hair, greeted them warmly, invited them to dry themselves in his cottage, served them hot punch, and left to fetch records from the church next door.

'Yvonne Bloch, you say. Here she is.' He handed the record book to Georges. The young woman had been baptized a few days after birth, seventeen years ago.

'I remember her well,' said the priest. 'I trained her for confirmation. A lively, pretty girl. She was unhappy at home.'

'Why?' asked Georges, draining the last drops of punch from his cup.

'Her father is a poor, shiftless, brute and considered her a burden. He might also have abused her. She feared him. Her best friend and older cousin, Renée, looked after her when her mother couldn't manage.'

Georges inclined his head as if puzzled.

'Madame Bloch was ill.' The priest tapped his temple in a revealing gesture. 'And she got worse as the years passed. A few months ago, Monsieur Bloch had her committed to the mental hospital in Paris, the Salpêtrière.'

Georges protested, 'But she wasn't a resident of the city.'

'I know,' the priest granted. 'An acquaintance with influence made the arrangements.'

'A man?'

'Yes. He came in a carriage and took Madame Bloch away. I don't know his name, but from time to time he has returned to visit Monsieur Bloch.'

Who could that influential benefactor be? Georges wondered, a suspicion rapidly growing in his mind. He sent his companion, the trooper, to fetch the portfolio from his saddlebag.

'Is this the man?' Georges asked, showing the priest Michou's sketch of Denis Grimaud.

'Why, yes, that's him,' replied the priest. 'He was here recently.'

'Before I leave, tell me, what prompted Yvonne to move to the city?'

'Her cousin found a job for her in a millinery shop, I believe. There was little for her to do here.'

'Do you know what has become of her?'

'No, I don't. Monsieur Bloch says only that she has run off with a man and disappeared. That would be sad. I wouldn't expect it of Yvonne. She seemed like a good girl, though lately perhaps a little free in her manner.'

That last remark made Georges question how well the priest knew Yvonne since her confirmation. Other villagers could fill that gap, probably best over a glass of wine. Georges's stomach had begun to tell him that suppertime was approaching. But he didn't want to impose on the priest's hospitality. A country curé was poorly paid, perhaps only 400 livres a year, whereas his bishop might receive 400,000. From the rundown appearance of the cottage and the church, Georges judged that this priest had very little to spare. So Georges asked, 'Is there an inn nearby?'

The priest frowned. 'Yes, there is. The food is edible, but I can't recommend the clientele. After dark, it's a dangerous place for strangers, even for armed troopers like yourselves. Your boots, your horses, your weapons, and the fine wool cloth of your uniforms would sorely tempt our poachers and desperate peasants. Sleep here, if you wish. I'll throw pallets on the floor.'

Georges thanked the priest for the offer. 'We might need to accept it.' He signaled his companion. It was time to learn what Yvonne's neighbours thought of her.

The inn was little more than a large hovel, a bar on one side, several long tables and benches on the other. A pair of sconces gave off a dim light, and tobacco smoke from clay pipes fouled the air. The clientele consisted of small knots of men, almost uniformly dressed in ragged, dirty woolen shirts and breeches. Their feet were either bare or shod with heavy wooden sabots.

As Georges and the trooper entered, all eyes turned toward them. A hostile silence descended upon the room. Georges understood that this inn on the edge of the royal forest must attract more poachers than honest peasants. Hoping to allay the anxiety of the men behind him, Georges proclaimed to the barman loudly enough for all to hear that he and his companion had come only to eat a meal and find information concerning a missing young woman. Could the barman be helpful?

The barman looked over Georges's shoulder to a group of young men drinking wine. With his eyes he signaled a question. In a cracked mirror behind the bar Georges saw one of the men nod.

Anticipating the barman's response, Georges ordered more wine for that table. He murmured to his companion to guard the horses, then joined the men. There were four of them, poachers all, Georges guessed, and armed with sharp knives hidden beneath their long, loose shirts. Their leader gave Georges a wary smile and asked, 'Just which young woman are you looking for? More than one is missing and for different reasons.'

The young man was a rustic Lothario. With his thick, curly, dark-brown hair, golden-brown dancing eyes, long lashes, and sensual lips, he *would* know all the pretty young women in the area. He appeared intelligent, if illiterate.

'I'm looking for Yvonne Bloch. Her friend in Paris is concerned, says Yvonne's missing, and wonders if she's returned to Barbizon. If not, would you know where she's gone?' Georges glanced the question to each of the four young men.

Wine arrived, together with bread, cheese, and sausage. Georges offered the food and drink to the young men. The Lothario shook his head, stared inscrutably at Georges for a long moment. Then, with a toss of his head, he sent his three companions to another table.

'She hasn't returned, nor do I know where she has gone.' He became silent, thoughtful, and drank deeply of the wine. 'We were lovers . . . until her odd cousin Renée seduced her with tales of fancy clothes and pleasure at the Palais-Royal. Last year, I worked in the Valois arcade for a short while and learned what Renée did for a living. I tried to tell Yvonne to beware, but she wouldn't listen.'

His eyes focused inward to the past. He emptied his glass. Georges signaled the barman for another. 'Yes,' murmured the young man, 'I nearly starved in Paris. Then I realized that I'd much rather poach quail in the king's forest.'

Suddenly, he became aware that his loose tongue had virtually confessed to a capital crime that could send him to a naval prison for life. His unsteady hand went towards the knife beneath his shirt. At the next table his three companions rose to their feet. But Georges quickly drew a small pistol and aimed it at a spot between the young man's eyes.

'I want you to slowly put both hands on the table and tell your friends to sit down. Otherwise we may have a serious accident. Now pay attention to what I say. I guard the king's highways, not his forests. Do you understand?'

The young man nodded, and obeyed Georges's command.

Georges lowered the pistol but kept it in his hand. 'I have another question. Do you recognize this man?' He showed the young man Michou's sketch of Denis Grimaud.

'He looks familiar,' he replied through trembling lips. 'Yes, he has come here off and on, visits Yvonne's father. I've wondered why? Once I asked him. He told me to mind my own business.'

'I, too, will ask him, and expect a better answer than that.' Georges put away his pistol, rose from the table, and bade the young man goodbye. Outside, he joined his companion. 'We'll sleep on the priest's floor. Keep your pistol at your side. Tomorrow we'll visit Monsieur Bloch.'

When they rose from their pallets shortly after dawn, the priest was at his morning prayers. They dressed quietly. He finished a few minutes later and greeted them. 'This is Sunday, so we'll have coffee and special sweet biscuits, baked by a kind woman of the village.'

While they enjoyed this unexpected breakfast, the priest asked, 'Did you sleep well?'

'Yes,' Georges replied, and the trooper nodded, his mouth full of biscuit.

'You had visitors during the night.'

Georges inclined his head in surprise. 'Oh?'

'About midnight the poachers sneaked up to your horses, hitched behind the cottage. You can imagine the evil that those rogues had in mind.'

Georges nodded. 'I think they intended, while stealing the horses, to lure us outside to meet their knives.'

'Fortunately,' the priest continued, 'I had put Hugo on guard. He growled and woke me up. I heard the poachers flee.' The priest set down his coffee cup and whistled. The back door was ajar. Hugo nuzzled it open, padded up to Georges, sniffed him, licked his hand. This was the largest, ugliest dog Georges had ever seen. His fawn-coloured body was marred by several old knife wounds. One eye was missing. His dark brown muzzle, nose, and drooping ears were also scarred.

The priest explained. 'Hugo is a mastiff. A few years ago, he engaged in combat with a vicious bandit who broke into the local chateau. The bandit did not survive. Hugo was badly injured. His owner, the countess, was going to put him down. But I asked for him and nursed him back to health. With children he's as gentle as a lamb, even when they pull his ears. Last night the poachers were lucky to leave with their hindquarters intact.'

Georges stroked Hugo's massive head. 'I see him in a new light. Beneath his battered skin, he has a better character than many humans that I know.'

The priest agreed, gazing into Hugo's eye. 'He may also have the gift that we clergy call the discernment of spirits, a rare power of perception higher than mere reason. He senses the presence of evil in men, and he reacts fiercely.' The priest tilted his head in a teasing gesture and glanced at Georges. 'Would you agree, sir?'

Tickling Hugo behind the ear, Georges replied in a fully rounded, professorial tone, 'Our philosophers have discovered that human thoughts are physical substances. When they turn evil, they produce a distinctive, very foul scent, like rotten eggs, which unfortunately we humans are not equipped to perceive. In contrast, thanks to this extraordinary olfactory organ, his nose, a dog can smell evil in men. Then, prompted by instinct, he either flees or, like Hugo, he fights.'

'A witty policeman! I count myself blessed.' The priest's face beamed with pleasure. He rose from the table. 'Good day, gentlemen, I'll prepare the church for today's Mass. And you have work to do, even on Sunday – the Lord will understand. Bloch will worship, as is his custom, at home.'

The Bloch cottage showed obvious signs of sloth and neglect. Weeds had choked all other growth in the kitchen garden. A wagon lacked a wheel. The chickens looked dirty and poorly fed. The cottage lacked paint and plaster. Georges asked the young trooper whether anything had changed since his visit months ago.

'No, it's the same. But we spoke to Monsieur Bloch outside. I have no idea what the inside looks like. And I didn't see Madame Bloch.'

Bloch opened for the two visitors but stood in the doorway, blocking their view of the interior. He clearly did not intend to invite them in. Georges pushed him aside and entered, followed by his companion.

A lean, bent, grizzled peasant with the bleary eyes of a man addicted to strong drink, Bloch protested that the police should pursue poachers and thieves and not abuse honest men, like himself, who eked out their living on small plots of land. Georges pointed him to a chair at the table and they all sat down.

'We're searching for your daughter,' Georges told him. 'Her friend Renée Gros has reported her missing.'

'Renée should let Yvonne run her own life.' Bloch explained that Renée, several years older than Yvonne, her first cousin, had presumed to play the role of her mother. 'She's weaned my daughter away from me, enticed her to the Palais-Royal,

corrupted her. Yvonne has come to her senses and fled from
Renée and Paris.'

'Why hasn't she come back home?' Georges asked.

With a wave of his hand, Bloch pointed to the poverty of
the cottage: dirt floor, unglazed windows, a decrepit hearth.
In the winter the room would be almost unbearably cold.
'After Paris she could never live here.'

'Do you believe that your daughter is still living?' Georges
asked, scanning the room. He took note of a fine pair of leather
boots standing in a corner and an expensive woolen cloak on
a peg fastened to the door. He also noticed the sharp new steel
blade on Bloch's scythe hanging on the wall.

'I can't say for sure whether she's dead or alive,' the peasant
replied. 'Neither of us can write, or would have any reason to
keep in touch. She never was much use to me, nor I to her.'

Georges leaned forward, his eyes caught the peasant's, and
he asked abruptly, 'How much does Grimaud pay you?'
Georges pointed to those expensive items among Bloch's
meager possessions. 'You couldn't honestly raise the money
to buy those things, not in a thousand years.'

Bloch's voice took on a defiant tone. 'I didn't break the
law, so it's none of your business how I paid for them.'

'Why has Denis Grimaud visited you several times since
Yvonne has disappeared? People in the village have wondered.'

Bloch averted his eyes, remained silent.

'Your daughter may have been murdered, that's the king's
business, *my* business. Unless you tell me the truth, I'll take
you to the Châtelet for interrogation. You won't enjoy that, I
can assure you. A serious crime is involved. You'll stay in
prison until you explain why Grimaud is paying you to conceal
your daughter's disappearance. There's no other reason why
he would come here. So you may as well tell me.'

The peasant had begun to perspire. His hands trembled. He
wet his lips and swallowed. A minute passed while he struggled with conflicting thoughts. Georges waited quietly, eyes
narrowed, staring at the man.

Finally, he blurted out, 'She *has* disappeared, and no one
knows why.'

'Tell me about it,' Georges demanded in a soft, low voice.

The peasant drew a deep breath, then explained that several
months ago Grimaud had hired Yvonne for an evening of

entertainment at the town house of the Marquis de Bresse. Late at night, she left the house, alone and drunk, and had not been seen since.

The marquis was desolated and also concerned about scandal, feeling that he would likely be blamed. So he offered the father a sum of money in compensation, plus a small monthly pension, if he would keep his daughter's mysterious disappearance a secret, even from the police. Bloch accepted the offer.

'Have you told anyone? Her cousin Renée?'

'No, you are the first. Renée has asked me several times, she's suspicious. But I tell her that my daughter is probably married, living outside Paris under a different name. For all I know, that might be true.' He scratched his head, reflecting. 'Of course, like any drunken whore, she might have been robbed and thrown into the river.'

'Really? I think it's more likely that she never left the marquis's house alive.'

Bloch's brow creased with doubt. 'Why would either the valet or the marquis want to kill her?'

'I ask myself the same question,' Georges replied. He studied Bloch's face. Throughout this conversation, it showed no sign of grief. How little his daughter meant to him. No wonder that she, like so many other young women, left a poor, loveless home to seek her fortune in the arcades of the Palais-Royal.

Five

The Investigation Widens

18 May

On this cool, wet Sunday afternoon at the Palais-Royal, the garden was deserted. Anne and Comtesse Marie struggled through dense crowds in the sheltered Montpensier arcade.

Anne was thinking of the next step in her investigation of Lucie's disappearance. It would be costly and involve Marie. Anne wondered how to present it to her. The financial issues at Château Beaumont preoccupied her mind and distracted her from Lucie's case.

In the morning, the countess had come to the city on business and met Anne at the town house on Rue Traversine. For the past two years Marie had entrusted its care to Anne. After morning coffee, they had walked through the rooms, discussing possible uses for them and the sale of some of their furnishings.

'Isn't it a shame,' the countess had asked, 'that the rich leave their town houses empty for months on end, while the common people must crowd into tiny decrepit rooms and the destitute live on the streets or under the bridges?'

'At least in this house,' Anne had replied, 'Michou and Sylvie make good use of the second storey. Now that I realize how strongly you feel, I'll look for suitable uses for the other rooms as well.'

As they entered the café, Anne surveyed the room and remarked, 'The place is packed. The rain has driven hordes of pleasure seekers indoors. Fortunately, I dispatched a servant to ask Bernard to reserve a table.'

The countess caught the eye of Bernard, her favourite waiter and occasional spy. He smiled discreetly, bowed slightly, and led them to a tea table, then left them for a few minutes to get settled.

'I have news,' said Anne, sitting opposite the countess and speaking softly. She went on to describe her meeting with Denis Grimaud on the Isle Saint-Louis and her search of Lucie's garret room. 'I doubt that the young woman has vanished voluntarily. She would never have abandoned her diary, nor the letters to her mother. I believe we're dealing with an abduction. She could be imprisoned in a brothel.'

'Or it could be worse,' added Marie. 'The young woman's life may be in danger – or already lost.'

'That's quite possible,' Anne admitted reluctantly. 'Yesterday, Paul recognized how serious her case had become and assigned Georges to join the investigation. At Inspector Quidor's office he and I determined that Lucie wasn't in the register of prostitutes or the file on missing persons. Her body wasn't at the morgue, either. I left a copy of Michou's sketch of Lucie with the inspector to show to his agents.'

Perplexity furrowed Marie's brow. 'It's astonishing that you haven't found even a trace of Lucie. How could she have simply vanished?'

'I have to conclude,' Anne replied, 'that the key to finding her lies with Monsieur Grimaud or his master. Yesterday, Georges searched in the criminal investigation department's records for information about Grimaud's companion Renée Gros and her missing friend Yvonne Bloch, then went to Barbizon to investigate Yvonne's family, friends, and acquaintances.'

Marie's concern was mounting. 'What could *we* do?'

'Carry out an investigation parallel to Georges's and learn more about our potential suspects, the valet and his master.' Anne gestured toward Bernard who approached them from the other side of the room. 'Could we enlist him in our search?'

Bernard Fontaine was the kind of man one hardly noticed. His appearance was nondescript, his manner self-effacing. But his hearing and his eyesight were unusually sharp, his memory retentive. He also read lips. And, so, for pleasure and profit, he had created an informal network of other waiters and domestic servants to work for him. Comtesse Marie had previously employed him in various delicate investigations. He also spied for other trusted clients.

Anne was astounded when she first met Bernard over two years ago. She knew that the police relied on spies. But what use did society have for private ones? Then she learned that aristocratic circles were continually plagued by charlatans and impostors, such as the gang who had recently stolen the queen's necklace. They would never have succeeded, if the Cardinal de Rohan – the chief victim of the plot – had engaged Bernard to investigate their credentials.

'A splendid idea!' Marie replied. 'I'll sound him out.'

Bernard took their order for tea and scones and was about to leave when Marie beckoned him to come closer. 'Would you have time for a project of mine? I need to know more about the Marquis de Bresse and his valet. Could we meet at my town house on Rue Traversine?'

'I'll give you an answer with your tea, Comtesse.' As he left, he glanced toward the door, stopped and stared for a second, then returned to their table. 'The object of your interest has just entered the café without his valet. Look.'

The marquis walked toward them with a mincing gait. About thirty, he looked younger, almost like a boy. His face seemed frozen in a heedless, ironic smile. Slender, well-proportioned, he wore a pink silk suit with elaborate silver floral embroidery and carried an ivory headed cane. His hands were small and thin. His complexion was fair; his features delicate, almost feminine; his long sandy hair was tied at the nape of his neck by a black ribbon.

'Though I've seen him many times,' whispered Marie, 'he still makes my skin crawl.'

'He has the same effect on me,' Bernard remarked, then turned to leave. 'I'll come right back with the tea.'

Acquaintances at a table a dozen paces away beckoned the marquis. In reply he waved his hand and flashed a wide gold band on his right ring finger. As he passed by Anne, he glanced at her. Their eyes met in a hostile encounter. He flinched and sauntered on.

'I'm afraid that he sensed my dislike. As an actress, I should have better control over the expression on my face. I've been too much influenced by the scandalous reports that I've heard about him and other libertines.'

'How you looked at him doesn't matter, Anne. His valet has told him about your investigation into Lucie's disappearance. He feels threatened.'

Anne continued to observe the marquis as he bantered with his acquaintances. After a few minutes, she murmured to Marie, 'Someone has said that "eyes are the mirror of the soul". I saw in his the hatred of an enemy.'

At that moment, Bernard returned with their tea and scones. Anne asked, 'Who are Bresse's acquaintances?' She cast a glance in their direction.

Bernard served Anne a scone. 'They're idle sons of powerful magistrates at the Parlement of Paris, like Bresse's father. They gather here often to ridicule the king's ministers.' Bernard turned to the countess and whispered as he served her, 'I'll be at your town house at six this evening.'

Anne and Marie were waiting in the front parlour. Promptly at six, a servant announced that a man was at the door, asking

for the countess. 'He wouldn't give his name,' the servant
added doubtfully. 'What shall I do?'

'Show him in,' Marie replied.

Bernard entered, taking off the cap that had concealed the
upper part of his face, except for the eyes. His scarf still
covered the lower half. Removing the scarf, he bowed to the
two women, and said, 'I must be cautious. I can't recall society
so agitated, especially at the Palais-Royal. Pamphlets vilifying
the queen pass openly from hand to hand. Cabals flourish like
weeds. Partisans of the Parlement, the royal government, and
the duke's faction snarl at each other while they fight over
the prostrate body of *la belle France*.'

Cap in hand, he took a seat and with a deferential tilt of
his head asked, 'What can I do for you, Comtesse?'

'Assist Madame Cartier. I'll ask her to explain.'

Anne briefly related the story of Lucie and the attempts to
find her. 'I suspect that she has come into harm's way. Her
tracks have led me to Denis Grimaud, valet of the Marquis
de Bresse. I must learn more about both the valet and his
master.'

While Anne spoke, Bernard asked a few questions but
mostly listened with keen attention. When she finished, he
said, 'The marquis dines regularly at the café and I've often
served him. He's an intelligent, cultivated, and elegant man,
a master of witty conversation. Like other libertines, he mocks
religion, women, the king's ministers, eminent critics of literature and art, and almost everything that ordinary people
respect or cherish. At least in the café, his taste in food and
drink, his manners, his conversation are exquisite. Elsewhere,
he might behave differently. I've occasionally heard troubling
rumours about his moral character but cannot vouch for their
accuracy. His valet is virtually unknown to me.'

'Could you learn more, particularly about the valet?' asked
Anne.

'I would have to engage my associates in the project.'

'This will help you.' Anne gave him Michou's sketch of
the valet from her observations at the millinery shop.

'Yes,' he agreed. 'I'll pass it around. Gaining the coopera-
tion of my associates might take time . . . and money.' His
eyes shifted to the countess.

'Do what you must,' she said, then smiled ruefully. 'Time

is a pressing problem, and money is in short supply. However, I'm growing worried about the girl and will spend what it takes to find her.'

Late that night Anne was at home in the salon reading a letter from her favourite relative, her grandfather André, the gunsmith in Hampstead near London. She recalled his many kindnesses, especially his generous acceptance of Paul, an officer in the service of the monarchy that had forced André and other Huguenots to flee to England.

Even though this was Sunday, Paul had left early in the morning for the royal palace at Versailles with Baron Breteuil and Lieutenant General Thiroux DeCrosne, chief of French police, to discuss with the king's council the growing unrest in the country. The provincial high courts, or parlements, had joined the Parlement of Paris in defying the government and demanding a meeting of the kingdom's traditional legislature, the Estates-General.

As a provost of the Royal Highway Patrol, Paul could speak with authority about the danger of civil disorder. Spread out across the entire kingdom, the patrol was better suited to take the pulse of the population than the royal governors and other high royal functionaries, who often lived at a great physical, social, and mental distance from their people. In command of the district surrounding Paris, Paul was responsible for public order in the most strategic area of the country.

Alone at supper this evening, Anne had missed him – there was much to report, but she was pleased that the highest levels of the government appreciated him. Their marriage had not hurt his career, as some of his acquaintances and relatives had feared – or hoped, as the case might be. At least not yet.

Anne now heard Paul's voice in the entrance hall below. She laid aside the letter from England, rushed downstairs, and met him in his office. They had scarcely begun their conversation when Georges returned from a tiring trip to the village of Barbizon. He looked hungry, as did Paul, so Anne called a servant and ordered supper for the two men and an herbal tea for herself.

While waiting for the food, Georges assessed his experiences in Chailly and Barbizon. 'Yvonne Bloch is a puzzle,' he reported. 'In the curé's eyes, she was still the innocent, naive girl whom he had trained for confirmation. To the rustic Lothario, she was a fickle lover. Her father considered her a thankless burden whom he was well rid of.'

'What was her relationship to Renée?' Anne asked.

'A mixed blessing,' Georges replied. 'She was Yvonne's best friend and took the place of her demented mother, but she also served as a bad example and enticed her into a life of vice in the Palais-Royal.'

'Have you learned how she disappeared?'

'I asked Yvonne's father that question. Grimaud paid him to say that she probably met an unknown man, got married, and left Paris. If so, I asked, why did she, like Lucie, tell no one and leave her possessions behind? In response Bloch conjectured that, alone and drunk late at night after leaving Bresse's house, she was killed by robbers who threw her body into the river.'

Paul sniffed. 'Either explanation sounds merely convenient.'

At that point, a supper of bread, red wine, pea soup, and cheese was served, and the two men set to eating. Sipping her tea, Anne reported her impressions of Bresse at Café de Foy. Whether irritated or intimidated, he seemed to resent her investigation. 'As if to say,' she added, 'that an elegant, cultivated aristocrat, such as himself, should be above suspicion of murdering a prostitute.'

Georges grimaced at the idea but continued eating. Paul paused to remark, 'I'm troubled to hear that the marquis seems hostile to you. Given his high rank and the prestige of his family, he could be a formidable enemy.'

'I've faced conceited men like him before,' Anne retorted. 'They count too much on their privileges and become careless. So I'm not surprised that Bresse would pay Monsieur Bloch to cooperate in concealing his daughter's disappearance, a deception that Georges easily exposed.'

Georges nodded. 'We should also note that both Yvonne and Lucie disappeared in a similar, mysterious way. Was that merely an unfortunate coincidence or part of a wider pattern of evil?'

'We may find the answer when we know Grimaud better,' Anne replied. 'To that end, Comtesse Marie has hired her spy Bernard and his associates. That may take a few days. In the meantime, I'll encourage Michou and Sylvie to fish for clues in the Palais-Royal.'

Six

Berthe

23 May

A lmost a week passed without word from Bernard. Anne had begun to think that her search had come to a dead end. She was also feeling lonely. Paul and Georges had left early in the morning and would be gone for four days inspecting posts of the highway patrol. The house seemed empty. Then at noon, while digging in the garden, she received a brief note from Bernard. He would meet her at the countess's town house at six in the evening. She was to come disguised as a male domestic servant. She read the note twice, wondering what kind of adventure Bernard had prepared that required such secrecy.

At six, she was waiting for him in the shadows of the town house's courtyard, dressed in a plain brown wool suit, her fair complexion darkened with powder, and a cap hiding her blonde hair. Bernard entered the courtyard, also in a servant's costume, and signaled her to follow him.

Out on the street, he whispered, 'We're going to a cheap wine tavern in the central markets near Saint-Eustache. One of my associates has found a prostitute, Claudette, who knows the marquis's valet Grimaud, but fears him. So we must not attract his attention.'

Anne's own apprehension grew as she sensed the tension in Bernard's voice, so unlike his cool demeanor in the restaurant. They cautiously picked their way through the narrow, congested streets near the markets. The evening light had vanished. Streetlamps were dim and far apart. Between them, specks of light from shuttered windows punctuated the darkness. Raucous shouts came from the wine shops along the way. Half-drunken men and women staggered toward Anne and Bernard and jostled them as they passed by.

Finally, Bernard stopped at an open gate to a small courtyard with tables for patrons of the wine tavern. Because it was convenient to the markets, it drew a loud, mixed crowd of ham-fisted, foul-mouthed fishmongers, hard-faced peasants reeking of garlic, and stout bakers' wives – not a respectable woman among them. Anne was happy for her disguise.

The evening air was warm and dry. For market people this was the end of a long, tiring day, and they were hungry and thirsty. Waiters bustled about, their trays precariously loaded with food and jugs of wine.

'She's inside,' whispered Bernard into Anne's ear. He nudged her forward into the tavern's large, noisy hall. At the bar, he ordered wine and mumbled a few words that Anne couldn't hear. The barman gave him a full jug and two empty glasses. As he took Bernard's money, he passed a key to him and nodded toward a hallway at the back of the room. Bernard led the way to a door and knocked. A weak, timorous voice responded. Bernard unlocked the door. 'Quick, get inside,' he ordered, as Anne slipped past him.

The room was tiny. A bed stood off to one side. A woman sat at a plain wooden table, a glass of wine in her hand. She stared wide-eyed, apprehensive, at the visitors, then waved them to the chairs facing her.

'Claudette,' she said, pointing to herself. She was perhaps thirty, Anne's age, but looked much older. Her eyes were brown, sad, and lusterless, her complexion gray, her cheeks hollow. Anne could see from the woman's fine facial bones that she had once been quite attractive. She was dressed in a thin, yellow, low-cut silk gown, frayed at the hem.

Bernard introduced Anne and himself. 'We've come to speak to you about Grimaud.'

The woman made a grimace, then held out her hand. Bernard gave her a coin.

'What do you want to know?' Her voice was dull, toneless. Suddenly, she fell into a fit of dry coughing.

Bernard waited until the coughing stopped, then asked, 'How did you come to know him?'

'I'll tell you my story,' she replied. 'I came to Paris from Abbeville, penniless and alone. I had been a domestic servant. My mistress accused me of stealing a linen napkin and discharged me without a reference. To survive I sold myself in the arcades of the Palais-Royal. One day, a man called Denis seemed to like me, told me to go to a millinery shop. I might find work there. The lady in charge seemed kind, heard my story, hired me, gave me some decent clothes. After a few days, Denis came back. The lady said she didn't need me anymore, but Denis knew of a position in domestic service. I jumped at the opportunity. The next morning, he took me to a marquis's house on the Isle Saint-Louis.

'The marquis seemed charming and kind and hired me. Later in the day, he demanded sexual favours, said it went with the job. I cried, begged him to treat me as a simple servant, not as a kept woman. He threatened to have his valet beat me. So I gave in.' She turned her face to the wall, coughed again, and began to weep.

Anne rose to comfort her. Bernard mouthed, 'No.' Anne hesitated, confused. Bernard signed, 'She's consumptive, perhaps syphilitic.' Anne sat down, feeling guilty, but thought that Bernard might know best.

In a short while, Claudette dabbed her eyes with a cloth and resumed her story. 'In the evening, the valet Denis took me to a room in the basement with thick stone walls. He left, then the marquis came. For hours he assaulted me, forced me to perform all kinds of unnatural acts. When I protested, he whipped me, said that a whore had no right to complain. The next day he did the same thing. He grew odd, said he would like to kill me. I thought for sure I was going to die. Later that day, the valet gave me some money and told me to leave. He warned me to keep my mouth shut. If I complained to the police, they wouldn't believe me. And the valet promised he'd punish me. I'd end up in the river, dead.'

'Where was the valet while the marquis was abusing you?'

'To judge from offhand remarks he made, I think he was watching it all. I don't know how.'

'Have you seen him since then?'

'No, I take care to avoid him. For the past two months I've been working here as a prostitute.' She slumped back in her chair, short of breath, exhausted.

'Did you see or hear anyone else in the marquis's house?' Anne was thinking that Lucie might be kept there.

'No, and that seemed strange. When I asked Denis, he said that the servants had the time off.'

'When the marquis said he wanted to kill you, was he angry about something you did? Had you provoked him?'

Claudette thought for a moment, her forehead creased with the effort. 'He didn't seem angry at all. I believe he expected to take pleasure from watching me die.'

Anne took a copy of Michou's sketch of Lucie from her pocket and showed it to Claudette. 'Have you ever seen this young woman, perhaps at the Palais-Royal?'

'Her face looks familiar.' Claudette studied the sketch, hesitated. 'Yes, she worked for a while at the millinery shop. I saw her later with Denis.'

'Have you heard if he has abused her?'

'No, I haven't. But then I haven't seen her in a month or more.'

'Do you know of any other women whom the marquis and his valet might have abused?'

'I've heard rumours about the marquis, that he has treated other women as he did me. But I don't know any names. His valet has a companion, a tough little woman named Renée. He wouldn't dare abuse her. She works in the Valois arcade and helps him recruit for his master and other rich men.'

'Who is Denis courting now?'

'I've heard that he has recently been seen with a young woman named Berthe. She's new to the business in Paris. You'll probably find her in the Valois arcade. She's unusually tall and strong, has raven black hair and a fair complexion, wears a dark red gown.' Claudette's voice had fallen to a hoarse whisper. She looked utterly dejected.

Bernard spoke up. 'You've been very helpful, Claudette. I think we should leave now.'

Anne took her hand, pressed a coin into it. 'I wish your life would take a turn for the better.'

'Do you think she told us the truth, Bernard?' Anne looked at him sideways. They had left the tavern and were walking toward the Palais-Royal.

'I think so. I suspect that Denis Grimaud and his marquis

are acting in a consistent pattern. And we'll know for certain if we can hear from more of their victims. It's late. Do you still wish to find the young woman Berthe?'

'Yes, by all means,' Anne said. They quickened their pace. Anne was struck by a change in Bernard. As a waiter, his manner was diffident, even servile. But this evening he moved with vigor. A hidden passion lighted up his eyes. She wondered how old he was. In the restaurant he looked and acted about forty. Tonight, she would have guessed he was ten years younger.

When they reached the Valois arcade, they found it crowded with men and women at various stages in the mating game.

'If Berthe's with Grimaud, we should be able to find her,' Anne remarked.

'And there they are!' Bernard pointed to a couple walking from the arcade into the garden. They rented chairs and sat side by side in the light of a nearby lamp. Their faces were fully visible. They began an earnest conversation.

Anne and Bernard took seats nearby among a diverse group facing Berthe and Grimaud. 'We'll try to read their lips without attracting their attention,' Anne whispered. 'Let's pretend to carry on a conversation between us while looking at them sideways. It will be difficult but we might catch snatches of what they say.'

As Claudette had said, Berthe was a tall, large-boned, and handsome young woman, rough though not vulgar in her manners, direct and simple in her speech. Her dark red gown was worn and patched. Necessity had forced her into prostitution. In her eyes Anne detected intelligence touched by anxiety.

'I went to the millinery shop today,' said Berthe to her companion, after a casual exchange. 'She has no work for me. I need money – more than I can earn selling myself there.' She made a contemptuous gesture toward the Valois arcade.

'Be patient, Berthe,' Grimaud said. 'I'm trying to find a position for you. Give me a few more days.'

'You've had "a few more days" before. This will be the last time.' She got up and walked briskly away.

A few minutes later, a foppish young man appeared and sat down in her place next to Grimaud. 'Denis, who was that handsome young tart? I've not seen her before. She must be

new to the Valois arcade. Would you introduce me?' The fop
spoke in a loud, bold voice.

'She lived in Amiens for years and recently came to Paris.
You don't need an introduction. Think of her as public property, like any whore. But take care, she's expensive and hard
to please, thinks of herself as an upstanding lady fallen upon
hard times, says her father was a heroic soldier in the king's
army. Unless she sees in you the prospect of a decent job,
she'll dismiss you with scorn.'

'Then I'll wait a week or two until she's had to play the
common tart and lost her pretensions.'

The two men rose from their chairs. Grimaud said to his
companion, 'Let's see what's available tonight.'

Anne and Bernard pieced together much of this conversation from what they could overhear and from reading lips.
The rest was possible to guess. The two men held women in
contempt, an attitude that was familiar to Anne. She had experienced it herself as a music hall entertainer in England and
it continued to incense her. She clenched her fists, swore
silently at their retreating backs.

Bernard leaned over and whispered, 'What's the matter,
Madame Cartier?'

'I'm too angry to talk about it, Bernard. I'd like to follow
Berthe.'

They set off for the Valois arcade. Berthe was standing at
the entrance to a brothel, a hand on her hip, attempting to
look seductive but appearing simply miserable. Finally, an
English gentleman approached her. They spoke for a minute,
then she nodded with a thin smile, and they went inside.

A wave of sadness and fatigue came over Anne. She turned
to Bernard, 'It's late, we can't do more tonight. I want to go
home.'

'I had better see you to the door.'

Anne's home at the provost's residence on Rue Saint-Honoré
was dark when she and Bernard arrived. Paul and Georges
would be spending the night in the highway patrol post at
Villejuif.

'Can I offer you tea, Bernard?'

He hesitated to reply, then agreed, adding, 'But I can't stay
long.'

They sat in a parlour near the front entrance. A young maid brought hot tea, fortified with a few drops of brandy, and withdrew.

Anne began, 'We haven't found even a trace of Lucie, but we've learned a lot about Denis Grimaud. He selects simple, comely, young country women, entices them with promises of good jobs, samples them, dresses and grooms them at the millinery shop, and delivers the best of the lot to the marquis, and perhaps to other aristocratic rakes. They abuse the women according to their perverted tastes, then Grimaud casts them off with a dire warning.'

'Yes,' agreed Bernard. 'I believe that Grimaud also promised Lucie a good job, not one in the kitchen – he lied to you. To judge from Claudette's experience, the marquis abused Lucie. But I wonder if he had Grimaud cast her off, as he did Claudette. I think we've come to the point of having to question the marquis.'

Anne paused to reflect. 'He would refuse to speak to us. This task should fall to my husband, Paul, perhaps in the course of a social visit.'

'In the meantime,' Bernard said, 'we should question other servants in the marquis's household who might have seen Lucie and would be more trustworthy than Grimaud. I'll return to my associates with this matter.' He finished his tea and rose to leave. 'I'll contact you as soon as I have more information.'

When the front door shut behind Bernard, a profound silence came over the house. Anne lingered in the parlour, sipping her tea. Her mind drifted over the events of the day and paused at the visit to Claudette. Her bleak, pallid face loomed up, accusing Anne.

Why had she listened to Bernard's warning and failed to heed the stirring of her heart? Because, Anne's mind replied, a compassionate gesture then could have brought on an illness that might endanger Paul, Georges, and others in this house.

Still, Anne's heart fretted, uneasy, over the prospect of young maids in the city. They were so vulnerable, their circumstances so precarious. Out of desperation they would put themselves in the hands of human predators and suffer great harm. There were hundreds if not thousands of Claudettes in Paris.

Anne slumped in her chair, her spirit sinking. She stared glumly into her cup.

'Will Madame be needing anything else?'

Anne sat up, gathered her wits. The maid who had served her and Bernard was at the open door. Suddenly, Anne realized that the hour was nearly midnight. The maid had been waiting for Anne to leave the parlour. Only then could the young woman retire. Her work next day would begin at dawn.

'No, that will be all. Thank you for the tea.' Yet for a long moment Anne gazed at the smiling, heavy-lidded maid in the doorway. She was the cook's niece from the country, perhaps sixteen and very pretty. Spontaneously, Anne asked, 'Are you happy here?'

'Oh, yes, Madame. You and the colonel are very kind. And I learn so much from my aunt and the other servants. This is a wonderful place.'

Anne felt immensely uplifted. 'Sleep late, my dear, I'll tell the cook that I kept you from bed. Good night.'

Seven
The Marquis's House

25 – 27 May

Two days after the visit to Claudette, on a fair, warm Sunday afternoon, Anne was alone in the garden, pacing impatiently back and forth on the paths among the roses. She was trying to recover her calm. She hadn't heard from Bernard who had promised to contact her.

Without the company of Paul and Georges, she was also prey to disturbing thoughts. Her search for Lucie had brought her deep into the lives of prostitutes. At quiet moments between household duties, she imagined herself in the degrading situation of Claudette and Berthe selling their bodies. She felt the contempt that society heaped upon them.

Now, suddenly, a painful memory surfaced in Anne's mind. Almost three years ago in Islington near London, Justice Hammer had falsely, maliciously condemned her, not only of assault upon a gentleman but also of lewd solicitation. A placard was hung on her chest declaring her a 'French whore'. She was paraded through the village market and tied to the scaffold, amid the insults and taunts of the crowd. Finally, Justice Hammer had cut off her long, golden hair. That was the darkest, the most humiliating moment of her life. Only the intervention of her friends had saved her from also being stripped and whipped.

A servant's steps roused Anne from her distress. He handed her a message from Bernard. She read it with relish.

> Disguise yourself as a common domestic maid and meet me in Notre Dame shortly before six o'clock in the evening

She banished her demons and hurried to her room to change.

Ten minutes before six Anne arrived at the west front of the cathedral, glanced quickly about to see if she had been followed. Grimaud was aware that she was investigating him and might try to thwart or even harm her. But now, reassured that she was safe, she entered the church. The light was low. She waited by one of the great pillars near the entrance and scanned the vast space. It was almost empty. Persons near the high altar at the far end seemed no larger than insects. They were preparing for an evening service at six.

'Madame Cartier.'

Anne nearly jumped out of her skin. Bernard had come from behind her.

'Sorry to startle you,' he said softly, as he escorted her down the main aisle to the transept. 'The marquis's cook will attend the service. I'll point her out. Afterward we'll follow her. Besides Grimaud, the cook is the only servant who lives in the house. She has a room off the kitchen. The other servants live outside and come in as needed.'

At the sound of the church bells a small congregation assembled in front of the high altar.

'There she is.' Bernard discreetly pointed to a short, stout, middle-aged woman entering by the north transept. She edged her way through the group to the front. Anne and Bernard also moved up to observe her closely. In contrast to many others who carried on private conversations or were otherwise distracted, the cook focused intently on the priest, especially when he delivered a brief homily. Fully engaged, she nodded to his exhortations, smiled at his bons mots.

Anne was not surprised when Bernard whispered in her ear, 'The cook is deaf.'

'I know,' said Anne. 'She's reading the preacher's lips.'

When the service ended, the cook left by the front entrance. Anne and Bernard followed her to the Rose d'Anjou, a wine tavern at the flower market.

Scarcely a five-minute walk from the cathedral, the tavern was a clean, decent, single room favoured by patrons of the market. The marquis's cook sat at a table by herself. With gestures she ordered a jug of wine and a lamb ragout.

'It's a meal she's accustomed to having here,' Bernard whispered.

Anne and Bernard waited until she was settled, then approached her. Fortunately, all the other tables were occupied. Anne signed to the cook, could they share her table. She cocked her head at a wary angle, and studied them carefully. Glancing around the room, she verified their need for two places, then moved over to free space for them. They also ordered the wine and ragout.

'How did you know I was deaf?' the cook signed to Anne, her eyes narrowing with suspicion.

'In church you were the only person paying attention to the homily – you were reading the priest's lips.'

The cook smiled tentatively. 'I'm happy to have company. My deaf friends aren't here tonight.'

The food and drink arrived and the conversation drifted from comments on the ragout, which was very tasty, to food in general, and then to the cook's own profession. Bernard, who could read the cook's lips with occasional help from Anne, fell into his usual nearly invisible mode and observed.

The cook explained that her father, a hearing man, had cooked for a noble family and had taught the craft to his daughter, deaf from birth. From her mother she had learned how to read and write. Thus equipped, she had managed to support herself after her parents died.

'How did you come to work for the Marquis de Bresse?' asked Anne.

Her expression darkened. She hesitated to reply. 'I cooked for a brothel in the Valois arcade. He was a frequent guest. When he mentioned needing a cook, the madam recommended me.'

Anne changed her tack. 'I hear gossip and rumours about him and his companions.'

The cook nodded. 'I dare not speak ill of him, or I'd lose my position. He finds my cooking to be satisfactory and my deafness to be convenient. Even if I wanted to, I could hardly spy on him or spread tales. He confines me to the ground floor of the house, mostly the kitchen, the pantry, and my own room. When he entertains in the dining room upstairs, he asks Grimaud to serve the meal and to clear the table.' She filled her glass, drank half of it.

Anne signaled the barman for more. 'From time to time the marquis must invite women to the house. Have you ever seen this one?' Anne handed the cook Michou's sketch of Lucie. 'I'm helping her mother to find her.'

The cook put aside her glass and studied the sketch, creasing her forehead with the effort. Then a mixture of surprise and concern came over her face. 'Yes, by chance I saw her. Over a month ago at midday, I had stepped out into the back garden for fresh air and sat in the arbor. Grimaud brought the girl through the garden to his rear entrance. They passed by without noticing me. She was a lively, pretty girl. Looked anxious. Grimaud had a firm grip on her arm.'

'Did you see her leave?'

'No, I didn't, but I probably wouldn't have. I'm usually in the kitchen or my room where I can't see people entering or leaving the house.'

'Grimaud claims that he never brought the girl there.'

The cook grimaced. 'I know what I saw. I'll not comment on Denis Grimaud.'

Anne understood from the rigid set of the cook's jaw that she thought ill of the valet.

Her meal finished, the cook signed that she would take leave of her companions. Having rejected Anne's offer to pay for her meal, she rose from the table, paid the waiter, and left the tavern.

'I believe her rather than Grimaud,' said Bernard. 'We know now that Lucie entered Bresse's house.'

'Could the marquis be holding her against her will?' Anne asked.

'He's a declared libertine and has no moral scruples,' Bernard replied. 'He must regard her, a prostitute, as belonging to a subhuman species, whose only value lies in the sexual pleasure that she offers. The police also care little for her or her kind. If the marquis were clever, he could do with her whatever he liked. Yes, he might be holding her.'

'Poor Lucie,' Anne declared. 'I'll inform my husband. We must act.'

The next morning near noon, Anne heard horses in her court-yard and looked out the window. Paul and Georges had returned from their inspection trip. She went to the front entrance to greet them. Georges set off on foot for the Palais-Royal to continue his systematic inquiry into the disappearance of prostitutes.

Paul embraced Anne with less vigor than usual, for he was tired and hungry and in low spirits. The situation in the countryside had worsened. Peasants had beaten a pair of estate stewards who had attempted to collect back rents and evict tenants.

'You're not going to solve those problems today, Paul. Cheer up. I've arranged a bath and a dinner for you.'

At two o'clock they sat down to eat. Anne patiently heard his complaints about landlords raising rents and fees and agitators stirring up trouble among the peasants. Finally, she waved a hand in protest.

'Sorry.' He smiled penitently. 'And what have you done while I was gone? Have you found any sign of Lucie?'

'Not yet,' replied Anne. 'With Bernard's help I've learned that Denis Grimaud enticed Lucie into the Marquis de Bresse's town house. The cook saw her enter. Lucie was probably abused and hasn't been seen since. According to the cook, Lucie could have left the house unobserved. Or she might still be there, dead or alive.'

While Anne spoke, Paul continued eating but listened

intently. When Anne finished her story, he laid down his knife and fork, leaned back, and reflected for a moment. 'I think you and I need to pay a visit to the Marquis de Bresse.'

The next day, Anne, Paul, and Georges approached the marquis's house on the Isle Saint-Louis, apprehensive as to the reception that they would receive. Paul had requested an invitation to tea, suggesting that they discuss the marquis's valet Denis Grimaud, implicated in a young woman's mysterious disappearance. When questioned, he had lied about certain important details.

The Comtesse de Beaumont was also concerned since the young woman was one of her tenants. Saint-Martin's message had ended with a warning: if the matter could not be resolved privately, then the police would become involved.

The marquis's response had been less than hearty, but he had agreed. Paul hadn't mentioned that he would bring his adjutant along and search the house.

Grimaud, clad in pink livery, opened the door and showed them into a nearby small parlour. 'I'll tell the marquis that you have arrived,' he murmured. For a moment, his bulging eyes held them in a cool, hostile gaze, then he left them standing.

'He's not a pretty fellow,' Paul said softly. 'His eyes are remarkable, quite intimidating. To judge from his expression, I'd say he resents being investigated.'

Anne shuddered. 'He's a man without scruples or pity. I hate to think of poor Lucie in his arms.'

In a whimsical mood she asked, 'What can this room tell us about the marquis?' The walls were painted a light yellow, free of decoration. The furnishings were remarkably simple – a half dozen wooden chairs and a table. A plain mirror hung on one wall, an ordinary clock on another.

'The parlour's appearance is deceptively modest,' Paul ventured to say. 'Like the exterior of the house, it masks its owner's hedonistic nature, his hidden wishes and desires. The marquis surely could raise the money to build and furnish his residence as lavishly as the great aristocratic magistrates who are his neighbours on this island. Think of Hôtel Lambert or Hôtel de Lauzun, how they reflect their owners' high office, their great power and magnificence. But instead the Marquis de Bresse keeps a low profile to the outside world, even hides himself. As a dedicated libertine, his main principle in life is to please himself, not to impress others.'

Anne heard steps nearing the door and cautioned Paul. In the next moment the valet entered. 'The marquis will see you. Follow me.'

Georges whispered to Paul, 'I'll wait here, Colonel, call me when you are ready to search.'

The valet led Anne and Paul into a hall, up a staircase to the next floor. At a doorway he scratched lightly. A faint voice came from within. The valet opened and motioned the visitors into the marquis's study. Bresse sat behind a highly polished brown mahogany writing table. His ivory-headed cane rested in a stand nearby. He rose to his feet and advanced with his mincing gait to greet them.

Anne recalled him from their fleeting encounter nine days earlier at Café de Foy. To judge from the hostile look in his eyes, he also recognized her. Even in private, he dressed with refined taste. Today, he wore a light green silk dressing gown, fastened at the waist with a dark green sash. His long, sandy hair was gathered at the back of his neck and tied with a dark green cord. He gave his visitors his characteristic ironic smile.

After seating them, the marquis ordered his valet to bring tea and sweetmeats. A casual conversation ensued between the marquis and Paul. The tea arrived. Grimaud poured, offered the sweetmeats, and withdrew.

This interlude gave Anne the opportunity to survey the study. In contrast to the parlour, this room was sumptuously furnished and decorated for the marquis's pleasure. Shelves of leather-bound, gold-embossed books lined one wall. In the middle of another wall was a fireplace. On its pale green marble mantel stood small white marble replicas of ancient Roman erotic statues. A French door opened to a balcony over the back garden. On the opposite wall, paintings and engravings depicted satyrs and nymphs in erotic scenes.

Bresse followed the trail of her eyes. 'Does my taste in art upset you, Madame Cartier?'

Her feelings of displeasure had registered on her face. But she assured him, 'Don't mistake me for a prude, Monsieur. Erotic art is like pepper, best taken in small doses. And they are most enjoyable when they are suggested, rather than blatantly proclaimed. In a few words, Monsieur, the erotic excess of your collection is simply too vulgar for my taste.' She observed with satisfaction that Bresse flinched slightly at the insult.

'And for mine, as well,' added Paul, heading off a defensive riposte from the marquis. 'But we've come here on other business, the missing young woman Lucie Gigot. At the request of Comtesse Marie de Beaumont, my wife has attempted to find Lucie, who disappeared more than a month ago.' He gestured for Anne to continue.

She briefly described the steps she had taken thus far, then remarked, 'Lucie was last seen entering this house with your valet, Denis Grimaud, who had promised her a position in your service. I find it troubling that he had earlier denied bringing her here.'

Paul waved a hand. 'I might add that Grimaud has solicited other women in a similar fashion. And they too have disappeared.'

These remarks about his valet didn't seem to perturb the marquis. 'Monsieur Grimaud is free to enjoy women in his room. I'm sure he pays them, so they have no reason to complain. You haven't accused him of forcing your Lucie or any other women to come here. I don't understand his denial. It wasn't necessary. Have you any evidence that he harmed this Lucie or any other prostitute?'

'At the present time, such evidence, if it exists, is beyond our reach, Monsieur. We would need your permission to look for it.'

'Oh, do you wish to search my house? How extraordinary!'

'I can appreciate your reluctance. But an unofficial, informal visit by my adjutant Georges Charpentier, my wife Madame Cartier, and myself, especially to your valet's quarters, might be more palatable to you than a search by Inspector Quidor and his agents.'

'You have put the matter in a clearer light, Colonel. You may come tomorrow morning, if you wish.'

'I prefer to search today,' Paul said firmly, 'since we've already disturbed you. I'll call my adjutant from the parlour.'

'While you hunt for your elusive Lucie,' said the marquis in an amiable, mocking tone, as if he enjoyed the prospect of seeing them look foolish, 'I'll be in my study. You will find nothing here that should concern the police. Nonetheless, my valet will show you around.'

They started on the garden side of the house, where Grimaud had a private entrance. His quarters consisted of a large ground-floor room with a sleeping alcove. In the centre of the room was a plain table with simple wooden chairs. A large, nonde-script cabinet stood against a wall. The room seemed curi-ously empty, devoid of any expression of personal taste – no books or mementoes in sight, no pictures on the walls. If Grimaud had a home at all, it wasn't here but in the brothels of the Palais-Royal.

Georges questioned him at the table. Anne and Paul sat to one side.

'You were seen escorting Lucie into the house through this back door. Why did you deny it when Madame Cartier asked you?'

'At the time I thought it was none of her business. I know better now. Yes, I did bring Lucie here. Like other female visi-tors, she came willingly. We made love in my room. I paid her. And she left.'

'How long was she here?'

'An hour or so.'

'We will now examine your room.'

Georges and Anne searched the cabinet's contents, a few ordinary suits and other clothes, shoes. No bloodstains. Saint-Martin studied a drawer in the table and found nothing remark-able – only a small amount of money and writing supplies.

Paul whispered to Anne, 'Where's his money?'

Anne replied in a whisper, 'Sylvie has heard that he gambles it away.'

Together they examined the floor and the walls for secret compartments. They still found no bloodstains, hidden messages, or any other evidence of violence. Nor, for that matter, of Lucie's presence.

'Show us the basement,' Saint-Martin ordered Grimaud.

They descended a stone stairway between the valet's quar-ters and the kitchen. It led to storerooms for wine, dried fruits and vegetables, and spare furniture and utensils. Again, no evidence of Lucie. Grimaud was about to lead them back upstairs when Anne glanced behind a faded fabric screen.

'What's this?' she called out and pulled the screen away, revealing a heavy oak door.

'A few empty rooms,' Grimaud replied reluctantly, momentarily embarrassed.

'Let's see them,' demanded Saint-Martin.

The valet unlocked the door and showed the visitors in. Most of the rooms were indeed empty. But one room housed a small laboratory.

Grimaud explained, 'The marquis belongs to a society of amateur chemists. Lest the gossips and rumourmongers accuse him of alchemy, black magic, and the like, he prefers to keep his experiments secret.'

While Saint-Martin gathered more information about the marquis's experiments, Anne studied the empty rooms, particularly the largest of them. Its walls were built of thick blocks of cut stone, studded with hooks for tools or utensils. Long, thick oak beams supported a rough wooden ceiling.

Georges joined her. 'This room goes back to the last century. It might have been used for slaughtering animals and fowl and to clean fish.' He pointed to a large drain in the centre of the room that could serve to rid the floor of offal and other debris. 'A sewer must run beneath us.'

'Still no sign of Lucie,' Anne remarked, frankly relieved.

They went upstairs to the first floor. The door to the marquis's study was open. He was sitting comfortably at his writing table and called them in, then taunted them. 'Look under the table. Your Lucie might be there.'

For a few minutes, the three visitors surveyed the room without detecting anything suspicious. Anne would have liked to ask the marquis to move, so that she could search the drawer in his table and read his secret papers. But this didn't seem to be the right occasion.

'Would you like to see the rest of my house while you are here?' he asked, with noticeable irony in his voice. 'I'll show it to you myself.'

'Yes,' Saint-Martin replied evenly. 'That would be helpful.'

The marquis left his valet in the hall outside the study and led the visitors into the dining room, a jewel of the Rococo style, the walls cream-colored with gilded floral decoration, the window drapes forest green. In one wall was a dumbwaiter to bring food up from the kitchen. Adjacent to the dining room was a lovely, comfortable sitting room. Still no sign of Lucie's presence.

On the second floor they visited the marquis's bedroom overlooking the garden, checked his wardrobe of expensive, well-tailored silk suits, and examined a guest room. At a locked door the marquis balked. 'This is my private cabinet. Only my friends may enter it.'

Saint-Martin frowned. 'What do you have hidden in there?'

The marquis yielded. 'I'll open the door so that you can see that the young lady isn't hiding in the room, but you may not enter.' He unlocked the door and pulled it open. Saint-Martin nodded, and Georges quickly surveyed the interior.

'She's not here,' he said. The marquis locked the door. As they walked on, Georges whispered to Anne and Paul, 'I saw enough to recognize a large erotic collection.'

Anne turned to her husband. 'Why didn't you defy the marquis and just walk in and search the room?'

'We aren't the morals police,' Paul replied, 'and I don't want to appear high-handed without good reason. The aristocracy, especially the magistrates in Parlement, charge the royal government with despotism and with arbitrarily violating traditional rights. We have come simply to find out if Lucie is here.'

They came to the stairway to the attic. The marquis addressed Anne. 'You will soil your gown if you go up there. It's quite dirty.'

'Thank you for the warning, but I'll have a look anyway.'

They climbed up and discovered a large storeroom of old, dusty furniture, trunks, spare roofing tiles, and pieces of guttering. They were about to descend when Georges pointed to a closed door at the far end of the room, barely visible behind a giant armoire. 'We should check that room too.'

The marquis shrugged, but he unlocked the door.

The room was cleaner than the rest of the attic and contained a bed, a few chairs, and a table. A large mirror hung on one wall. The other walls were bare. A large window admitted late morning sun rays into the room and offered a view over the Seine to the Quai de la Tournelle on the Left Bank.

'What's the purpose of this room?' Saint-Martin asked the marquis.

'I never come up here,' replied Bresse. 'You will have to ask my valet. He might use it as a guest room.'

Anne pulled the bed away from the wall and studied the exposed floor. Something glittered there. She bent down and picked up a piece of jewelry, a little gold cross on a thin broken gold chain.

She showed the piece to Georges and Paul, then pulled Michou's sketch of Lucie from her bag. 'Look,' Anne said, 'this is the necklace that Comtesse Marie gave to Lucie on the occasion of her confirmation. She would not have left this house without it. Examine the broken chain. It was torn from her.' Anne handed the necklace to her husband. Bresse looked on, a distressed expression on his face.

'Monsieur,' said Saint-Martin, 'shall we return to your study? We must discuss this discovery.' He put the necklace into his pocket.

Anne, Paul, Georges, Grimaud, and the marquis gathered in the study. The marquis leaned back, irritably stroking his chin. As Saint-Martin began to question Grimaud, the atmosphere in the room grew tense. The valet sat on the edge of his chair, attempting to appear nonchalant.

'Earlier, Monsieur, you said that you and Lucie had sexual intercourse in your room for about an hour or so. Explain how her necklace found its way into the attic room.'

Grimaud glanced toward the marquis, who was staring at him. 'Well, she stayed in that room, rather than return to her home late at night.'

'So she was here all day with you, not just for an hour or so, as you previously said.'

The valet nervously turned again toward the marquis, whose ironic smile had vanished. His lips were straight and tight.

'Correct,' Grimaud stammered.

'And now you will most likely claim that Lucie left this house early the following morning.' Paul's voice was thick with doubt. He addressed the marquis. 'Can you see, Monsieur, that your valet's explanation lacks credibility? How shall we arrive at the truth?'

The marquis's frown had turned into an ugly scowl. 'The truth is, Colonel, that your Lucie isn't here. And you haven't discovered any evidence that she was mistreated. The young woman broke the chain herself, mislaid her necklace, and left without it.' He glared at Grimaud. 'My valet fears that he will be punished for bringing a prostitute into this house and keeping her overnight. His clumsy explanations are merely inept attempts to escape his guilt. I told him long ago to confine his whoring to his own room. For this and other reasons he shall hear severe words from me. So, Colonel, as far as I'm concerned that's the end of the affair. You must pursue your missing Lucie elsewhere.'

Eight

A Lost Necklace

28 May

At the house on Rue Traversine, Georges sat down for breakfast in the studio with Michou and Sylvie. For almost two weeks, together with their friends, they had diligently searched for Lucie. This morning they had to admit, sadly, that they couldn't find her.

Nonetheless, Georges felt proud of them. For they had also cast a wide net for news of other young women, associated somehow with the millinery shop, who had disappeared during the past year, under circumstances similar to Lucie's. With remarkable guile and a disarming manner, they had pulled useful information from many prostitutes who feared the police and would never willingly speak to them.

At a nod from Georges, Sylvie reported their findings. 'We received the names of several missing young women, besides Lucie and Yvonne Bloch. Then we verified and shortened the list to two additional possible victims, Antoinette Minard and Josephine Bourget. Both were penniless, attractive country women, new to the city and last seen with Grimaud. They disappeared about a month or more after Yvonne and before Lucie.'

'I assume,' said Georges, 'that Renée Gros knew them. Was she aware of their mysterious disappearance?'

'She knew them,' Sylvie replied. 'But she hadn't noticed that they were missing.'

With Sylvie translating, Michou added, 'The milliner Madame Tessier had also employed them. At first when we questioned her, she accused us of bothering people. "Mind your own business," she said, "or you'll be sorry." We told her anyway about Minard and Bourget. Her attitude changed. Their disappearance seemed to surprise, even disturb her.'

'How much do you think Madame Tessier knows?'

Michou and Sylvie exchanged glances, then signs. Sylvie replied. 'We can only guess that she might not know precisely what Grimaud was doing with these women.'

'And she might not want to know,' Michou signed. Sylvie translated and nodded.

'Why?' Georges asked.

Sylvie replied, 'Grimaud found out her secret and would expose her if she were to accuse him of wrongdoing. As a young woman in Lyons under a different name, she was convicted of theft from a millinery shop where she worked. After several years in prison, she moved to Paris, changed her name to Tessier, and started her own small millinery business. A few years ago, she moved into the new Valois arcade and prospered, even bought property near Château Beaumont.'

Georges tilted his head, puzzled. 'How could she "prosper" as a milliner? Honest women in that trade can barely earn a living.'

'Correct,' Sylvie agreed. 'Tessier has always earned extra money from vice, as a part-time prostitute when she was young in Lyons, and as a procuress in Paris, supplying choice, young, pretty girls to rich men. About a year ago, Grimaud discovered the scandals of her past life and has forced her to share her illicit business with him. As a result, her personal income has dropped and she's unhappy.'

'How did you find out all this about her?' Georges was beginning to grow skeptical.

'From the same person who probably told Grimaud, a woman who had been in prison with Tessier in Lyons and moved to Paris a few years ago. She now lives in misery. When Tessier refused her pleas for help, she became resentful.

She spoke to us while under the influence of too much brandy, then regretted it, begged us to tell no one, or Grimaud would punish her.'

'But,' signed Michou, 'we brought her here with the promise of a good meal. The cook is feeding her in the kitchen. She's probably finished by now. I'll fetch her.'

A few minutes later, Michou returned with a wizened, middle-aged woman with stringy white hair. When she saw Georges, she began to shake. He calmed her down with kind words and a copper coin. Her story repeated what Michou and Sylvie had told.

Then Georges asked her, 'How does Madame Tessier control her prostitutes?'

'She lends money to them, or if they happen to work for her in the millinery shop, she'll give them fashionable clothes, or drugs, or an advance on their salary – always at a high rate of interest. They are usually unable to repay her. She then warns them to obey her commands, sell their bodies, and surrender part of their income to her. Otherwise, she'll betray them to the duke's guard or the police.'

Michou added, 'These prostitutes become her slaves. Grimaud treats his women in the same way.'

Georges had heard enough. He thanked Sylvie and Michou. 'I shall have a serious talk with Tessier and find out what she really knows about these missing young women.' He picked up his hat and left for the Palais-Royal.

Accompanied by a young trooper, Georges stood outside the millinery shop pondering the approach he should take. Madame Tessier would not be easily intimidated. For a start, she must be paying the duke's captain of the guard to protect her, or he would have closed down her shop long ago. And her character was hard. Many years in the brutal environment of a prison and much exposure to the depraved conditions of the Palais-Royal had given her a thick skin, a slippery conscience, and, above all, a keen, if narrow perception of her own best interest.

Georges decided on a bold, brusque confrontation. He soon found an opportunity. Tessier was in the habit of closing her shop for an hour at about three o'clock in the afternoon and resting in her room upstairs. Promptly at three, she left the shop. Georges beckoned the trooper, and they followed her quietly. Georges gave her a minute, then knocked on the door.

There was no response.

'Open up, Madame. It's the police.'

The door opened a crack. Georges showed his identification.

'What do you want?' came a skeptical voice.

'I have questions for you concerning two missing young women, Minard and Bourget.'

'Go away. You don't have authority here. I'll open only for the duke's men.' She tried to shut the door. But Georges leaned his shoulder into it and burst it open. Madame Tessier went staggering back across the room and came to rest, fortunately, in an upholstered chair. Her bonnet was askew, her face purple with rage.

'How dare you!' she sputtered. 'The duke will hear of this outrage!'

'I've come here on the king's business to investigate a series of murders.' He was overstating the reach of the evidence thus far, but he was confident that further investigation would confirm his claim.

The trooper closed the door and Georges pulled up a chair facing the woman. 'Now let's speak seriously,' he said. 'A few months ago Antoinette Minard and Josephine Bourget were seen working in your shop. Tell me ...' Georges paused, looked her in the eye. 'Did Denis Grimaud bring them to you?'

'Well, what if he did?' Tessier replied, distracted, fussing with her bonnet.

Georges remained silent, staring grimly at her.

'Yes, he did. What of it?'

'How long did they work in your shop?'

'A couple of weeks. I had to let them go. Business was slack.'

'In other words, they owed you money and couldn't pay. You called Grimaud and he took them to a certain rich client . . . as he had earlier taken Yvonne Bloch and later was to take Lucie Gigot. The client's evil reputation frightened them, so Grimaud promised them well-paying jobs. If they refused, he threatened to report them to the police as prostitutes. Right?'

Tessier's composure remained intact, except for her eyes.

They flickered anxiously. She began to shrug her shoulders. 'How should I . . .?'

Georges cut her off. 'An eyewitness saw Grimaud take Lucie into the Marquis de Bresse's house. She was never seen again. We believe that the other three young women suffered the same fate. Are you beginning to see how you fit into the picture?'

She now looked confused as well as anxious.

'You helped Grimaud entice four young women to their deaths. Neither you nor he killed them, but you were accomplices, fellow conspirators. For such a monstrous crime you will pay dearly . . . Unless you cooperate with me.'

'I honestly didn't know what Grimaud was up to. When I asked about the women, he always said they hadn't liked the jobs he had found for them, and they had gone back to where they came from. I first became suspicious when Lucie's mother arrived in my shop looking for her. From rumours about the marquis, I suspected that he might have harmed her. And Grimaud must have known. Then Madame Cartier began to investigate her disappearance.' Tessier now looked distraught and dabbed a kerchief at her eyes.

'Why would Grimaud have known?'

'Because he lives in the marquis's house and is an inquisitive bastard, loves to pry into other people's business.'

'As he has pried into yours. I too know about the prison in Lyons and your part-time prostitution. He has a hold on you. But if you don't break loose from him, you will share in his ruin.'

Tessier began to cry, shaking her head in despair.

Georges studied her. Was she putting on an act? He couldn't be sure.

'What can I do?' she asked piteously. Her tears had created gullies in the heavy cover of cosmetics on her face, revealing pox scars.

'I'll write a summary of this conversation and you will sign it. I may have more questions for you later. In the meantime, you will no longer do business with Grimaud. Do you understand?'

She nodded, mumbling her agreement.

Georges wasn't sure of its sincerity.

*   *   *

That afternoon, back at the provost's residence on Rue Saint-Honoré, Anne sat restlessly in the shade of a tree in the back garden. The shifting, grey clouds in the sky above matched her mood. Yesterday's visit to the marquis's house had frustrated and angered her. True, she had found Lucie's necklace. But the marquis dismissed the discovery in his typically supercilious way. Recalling the incident, she struggled to keep her feelings under control. The porter's terrier came by, licked the hand that she extended to him, then lay at her feet. Anne felt a little better and sent a servant to fetch Paul and Georges. They should have a discussion.

'I don't believe the marquis,' she began, when they had pulled up chairs. 'I'm convinced that Lucie never left Bresse's house. Something dreadful has happened to her. She would not have abandoned her confirmation necklace in that attic room, any more than her diary and letters in her room on Rue Saint-Roch.'

Paul nodded. 'I share your doubts. Under the best of circumstances, the word of a libertine such as the Marquis de Bresse should not be trusted. But our doubts aren't enough to bring him before a magistrate. He would want convincing evidence that a crime had been committed. He could also argue that, in fact, Lucie might have left the marquis's house, physically unharmed. She might now be drugged, hidden in a brothel somewhere in Paris, her diary and her necklace notwithstanding.'

'Your magistrate's theory might be true, Paul, but that doesn't make me feel better. What can we do now?' She leaned forward and petted the terrier. It rolled over for more.

Paul cautioned her. 'Lucie's case must yield to an order from the lieutenant general. He is sending us to Saint-Denis to inspect the highway patrol post and the surrounding area. It's one of the districts where he expects trouble this summer. We must leave early tomorrow morning.'

'How long will you be gone?' asked Anne, disappointed though not surprised. She knew that a missing prostitute could have little claim on the scant resources of the police.

'A day at least, more likely two,' he replied. 'While we're away, learn as much as you can about the marquis and his valet. If you find strong evidence of a crime against Lucie, take it to Inspector Quidor. Then she will become his problem as well as ours.'

'I shall also speak to the cook again,' Anne said, 'and ask Michou and Sylvie to check a few brothels where Lucie might be kept.'

Georges added, 'Eventually, we should investigate the Bresse chateau, where the marquis's parents live. It's near Paris. If he has abducted Lucie, he might have secretly moved her there.'

'For now, Georges, instruct a pair of troopers to visit the estate and inquire among the servants for a missing young woman, reported to be travelling in that direction. Give them Michou's sketch of Lucie.' Paul breathed out a sigh of hope. 'If we cast our nets widely enough, we may catch a clue.'

'Michou, Sylvie, and I have caught a few clues in the Palais-Royal, sir.' Georges described their discovery of two more missing prostitutes. 'Madame Tessier's confession to me this morning strengthens the theory that the disappearances of the four young women were not isolated events but part of a criminal conspiracy. The Marquis de Bresse and his valet are at the heart of it.'

That evening, while Paul and Georges prepared for their trip, Anne dressed in a simple muslin gown and scarf, tied on a bonnet, and went to the cathedral for the six o'clock service. As she had hoped, the marquis's cook arrived, participated in the service in her usual attentive way, and left for supper at the Rose d'Anjou.

Anne followed her and, after a suitable interval, entered the tavern. The cook sat at a rear table with a slightly younger woman. The cook looked up, recognized Anne with a smile, and beckoned her.

In the introductions, Anne learned that the cook's companion was her niece and best friend. Several days a week, she left her room in the Marais to clean the marquis's house and to help in the kitchen. The maid was a hearing person but had learned the common Parisian sign language from her aunt.

Over a bowl of pea soup, the cook remarked in conspiratorial tones, 'I told my niece about meeting you here last night.'

Anne smiled, but she feared that her conversations with the cook might come to the ears of Grimaud and the marquis, who would harm the cook and her niece.

'You might be interested in what she has to say,' the cook went on. 'She had dinner with me today in the kitchen and told me about an interesting conversation she overheard.' The cook gestured to the maid to continue.

'When I work at the house,' the maid said, 'I pretend I'm hard of hearing. The marquis leaves me alone, hardly notices me. Well, early this afternoon, just before dinner, I was cleaning upstairs in the hall outside his study. Monsieur Grimaud went in to speak to the marquis and didn't shut the door. The marquis was upset about something. Grimaud had hardly entered the room when the marquis raised his voice – I've rarely heard him do that.

'"You've become careless, Grimaud," he said. "The colonel's wife found the girl's necklace in the attic room. You should have made sure that not a trace was left of her visit to this house nor of any other women that you brought here. I am very displeased, do you understand?" Grimaud then replied, "I'm sorry, it won't happen again, certainly not tonight." "I'm sure it won't," said the marquis, "because you will not have the opportunity. I'll make my own arrangements. You see, I've been studying my financial accounts and have concluded that you've been cheating me. You are herewith discharged from my service and must leave this house within an hour. I'll bring this matter to the financial police tomorrow." That's all I heard,' said the maid. 'I guessed that the conversation was nearly over, so I hurried away.'

This news stunned Anne. She reflected for a moment on the likely repercussions, then asked the two women, 'How has Grimaud reacted to his dismissal?'

The cook had followed the conversation closely. Now she signed, 'After that conversation in the study, Grimaud came down to the kitchen. His face was red, he was so upset. He told me that I should prepare supper for a female guest. The marquis would arrange somehow to have it served. I must have looked surprised. Usually, Grimaud serves the meal. He turned on me as if I were the cause of his misfortune. "Stupid cow!" he shouted. "I have just left the marquis's service and will move out of the house in the next few minutes".'

The cook met Anne's eye and signed with careful emphasis. 'I'm to keep away from the house until tomorrow.'

'How will you manage?' Anne asked.

'I usually spend the evening here at the tavern, play cards with friends, then sleep in my niece's room. I followed the same procedure when your young woman came here.'

Anne's curiosity about the evening's female guest had grown to the point that she considered lurking near the marquis's house until the guest arrived. But she couldn't see how that would advance her search for Lucie. It might be a better use of time to follow Grimaud. His resentment at being discharged might persuade him to reveal the marquis's secrets, including what happened to Lucie.

Anne asked the cook, 'When did Grimaud leave the house?'

'A couple of hours ago,' the cook replied.

'I'll try to find him. I still hope to save Lucie. You both have been very helpful. On my way out I'll pay for your supper. Please keep what we've said confidential. Enjoy the rest of the evening.'

As Anne paid the barman, she noticed that the cook was already dealing out a deck of cards.

About eight o'clock Anne reached the Palais-Royal. There was an outside chance that she might find Grimaud and follow him. He was probably still pursuing Berthe, the reluctant young prostitute in the dark red gown. Anne recalled that she worked at a brothel above the Valois arcade.

At the brothel's entrance in the arcade, a knot of prostitutes and potential customers had gathered to negotiate, blocking Anne's way in. One of the men noticed her, began giving her side glances, then winks. She backed away and waited until the group dispersed.

While no one was watching, she quickly climbed a flight of stairs to the brothel's door. The porter gave her a searching look, then admitted her to a parlour and agreed to announce her to the madam in charge.

Seizing the opportunity, Anne appraised her surroundings. The door was open, allowing her glimpses of a large well-appointed room where the women and their customers gathered for drinks and food and then dispersed. This was her first visit to a brothel, but she had heard enough about such establishments from acquaintances to realize that conditions in them varied greatly. Thus far, this one at least seemed clean and well-managed.

In a few minutes the madam arrived, traces of curiosity and wariness in her eyes. A large, agile, middle-aged woman with black flashing eyes and a steady gaze, she inspired confidence. Her beauty had faded, but she had gained poise from years of adroitly managing men and women at a contemptible activity in a sublegal environment.

'What brings you here?' she asked, a note of skepticism in her voice.

'I'd like to speak to Berthe. I'm searching for a missing person whom she might know.'

'She didn't come in tonight. Sent a message that her father was ill.'

'Was Monsieur Grimaud here earlier in the evening?' Anne was confident that the valet would be known at the brothel.

'Yes, he too was looking for Berthe, but he's not welcome here. I don't allow my girls to deal with him, and I've warned Berthe in particular. If you need to talk to him, you will probably find him in the arcade, trying to pick up a girl.' The madam had begun to look uneasy. 'Why are you asking about him? Are you from the police?'

'No, I'm working for the Comtesse de Beaumont, trying to find one of her tenants, a young woman called Lucie, Lucie Gigot. Berthe might know her. Lucie could have worked here for a while.' Anne showed the madam the sketch of the young woman. 'She was last seen in the company of Monsieur Grimaud several weeks ago. He took her into the house of the Marquis de Bresse.'

The madam seemed to blanch beneath her rouge. 'I recall her, a simple, pretty, young woman. I got her through the millinery shop. She didn't stay long. Thought I was too demanding and didn't pay her enough, so she left. She didn't know what was good for her. I pay as much as I can and still provide a clean, safe house, medical services for my girls, protection from the police.'

Anne raised an eyebrow. 'How do the police threaten you? I thought they tolerated brothels that operated within certain limits of decency.'

'The duke's guards who patrol the arcades demand bribes from me. If I weren't able to pay, they would invent an excuse to close this place, arrest me and the girls, and turn us over to the Paris police. The lieutenant general would confine us to a workhouse like the Salpêtrière.'

'How unfair!' Anne exclaimed with genuine sympathy, having personally experienced injustice at the hands of Mr Hammer in Islington.

The madam agreed with a shake of her head, then went on. 'I warned Lucie that she would be exposing herself to great danger if she worked on her own in the arcades. The police would pick her up unless a shark like Grimaud got to her first. Unscrupulous men easily fool young country women like Lucie who are often poor, hungry, and desperate. The marquis pays generously, presents a charming appearance to entice such women, but he acts like a monster when he's aroused. He believes that he can do whatever he likes to a prostitute as long as he pays and doesn't kill or maim her. I don't allow any of my girls to go to him nor to any gentlemen like him. A girl who broke my rule would come back here, beaten or in shock, useless to me.'

Anne thanked the madam for much useful information and advice. At the door the madam said with sincerity in her voice, 'If you find Lucie, say that I think of her. She's welcome back for a visit.'

At the foot of the stairs, Anne took a deep breath, arranged the scarf over her shoulders, then stepped out into the roiling crowd in the arcade. She was still looking for Grimaud. After a few minutes she saw his foppish acquaintance in conversation with a prostitute. Anne lingered at a distance, increasingly uncomfortable in these surroundings. Men brazenly scanned her. One elderly intoxicated gentleman asked her price.

'More than you could afford,' she replied and turned her back to him.

Finally, the fop and the prostitute broke off negotiations. Before he could approach another woman, Anne hurried up to him.

'May I have a word with you, Monsieur?'

Taken by surprise, he took a step back, his eyes wide, astonished. 'Who are you?' he exclaimed. For a moment he stared at her. Then he regained his footing. 'You look familiar. You've been asking questions about Lucie.'

'Could we get away from this crowd?' Anne asked. Passersby were jostling them.

He pointed toward the garden. They found chairs and sat down.

'I'm looking for Denis Grimaud,' she began. 'This afternoon, the Marquis de Bresse discharged him and ordered him out of the house. I want to talk to him. I've just learned at a brothel that he was here an hour ago but seems to have disappeared.'

The fop nodded. 'I spoke to him then. He was very angry but wouldn't talk about it. Now I know why. What had he done?'

Anne ignored the question. 'Was he with a woman?'

'Yes, with the little wild one.'

'Who?'

'Renée. She's his partner in a manner of speaking. They left the Palais-Royal together.'

Anne was relieved to learn that Grimaud's partner for the evening was not Berthe. She encouraged the fop to carry on. He described Renée as a little younger than Anne's age, and much smaller. 'A fearless little firebrand,' he called her. 'She lives in a room near the Louvre and helps Grimaud find healthy, attractive young women for rich men. Since the marquis has thrown him out, he'll probably seek refuge with Renée.' He waved a hand in warning. 'But you wouldn't want to meet him there tonight. He'll still be in a foul mood. And Renée might not welcome him. They're companions, but I doubt that they like each other. You might find yourself in the midst of a fight.'

This new light on the relationship between Grimaud and Renée intrigued Anne. In the morning she would approach 'the little firebrand' first, then pursue Grimaud.

For this evening, Anne decided that she had done as much as she could. The fop gave her directions to Renée's room. Anne thanked him and rose from the bench. Before she could leave, he took her hand. 'Wait,' he said. 'May I buy you a drink?' He had the look of desire in his eyes.

'No,' she replied, gently but firmly withdrawing her hand. 'You will have to find someone else.'

Nine
Missing Persons

After breakfast, Paul and Georges went off on their mission. Anne then dressed in common street clothes and set out for the address near the Louvre that the fop had given her. She hoped to find Grimaud's companion, Renée, the wily, odd little prostitute.

The fop had said that she lived in an old, shabby building on Rue Payenne, a short, narrow street off the Place du Palais-Royal. On the ground floor was a small, seedy tavern. Anne peeked in. The bar occupied one side of the room. On the other side were a few tables and benches. Stairs at the back of the room led to the upper floors.

She joined a line of women at the bar, buying wine for the day. While waiting her turn, she studied the portly, red-faced, jolly-looking barman. He chatted easily with his customers, a couple of whom went upstairs with their wine. Anne grew anxious. She would stand out as a stranger in this place and arouse suspicion.

'New in the area?' the barman asked in an affable voice and still smiling. But his eyes had narrowed and searched her closely.

'Yes,' she replied with the Norman accent that she had learned as a child from her Huguenot family in England. 'I'm looking for a young woman, Lucie, an acquaintance of mine from the country. She moved to Paris a few months ago. Worked in this area.' From her bag Anne drew out Lucie's sketch and showed it to him.

He held it up, nodded with approval. 'I can't say that I've ever seen her. Still, in the course of a few months I serve wine to more women, even pretty ones, than I can remember.' He paused, gave Anne a piercing look, and said, 'Now Renée upstairs knows a great number of young, pretty women. If you'd care to get into her line of work, she might be able to help you.'

Anne tilted her head, put on a puzzled expression.

He leered at her and said, 'The oldest profession in the world. Giving pleasure to gentlemen and getting paid for it.'

'I see,' said Anne noncommittally. 'How can I meet her?'

The barman rubbed his chin, called upon his memory. 'She bought wine from me a half hour ago and took it to her room. She should still be there.'

'Is she alone?' Anne wanted to speak to Renée apart from Denis Grimaud.

'A gentleman often visits her, but he left just before you came. Yes, she should be alone.' With a wave of his hand he directed Anne to the stairs. 'Go to the top floor. Turn right.'

She climbed the stairs with growing trepidation. Her mind conjured up the image of a small, wiry young woman of loose morals and wild temperament. The fop had called her 'a fire-brand of a girl'. How could one pry useful, perhaps compromising information from such a person?

Anne thought it best not to appear prim. So she loosed the kerchief from her shoulders and tied it around her waist, offering a glimpse of her bosom. She took off her bonnet and allowed her blonde hair to fall free. She knocked hesitantly.

The door swung open, revealing a young woman with thick, black curly hair, a gamin or a street urchin, much like Anne had imagined her. What Anne hadn't expected was the shrewd, disconcerting intelligence in Renée's bright staring eyes. She was probably twenty-five, but her thin, pale green silk house dress revealed the slim body and small breasts of an adolescent girl.

'What do you want?' Her tone was unfriendly, her posture tense, defensive, as if expecting trouble. But as she swiftly scanned the visitor, she seemed to lower her guard.

Anne felt encouraged to say, 'I'd like to ask a few questions concerning an acquaintance of mine, who came to the city looking for work. I've heard that you know the situation for young women at the Palais-Royal better than anyone.' Anne used her Norman accent and simple, natural gestures.

'Come in,' said Renée, giving Anne a thin smile. 'The room's a mess, but it never gets better than this.'

It was a large, rather comfortable old room. The walls needed paint, the plaster was cracked. But morning sunlight poured through a pair of dirty glass windows. A third window was open. A woman's newly laundered blouse and an apron hung outside. The remnants of breakfast still cluttered a large battered table in the middle of the room. Anne's eye lit upon a pistol resting on the mantel above the hearth. In the sleeping alcove was a jumble of blankets, pillows, and bedclothes.

Renée offered Anne a chair at the table. 'Well, what do you want to know?'

Anne displayed Michou's sketch of Lucie. 'Have you seen this young woman? She was last seen entering the house of the Marquis de Bresse more than a month ago.'

Renée's eyes widened, her lips parted. 'That's Lucie!' she exclaimed. 'I liked her. A lively, cheerful girl, too simple and trusting to last long in Paris. Denis – he's my partner – he tried to find her a job. The best he could offer was in the marquis's kitchen, and she didn't want it. Last seen . . .?' Renée repeated Anne's words, her brow furrowed with confusion. 'Do you mean she never left the marquis's house?'

'If she had, wouldn't you have heard of her? She would have returned to the Palais-Royal. Had nowhere else to go.'

Renée became oddly still, reflecting. 'Denis had me secretly collect her things, so that she could escape from her landlord who claimed she owed rent. I thought that she went home.' There was a tone of doubt in her voice.

'No, she didn't. I've heard from her mother.' Anne paused, lowered her voice, affected a naive concern. 'You don't think that the marquis could have done her harm, do you?'

A cloud appeared on Renée's brow, her eyes darkened. 'There's always that risk for women like us. The men we serve are a mixed lot. Some are generous and kind, most are rutting pigs, a few others like the marquis are vicious brutes who should be . . .'

She hesitated, as if unsure how much to say to a stranger. Finally she remarked, 'There are scary rumours about the marquis. Recently, a couple of women have asked me and others I know whether we were missing any of our acquaintances who were last seen going to the marquis's house? When we discussed the question, we could think of a few – like Lucie. If I want to say any more on the subject, where can I find you?'

Anne didn't dare give her home address – the residence of the Provost of the Royal Highway Patrol. So she said, 'Bernard, a waiter at the Café de Foy, knows me.'

'What's your name? I forgot to ask.'

'Anne, Anne Cartier.' She rose from the table, shook hands with Renée, and left her on the landing, pensive, watching Anne descend. She had the strong impression that something weighed heavily on Renée's mind.

Better informed by her visit with Renée, Anne now wanted to meet Grimaud. He most likely resented having been forced to leave Bresse's service. He might be willing to speak more freely about Lucie's fate. If confronted, he wouldn't want to incriminate himself, but he might implicate the marquis in whatever harm was done to Lucie.

With help from a watchman, Anne found Grimaud outside the puppet theatre in the Camp of the Tatars, a low, temporary gallery of wooden shops and stalls, at the palace end of the garden. Benoit the puppet master, a friend of Anne's, was playing a farce with hand puppets to catch the interest of passersby. Among the small group of the curious who had gathered to watch was Grimaud and a young woman. To judge from her plain woolen dress and stout leather shoes, she was fresh from the country. The puppets fascinated her. Her thin, pretty face glowed with pleasure. Grimaud hardly paid any attention to the show. He was studying her from top to toe.

At the end of his show, the puppet master invited the crowd to enter the little theatre for a presentation of Punch and Judy. A few joined him. Most shuffled away, among them Grimaud. But his female companion was reluctant to go with him. They exchanged words. Finally she left him and returned to the theatre. He walked on, not noticeably disappointed, his eyes already searching the milling crowd for other prey.

Anne closed in on him before he could attach himself to another female. 'May I speak with you, Monsieur Grimaud?'

He stopped, turned to her with a look of surprise. Then, recognizing her, he frowned. 'I have nothing more to say to you.' He began to walk away.

'Would you rather speak to Inspector Quidor?'

He stopped again, glared at her. 'What do you mean?'

'I know why Bresse discharged you yesterday and that he intends to accuse you of embezzlement today . . .' She paused, met his eye, and added, 'If he's still alive.' The words surprised her, simply came out of her mouth for no apparent reason.

Grimaud gasped, his jaw dropped. For a long moment he sputtered nonsense.

What an extraordinary reaction, Anne thought. It was as if the marquis's death preoccupied his mind precisely at that moment. Anne's remark must have seemed prescient and threatening. She pressed him, 'You no longer have any reason to conceal what he did to Lucie, have you? And why should you take *any* of the marquis's blame?'

His eyes drifted away from hers, inward. He was calculating his options. His reaction had begun to attract the attention of curious passersby. Anne pointed toward the garden. 'Shall we go to a more private place?'

He nodded, followed her to an isolated, shaded bench in the garden, and began to speak in a low, halting voice. 'I'd be a fool to tell you what happened. You would take my story to Inspector Quidor. He would hold me in the Châtelet and inform the magistrates. They would question the marquis, who would contradict me and accuse me of slander. Who do you suppose the magistrates would believe, me or him? I would be soundly whipped and put in the stocks. If I had sufficiently annoyed him, he might even hire a pair of thugs to throw me in the river. So, if you want the truth from me, you are going to have to pay dearly for it.'

Hard as it was to admit, Anne thought that Grimaud had a point. Still she couldn't bring herself to trust him even when he might be sincere. Paying him for telling the truth seemed out of the question. Grimaud might already regret even speaking to her.

Anne tried one last desperate question. 'Where's Lucie's body?'

'I have no idea.' His reply lacked conviction.

Anne sensed that Grimaud was regaining control of himself. He knew that without Lucie's body it would be difficult if not impossible to prove that she was dead, not to speak of murdered.

He rose from the bench. 'Our conversation, Madame Cartier,

can't be of much use to your Inspector Quidor.' With a slight bow, he turned and walked off in the direction of the Valois arcade.

For a few more minutes, Anne sat there, frustrated by the little she had learned. Suddenly, she felt profoundly depressed. She had grown fond of the young woman, despite her faults, and had hoped against hope that she might somehow have survived. Now that hope seemed vain. She buried her face in her hands and began to weep.

In the evening, Anne went again to the cathedral. She noticed that Bresse's cook seemed distracted, as did her niece who had come with her. Anne followed the pair to the Rose d'Anjou, gave them a minute to get settled at a table.

They were engaged in a lively exchange when Anne entered. Both of them beckoned her and together signed the news, 'The Marquis de Bresse has disappeared.'

Anne was stunned, then immediately recalled her impromptu remark to Grimaud. At the time his reaction appeared strange. It now seemed suspicious.

The cook continued the story. She had spent the night with her niece. This morning they had returned together to the marquis's house in time to prepare a late breakfast, as was the custom when there had been a guest. However, no one rang for the trays of coffee and bread.

Their concern mounted as the hours passed without the marquis or his guest appearing. As the niece went about the house cleaning as usual, she saw no sign of life. The door to the marquis's study was closed, as was that to his bedroom. Finally, with great trepidation, the niece tried the doors. The study was locked. She knocked. No answer. She tried the bedroom and found it empty.

She and her aunt then searched the entire house, but could not find either the marquis or his guest. The remains of last night's supper were still on the table. Oil lamps and candles had burned out. There was no sign of violence.

Near panic, the cook and her niece decided that for whatever reason the marquis and the woman had left during the night, perhaps for an orgy with friends. They agreed that the marquis would not want anyone to call the police into his house in his absence.

At the conclusion of her narrative, the cook asked, 'Did we do the right thing?' Her signing was so agitated that Anne could barely understand her question.

'Has the marquis ever done this before, abandoned the house and gone out carousing?' she asked.

The two women stared at each other with wordless questions. Finally the cook signed, 'Yes, occasionally. Once he and his valet went to the marquis's chateau for three nights when his parents were away. The men looked dreadful when they returned.'

The niece broke in, 'Someone told me that the marquis has a secret cottage outside the city for his orgies.'

That could be true, Anne thought, then said to the maid, 'Go back to the house, stay overnight with your aunt. Be sure all the doors are locked. I'll talk to Inspector Quidor in the morning. He'll know what to do. Then I'll get in touch with you. In the meantime the marquis might return.'

Anne was halfway home when she wondered who the marquis's female guest might have been. The valet told the brothel madam that he would pick up a girl in the arcade. After he was discharged, had he nonetheless sent her on to his former master? Or, had Bresse found another woman on his own? Who was she? Where was she now?

Ten

Evidence of a Crime

30 May

Anne waited restlessly in Inspector Quidor's ante-room in the Hôtel de Police, wishing she could discuss the meaning of Bresse's disappearance with Paul and Georges. Had the marquis and his female companion left the town house to carouse somewhere else? A plausible theory. But her doubts grew. Yesterday, Bresse was to report his disgraced, former valet to the police. The marquis's disappearance was suspiciously convenient for Grimaud.

When Quidor finally arrived, he was red-eyed, hadn't slept much. Ill-humoured, he snapped at his clerk. Then he saw Anne and brightened a bit, beckoned her into his office.

'The day's off to a bad start,' he complained. 'I spent the early morning hours in the morgue. We had fished a man out of the river. An ugly sight.' He went to the window, threw it open, breathed deeply, returned to his writing table. 'Madame Cartier, I think you have news for me. What is it?'

'Yesterday evening, I learned that the Marquis de Bresse had accused his valet of embezzling funds, ordered him out of the house, and threatened to report him to the financial authorities. But before the marquis could act, he has vanished.'

'Really!' the inspector exclaimed. He leaned forward, arms resting on the table. His eyes were heavy-lidded but focused intently on her.

'Yes, together with a female companion, most likely a young woman from the Palais-Royal, engaged for an evening's pleasure.'

'And how did you discover his absence?'

'I've spoken to Bresse's cook and her niece, a maid. They had found no sign of violence in the house.'

When she finished, he straightened up. 'Madame Cartier, have you considered that the marquis and the woman may have left the house to carouse elsewhere?'

'Yes, Inspector. I've looked into that possibility. The marquis's horse and carriage are still at home. And the local livery stables have had no contact with him. Of course, he and the woman could have walked to a nearby location. Your agents could ask the neighbors.'

'Good work, madame. I'll record what you've told me and pass it on to my agents.' He glanced at his list of appointments. 'Later in the day, I'd like to speak with the servants.'

'The cook is deaf, sir, and her niece seems to be rather simple. If you wish to question them, I'd be willing to translate.'

'I accept your offer.' He lowered his voice. 'Just between you and me, if Bresse were to vanish forever, it would be a very small loss to the country, even a blessing. Still, if he were the victim of a crime, we couldn't allow the perpetrator to go unpunished.'

'Don't you think that you should secure the house?' Anne asked in a deferential tone. 'Right now it's cared for by the middle-aged cook and her niece. There might be valuable property inside, not to speak of records that could be of interest to you, should the marquis be found dead.'

'Thank you for the suggestion, Madame Cartier.' Quidor gave her a gruff, good-natured smile. 'I'll assign a pair of agents to the house. Perhaps you could show them around and introduce them to the cook and her niece.'

'Gladly.' Anne was pleased that Quidor trusted her. Then she thought, why shouldn't he?

At the marquis's house, Anne introduced the agents to the two servants and gave them a tour of the house. The agents then made themselves comfortable at a table in the front parlour. One of them brought out a deck of cards.

Anne seized the opportunity to search again for traces of Lucie. The marquis's study was her prime target. The door was locked. She had set out this morning with burglar's tools that Georges had given her. Now she applied the skill he had taught her. It was a simple lock. She picked it easily, entered the study, and locked the door behind her. She didn't want to be disturbed.

She began with the writing table, quickly scanning the loose sheets of paper piled neatly on top. Nothing of interest. She studied the wide, flat drawer beneath the table. Locked. She picked it open and found a ring of keys, probably duplicates for all the locks in the house. The marquis could have hidden his secrets anywhere. She searched through the shelves of books lining the walls, looking for a box disguised as a book. She also tested the panels behind the shelves. Again, nothing. Finally, she went back to the writing table, pulled the drawer all the way out, and revealed a hidden compartment. One of the keys opened it. Inside was a small, leather-bound book.

As she lifted it out, she heard footsteps in the hall outside. A sudden fright struck her. Was Bresse returning? She hid behind the door. The steps passed. Probably the maid was doing her routine cleaning. With trembling hands Anne opened the book on the writing table. It was Bresse's diary.

Unfortunately, the script was tiny, abbreviated, and crowded. Some pages were in code. She took a magnifying glass from the drawer and began to read.

The clock on the mantel struck noon and gave Anne a start. She had been reading for more than an hour, beginning with the entries at the end of March, about the time of Lucie's disappearance. She felt soiled and nauseous. In clear, precise, and sordid detail, the marquis had described his pleasures with women. His utter lack of respect shone through on every page.

She was about to give up when she found what she was looking for, a lengthy, detailed description of Lucie's visit. Bresse had concealed the identity of most of his women with pet names. But here was Lucie undisguised. He was attracted as much to her simple innocence as to her physical beauty. Grimaud had enticed her into the house with the prospect of a well-paid maid's position. A supper was set up. She dressed in finery as a female guest. The marquis himself waited on her to show how it should be done. He also demonstrated proper table manners and taught her a few polite phrases that a maid should know. Afterward they played a game of cards. At the close of the evening Grimaud showed her to the room in the attic.

The diary recorded that the young lady 'was enchanted'. There was no mention of an assault. Lucie's necklace might have broken accidentally. Anne surmised that the marquis raised the young woman's expectations in a deliberate and cruel deception. The 'entertainment' was to take place on the following day.

At breakfast the marquis laced her coffee with an aphrodisiac that he had specially prepared. She noticed a strange taste but drank it anyway. Within minutes she was convulsing and died. The diary reported the incident in clinical detail. The marquis wondered what might have gone wrong. He had used the recipe successfully several times earlier. On this occasion, unfortunately, the young woman probably had a natural defect, perhaps a weak heart, that could not tolerate the drug. Or, she had had too much wine the night before.

The diary expressed no remorse. The marquis's sole concern was that he might be prosecuted, and possibly executed, as a poisoner. He recalled that the Parlement at Aix had condemned his friend, the Marquis de Sade, to death for poisoning several prostitutes who had survived. Only his family's intervention had saved him.

Anne set the diary aside, walked to the window, looked out over the garden. She could hardly breathe. It felt as if a stone lay on her chest. She wanted to cry but the tears wouldn't come. While searching for Lucie, she had grown deeply concerned about her fate. Even after weeks of fruitless effort, Anne retained a sliver of hope that the young woman might be found alive and healthy. That hope was now dashed.

Anne returned to the diary and read on. Bresse ordered his valet to dispose of Lucie's body and to remove all evidence of her presence in the house. Anne tried in vain to discover where Grimaud might have disposed of the body. She couldn't afford the time to read the entire diary carefully. The coded passages were impossible. So she jumped to the most recent entries. They might yield clues to what happened here last night.

She learned that the marquis had planned a supper, followed by 'entertainment'. The female guest was identified only by her pet name, Lola. The marquis did not mention leaving the house. That could have been decided on the spur of the moment.

'Enough,' Anne said aloud. She had evidence of a crime. Bresse had poisoned Lucie, a capital offense, even though he might not have intended to kill her. Grimaud was almost certainly an accomplice. She must show the diary to Inspector Quidor.

'This puts Lucie's disappearance in another light,' said Inspector Quidor, as he arrived at the marquis's house. 'I'll present the new evidence to a magistrate. Bresse will be charged with homicide.'

Anne had sent one of the agents to fetch the inspector and had met him at the door. They sat in the parlour while the inspector read the diary's pages concerning Lucie. When he finished, he looked up and tapped the diary. 'I'll put this under the eyes of one of our experts for a thorough analysis. That should give us a full picture of the marquis's crimes.'

Quidor met Anne's eye. 'His assault on Lucie leads me to wonder if he might have likewise killed his latest female companion, then panicked and tried to hide somewhere in the city. I'll give new instructions to my agents to regard him as a fugitive from the law. And I'll order them to bring his valet in for interrogation. In the meantime I would like to search the house and question the servants. Will you come with me?'

'Gladly.'

Quidor's entry into the kitchen terrified the cook and her niece, seated at the table. They leaped to their feet and bowed. A burly, stern-looking man who lacked social graces, Quidor had an intimidating way of lunging into a room.

As she translated for Quidor, Anne tried to comfort the two women. 'The inspector isn't as rough as he seems,' Anne signed to the cook. She calmed down and gave the inspector a reasonably clear picture of life in the house from her limited perspective in the kitchen.

'I understand that the supper table wasn't cleared,' Quidor remarked.

The cook pointed to Anne and signed, 'She told me to leave it until later.' Indeed Anne had told the cook and the maid to leave everything exactly as they found it. The police might need to investigate the house.

'We'll begin with the dining room,' Quidor said and nodded to Anne to lead the way. The maid and the two agents followed.

Plates of half-eaten food remained on the small circular table. All the wine glasses were empty, except one that was half full. Quidor studied it, lifted it to his nose. 'Brandy. A bit off.' He found two brandy carafes on the sideboard and tasted a few drops. 'As I suspected,' he said holding up one of the carafes, 'laced with laudanum.' He turned to Anne. 'I assume the marquis served this to his female guest.'

'Unbeknown to her,' Anne added.

'Most likely,' he agreed. 'Now I would like you and the maid to take me and my agents through the house. We'll look for bodies: Lucie's, the marquis's and his guest's. Disposing of them isn't easy. They might have been thrown into the river. But, after a month, at least Lucie's would most likely have surfaced. I'm guessing that it's hidden in this building.'

'Two days ago, my husband, his adjutant, and I searched in all the obvious places,' Anne remarked. 'There still might be a cleverly concealed chamber.'

For a couple of hours they studied walls and floors and

looked at the house from all possible angles, working their way from the dining room to the upper floors. On the second floor they came to a locked door. Quidor glanced quizzically at Anne.

She explained, 'That's the marquis's secret cabinet where he keeps his erotic materials. Georges briefly examined the room.'

Quidor turned to the maid. 'Do you have a key?'

She shook her head.

Anne replied, 'I took keys from the marquis's writing table. One of them will fit.'

On the third try the door opened and they went in, except for the maid, embarrassed by the room's contents. Even Quidor, whose long career had exposed him to all possible varieties of vice, stood still for a moment and stared. The marquis's collection of instruments, sculpture, paintings, and engravings reflected a single-minded preoccupation with abnormal sexual activity.

Anne and the inspector began to search the room, checking floorboards and walls. Anne pushed against a cabinet. It moved. More shoves exposed a trapdoor in the floor. Quidor lifted it and revealed a stairway going down.

Quidor glanced doubtfully at Anne. 'The colonel would be very angry at me if you were to be hurt down there.'

'You go first, I'll follow.'

Quidor's agent brought oil lamps and they started down. The stairway ended at an open door to an empty, windowless chamber in the basement.

'Two days ago, we came to this room by a different stairway.' She pointed to the sword, the chains, whips, and other instruments of torture hanging on the thick stone walls. 'These things weren't here then.'

'I suppose they indicate the kind of "entertainment" that the marquis had in store for his guest.' For several minutes the inspector examined the instruments, pulled the sword from its scabbard. 'But I don't believe that they were used.'

Meanwhile, Anne knelt down and closely inspected an iron hammer on the floor leaning against a wall. 'This tool *has* struck someone's head recently. It hasn't been cleaned, I still see hairs and flecks of blood.'

Quidor bent down beside her, studying the hammer. 'You're

right. It could have killed a man, or a woman.' He rose, surveying the chamber. 'Where's the body?'

Anne pointed to the drain in the centre of the room. 'There's a tunnel below that serves as a sewer to the river.'

'I think one of my agents should explore below.' Quidor removed the grate over the drain.

The agent grimaced but climbed down with his lamp into the tunnel, then disappeared. A few minutes later, he re-appeared none the worse for his experience. 'The tunnel is in good condition. It collects from several drains and leads to the south branch of the river. The grate there is unlocked.'

'Could a body be hauled through the tunnel and thrown into the river?' asked Quidor.

'Easily now when it's dry,' replied the agent, as he climbed back into the chamber. 'But it would be difficult, or nearly impossible in rainy weather when the tunnel would be full of rapidly moving sewerage.'

Quidor picked up the hammer and pensively stared at it for a long moment, then turned to Anne. 'Who was hit by this? The female guest? Or the marquis?'

'The marquis,' Anne replied. 'I've studied the hairs closely enough to determine that they are fine and light-coloured, probably sandy, like his.'

The inspector shrugged, then gave the hammer to the agent. 'Take it to the marquis's bedroom, compare the hairs with any hairs you might find in his wardrobe.' He turned back to Anne. 'If the marquis were the victim, who would have killed him, the female guest or his valet?'

'The latter,' Anne replied. 'He has a strong motive for the deed. In the most recent pages of the diary the marquis writes that Grimaud was stealing from him. The maid overheard him warn his valet that he had found discrepancies in the finan-cial accounts.

'That confrontation resulted in the marquis discharging Grimaud, ordering him out of the house, and threatening him with legal action. To stop the marquis from following through on his threat, Grimaud could have stolen back into the house while Bresse was entertaining the woman and no one else was here, killed him, and sent his body into the river. He might also have killed the woman if she witnessed the crime.'

'That's a plausible theory, madame. Unfortunately, we

haven't found evidence yet to support it. But I'll try it out on Grimaud when my agents find him. By the way, madame, would you happen to know where he has gone?' Quidor gave her a teasing smile.

She replied in like spirit. 'Why, of course, Inspector, he's living with his female partner, Renée Gros, in a cheap room above a wine shop on Rue Payenne near the Louvre. But at this time of the day, midafternoon, I believe that he and Renée can be found at work in the Valois arcade of the Palais-Royal.'

Quidor stroked his chin thoughtfully. 'I'd like to talk to them now, separately, away from the bustle and distractions of the Palais-Royal.'

'May I suggest, Inspector, a parlour in the town house of the Comtesse de Beaumont on Rue Traversine, just a stone's throw from the Palais-Royal?'

'That would do nicely. I'll instruct my agents to pick them up.'

An hour later, an agent showed Grimaud into the parlour and stood by the door. The second agent waited with Renée in an adjacent room. Anne sat off to one side at a small writing table prepared to take notes. At another table Inspector Quidor leaned back comfortably in his chair and told Grimaud to sit facing him.

'Why have you brought me here, Inspector?' The ex-valet attempted to appear only casually interested in this meeting, as if he were accustomed to being collared on a daily basis by a police agent. But his voice trembled, and his bulging eyes glistened with apprehension.

'Where were you the night before last, Grimaud?'

The former valet hesitated for an instant before replying, 'Early in the evening, I went to a gambling den. Afterward I returned to my companion's room near the Louvre and spent the night there with her. Why do you ask, Inspector?'

'The Marquis de Bresse has disappeared.'

'I heard the rumour just before I met your agent. So it's true?'

'Yes,' Quidor replied, then leaned forward and met Grimaud's eye. 'Could you tell me where the marquis might be? What could have happened to him?'

'Honestly, I don't know.' His brow creased with the effort

to answer the questions. 'As you've probably discovered, I withdrew from his service, and his house, at midafternoon, the day before yesterday. Since then I've had no contact with him. On previous occasions, he has left the house at night to carouse elsewhere with friends. He may return in a day or two.'

'You have provided him with female entertainment in the past. Did you arrange a companion for the evening in question?'

'No, I didn't, and I don't know who, if anyone, joined him.'

'While I have you here, I want you to tell me what you refused to tell Madame Cartier in the garden of the Palais-Royal concerning Lucie Gigot's death a month ago. You hinted that the marquis poisoned her at breakfast in his house.'

For a moment Grimaud appeared taken by surprise. He averted his eyes, mumbled.

'Speak up, man,' the inspector roared. 'You were an eye-witness, you ought to know. The marquis's diary describes in detail the entire incident. I want to hear your version.'

Grimaud exhaled a deep sigh, then repeated the diary's account, except on one point.

The inspector tilted his head skeptically. 'You say that the marquis disposed of the victim's body. In the diary the marquis writes that he told you to do it.'

'The marquis changed his mind and buried her by himself. I don't know where she is.'

The inspector stared at him in disbelief, then said, 'That will be all, today, Grimaud. Sign the statement that Madame Cartier is preparing. Remain in the city until I say you may leave. I'll have more questions for you.'

In a few minutes Anne had a brief statement ready. Grimaud glanced at it, signed it. Anne and the agent by the door witnessed it.

After Grimaud left the room, Quidor turned to Anne. 'What do you make of him, Madame Cartier?' He leaned back in his chair, folded his hands.

'I know him as a practiced liar,' she replied. 'But Bresse's disappearance seemed to puzzle him, perhaps as much as us. So, I wonder why he was so apprehensive? Also, I'm sure he knows where Lucie is buried, but he won't admit that he obstructed justice.'

'I too sensed that he hid something from me.' He went to the door. 'We shall now hear from his companion.'

Renée Gros entered the room and took the seat facing Quidor. Like Grimaud, she appeared apprehensive, in spite of an obvious effort to conceal it. Her eyes gleamed with excitement.

'Mademoiselle Gros, where were you the night of May twenty-eighth?'

'I was in my room from nightfall until dawn, with my partner, Denis Grimaud.'

'Did he remain in the room all night?'

'At least as long as I was awake.'

'So he could have slipped out.'

'I suppose he could have, though I would have awakened.'

As Anne was taking notes, a question lurked in the back of her mind. Then suddenly it became clear. She waved a hand and caught Quidor's attention. 'May I ask a question?'

He nodded.

'Renée, have you ever been to the marquis's town house?'

The young woman's eyes narrowed, her face flushed. 'I've visited Denis there many times. Why do you ask?'

The inspector seized the word. 'Can you offer any proof that *you* were in your room all night?'

'Have you found anyone who saw me leave?' Her tone was quickly growing combative.

Quidor spoke gently. 'No, we haven't, mademoiselle. You are free to leave as soon as you sign the statement concerning your movements on the night the marquis disappeared. Please remain available. I may have more questions.'

'I can't write.'

'Then make your mark and we'll witness it.'

After she left, Anne and the inspector remained in the room. She handed him the notes of the interrogations.

'Thank you, madame.' He put the notes in his portfolio, then glanced up at her. 'Your question to Mademoiselle Gros was well put, gave her a jolt. She could have been in the marquis's house that night.'

'And she has a possible motive to harm Bresse,' Anne added. 'She strongly suspects that the marquis killed her cousin Yvonne several months ago.'

The agents appeared in the doorway, ready to leave. Quidor

rose, bowed to Anne, and said patiently, 'At this point we lack evidence that would place either of our suspects in the marquis's house. For the time being, we must wait until at least one of the missing persons surfaces.'

From the countess's town house, Anne walked the short distance to the Palais-Royal. She had to wait several hours before Paul and Georges would return home. Her plan was to wander in the garden and the Valois arcade, her senses open to the sights and sounds and smells of the place. A woman walking alone was likely to attract unwanted attention, but her plain attire helped lessen the risk.

On her way she passed by the little puppet theatre in the Camp of the Tatars. Her friend Benoit, the puppet master, was sitting on a bench out front and hailed her. She joined him.

'Have you heard the news?' she asked. He was one of her most trusted informants. She had introduced him to Lucie's case and had asked him to keep track of the chief suspects involved in her disappearance. 'The Marquis de Bresse has vanished.'

'Yes, I know.'

'He killed Lucie. We just found out for sure.' Anne briefly described the investigation thus far. 'His valet Grimaud helped him, but we don't know how much. And Grimaud's partner Renée might also be involved.'

'I'm sorry for Lucie,' Benoit remarked with feeling. 'She enjoyed the puppets. Grimaud is a bad character. Renée is strange but wouldn't hurt Lucie. They walked past me a few minutes ago and appeared to be quarreling.' He gestured toward the garden.

'I'll try to learn what the quarrel's about.' Anne thanked him and hurried into the garden.

A few minutes later, Anne saw them near the Circus, the large building that the duke recently erected in the centre of the garden. An equestrian show was about to begin. While Grimaud walked inside, Renée turned away toward the Valois arcade. Anne intercepted her.

'Could we talk, Renée? I have news.'

The little prostitute scowled. 'I'm in a hurry. Must get to work. Gave Grimaud my last copper coins so that he could watch a stupid horse show.'

Anne sensed that the coins weren't the only reason for the quarrel. 'Renée, our friend Lucie is dead. The Marquis de Bresse poisoned her weeks ago. I read the whole story this morning, when I discovered his diary. I think Grimaud witnessed her death and probably helped dispose of her body.'

Renée stopped in her tracks, stared at Anne. 'I've begun to suspect as much, but up to now I've not dared to confront him. I owe him money and I need his protection. He would have lied to me anyway. I'm sorry for Lucie. It's a pity – and it happens too often. Someone should avenge her death.' She paused briefly, and gave Anne an enigmatic smile. 'The rumour of the marquis's disappearance is all over the Palais-Royal. Do you have any idea what could have happened to him?'

'I can only conjecture. He might have gone off on an orgy. Or, he might be in the river.'

The young woman lingered thoughtfully for a moment, then excused herself and started walking rapidly toward the arcade. 'I really have to go now.'

Anne walked with her. 'One last question, Renée. The marquis had a female guest that night. The police don't know who she was or what happened to her. Would you know?'

She shook her head, and hurried away.

Late that evening, Anne was at home upstairs in the salon overlooking the courtyard. At the sound of horses' hooves on the paving stones, she dashed to the window and recognized her husband and his adjutant. They had returned from their inspection mission. She rushed downstairs to the entrance and greeted them.

Tired and hungry but still wanting to hear the latest news, they gathered with Anne in the provost's office. She described the progress of her search for Lucie and her death from poisoning, apparently unintended. Her body was still missing.

'Late yesterday, we also learned that the marquis and his female guest had disappeared. Inspector Quidor thinks that they may be in the river. As for Lucie's body, Quidor's men will search the back garden of the town house.' Anne addressed Paul. 'And he wants you and Georges to look for her at the family chateau. It lies in your jurisdiction.'

The two men listened to Anne attentively. When she finished, Paul turned to Georges. 'It appears that Lucie Gigot's

disappearance is now a criminal case, our problem, as well
as Inspector Quidor's. Arrange a trip to the Bresse chateau.'

'Have you ever been there?' his adjutant asked.

'A few years ago, I went briefly to speak to his father, a
magistrate on vacation, a shameless old roué. Several peasants on his estate complained that he harassed their daughters. I spoke to his wife, the countess, a formidable lady, with
a distant, obscure connection to the royal family. She said she
would tell him to desist. I believe he obeyed her, or at least
turned his attention elsewhere. The peasants seemed satisfied
on that point, if not concerning rents and fees.'

'This will *not* be a pleasure trip,' Anne remarked. 'What
kind of parents could produce such a monster of a son? I
dread meeting them.'

Eleven
A Missing Woman Found

31 May

The following morning, Anne and Paul travelled by coach
to the Bresse estate. Georges rode alongside on a horse.
A pair of mounted troopers followed. The sun shone brightly,
but rain-laden clouds drifted in from the west.

Anne's feelings were also mixed. She feared what might
lie ahead. They could find Lucie's body. By now, a month
after death, her beauty would be long gone. Anne's imagina-
tion balked at the horrid prospect that she might face.

Still a part of her was looking forward to this visit. It could
close the investigation. For more than two weeks she had
searched for the young woman, grown to know her. Moments
of hope alternated with troughs of despair. The conclusion
today might be bitter, but it should at least be final. She couldn't
bear the thought of endless uncertainty.

The Bresse family estate was only a few miles south of Paris. Its fields appeared devastated and deserted, like those of other estates in the Paris region. A large rectangular, three-storey stone structure with a mansard roof, the chateau reflected the grand pretensions of its aristocratic owners. A groom met the coach as it drove up to a porticoed entrance. Anne and Paul left the coach and were led by a servant into a parlour. Georges and the troopers rode around the chateau to search its farm buildings and gardens.

The Comte de Bresse came to the parlour in a shabby dressing gown. 'What's the meaning of this unannounced visit, Colonel? Two of your troopers were here only a few days ago looking for a missing young woman. What's going on?'

The count was a short, stout, middle-aged man with the hanging jowls, the bleary eyes, and the jaded expression of an old, worn-out libertine. Anne saw in him the worthy father of his son the marquis. There was even a distant physical resemblance.

Paul replied, 'I'm sorry to disturb you, sir, but I've come to tell you that your son has disappeared under suspicious circumstances. We fear that he may be dead. Have you had any recent contact with him?'

At this news the count took a step back and shook his head in disbelief. 'I haven't seen him in more than a month, Colonel. He was here then on a short visit. In the meantime we've exchanged a few messages, the last one about a week ago.' The count rubbed his brow with the back of his hand in an effort to recall. 'My son would occasionally go off on a lark for a few days. No one would hear from him. But he would return, not much the worse for a little debauchery. Perhaps that's what he's done in this case.'

'For a short while, the police shared your view. But they've searched his house and found evidence of violence. The young woman who entertained him on the night of his disappearance has also vanished. Furthermore, they've discovered in his diary strong reasons to believe that he killed a young woman about a month or more ago. Her body is still missing. He could have hidden it here. Therefore, we must put this chateau and its estate to a thorough search. I apologize for any inconvenience that it causes you. My wife will assist me, if necessary, in the interrogation of your wife and your female servants. I would like you to show us through the chateau.'

These revelations appeared to stun the count. He sought a chair and sat down. 'I'll ring for the steward. He has the keys and should accompany us.'

'That would be helpful,' Saint-Martin agreed.

A few minutes later they set out on the investigation, fully realizing that they wouldn't find the missing marquis or his female companion sleeping in bed or lounging in upholstered chairs. Later, if need be, Georges could look for hiding places in the floors and walls. Anne and Paul stopped before portraits of the marquis at different stages of his life and used these opportunities to question the count about his son.

In front of a picture of him as a schoolboy, his father said with pride, 'He was a precocious lad, an atheist at thirteen. And he made love to his first woman at about the same time.' Anne supposed acidly that his 'conquest' was a poor servant girl.

Their tour of the chateau ended in a drawing room where the Comtesse de Bresse had arranged for tea and sweetmeats. The walls were covered with portraits of distinguished noble ancestors.

'They are mostly hers,' Paul whispered to Anne. 'I've heard that the countess is inordinately proud of her distant connection to the great Condé family, which in turn is related to the king. Absurd as her attitude may seem, she has succeeded in gathering considerable power and privilege. When in trouble, her son fled for protection under her wings.'

The countess was a tall, thin woman a few years younger than her husband but older in appearance. Her dark, wrinkled face resembled a dried prune. She looked at her visitors down a long, large nose and greeted them with a high-pitched, nasal voice.

Paul introduced himself and Anne.

The countess looked annoyed, ignored Anne as if she were beneath notice. She took the slight in stride. But Paul bristled. 'My wife is helping the police search for a missing young woman named Lucie Gigot, last seen in your son's company. He has recently disappeared along with a female guest.'

'I should think, Colonel –' the countess let out a deep sigh

– 'that the police had more to do than to pursue a spirited young man simply enjoying himself. He will return to his house in a day or two. We should applaud if a couple of prostitutes have gone missing. Vipers! They serve only to debauch our young men.'

'In fact, madame, we are pursuing him because of a well-grounded suspicion that he murdered at least one of the prostitutes, the young woman Lucie Gigot. He may have hid her body on this estate a month ago.'

The countess gasped. A shocked expression came over her face. 'That's quite impossible. My son is not a vile common murderer. Killing prostitutes is beneath him.'

'We shall see, Comtesse.'

At that moment, Georges appeared at the entrance to the drawing room, followed by a breathless, indignant servant who was attempting to stop him. Anne warned her husband. He turned and beckoned his adjutant into the room.

'What is it, Georges?'

'Sir, I believe we have found Lucie.'

Meanwhile outside the chateau, Georges and the troopers had searched the estate's farm buildings and examined the gardens, fruitlessly. Then Georges questioned the servants about the marquis's visit to the estate a month or so ago. Only an elderly gardener appeared to know anything, but he was reluctant to speak. His master the count, a magistrate of Parlement and strong critic of the royal government, had warned the servants to tend to their duties and not give information to the troopers.

Georges took the gardener aside, pressed a coin into his hand. 'Do you remember the young marquis and his valet arriving by coach with a large trunk?' Georges was guessing. They were likely to use an innocuous container that was at hand, rather than build one.

'Yes, I recall them unloading the trunk behind the main barn. It seemed odd, they acted like a pair of thieves.'

'What happened to the trunk?'

'They put it on a mule cart and drove off down the back road. I lost sight of them.' He paused for dramatic effect. 'They returned to Paris without the trunk that same day.'

'Can you guess where they might have left it?'

The gardener scratched his head for a moment. 'As a young

fellow, the marquis often went to a secret place in the lime-stone ridge about a mile from here. I followed him a few times. His father wanted to know what the boy was up to. He used to carouse with girls from the neighborhood. The father said, "Let him be. He's sowing his oats".'

'Take me to that place.' Georges and a trooper set off on horseback with the gardener on a mule leading the way.

Anne and Paul left the count and countess in the sitting room – staring at each other, speechless – and followed Georges outside. A mule cart was waiting.

Paul spoke gently, 'You should come with us, Anne. You knew the young woman and can identify her body. I'm sorry to put you through this. I know how repugnant it is to you.'

'I'll do it for Lucie. I can't turn away from her now.'

The limestone ridge's eastern slope consisted of a steep rocky escarpment. Tall brush masked its base. The gardener pointed to a narrow path to the door into a cave. It was locked, but Georges opened it with his tools. 'I've been inside and seen the trunk but I haven't opened it.'

Inside was a room with paneled walls, tile floor, and vaulted ceiling. It was furnished with a table, a cabinet, chairs, and a bed. Light came from a shaft in the ceiling. The air inside was pleasantly cool and dry, though outside it was warm and humid.

In a corner against the back wall stood a trunk. It was locked.

'This is going to be unpleasant,' said Paul, offering Anne a scented kerchief. 'Open it, Georges.'

In a minute the trunk was unlocked, and Georges threw open the lid, releasing a powerful odor of death.

Anne approached the open trunk.

'Is it she?' Paul asked.

'Yes,' Anne replied, nearly gagging. Despite the body's decomposition, she could recognize the young woman's features.

Anne felt glued to the spot until Paul took her under the arm and led her outside.

'Stay here, breathe fresh air. You've done your part. We can finish the investigation of the cave without you.'

*   *   *

Paul ordered one of the troopers to take the trunk and its contents to the morgue at the Châtelet, while Georges and the other trooper continued to search the estate for more evidence. Paul and Anne returned to the chateau and met the count in his study.

'Comte de Bresse, we've discovered the murdered woman's body in your son's secret hiding place.'

The count turned pale at the news, lowered himself heavily into a chair. Paul faced him. Anne sat off to one side taking notes.

Paul was livid with anger, but he kept his temper under control. 'You told me, Comte, that your son was not a violent man. What do you say now?'

'Her death must have been accidental. Unwisely, he has tried to conceal it.'

'That may be,' Paul granted, 'but a magistrate will most likely accuse him of manslaughter. In his diary your son admitted to having surreptitiously given the young woman a dangerous drug, an aphrodisiac. A medical examiner may also verify the cause of death.'

'Is that all, Colonel?' The count appeared to be growing tired.

'Unfortunately not,' Paul replied. 'While carefully searching the secret room, we discovered many traces of old blood on the walls and on the floor. To your knowledge was Lucie the only person he has seriously injured or killed?'

The count hesitated, then mumbled.

Saint-Martin glowered at him. 'Speak up, sir! I know about the animals and the neighbour's daughter.' The gardener had told Anne and Paul that as a boy the marquis had gruesomely killed farm animals for pleasure. The gardener had protested to the count who said he would put a stop to it. The gardener had also mentioned that a country girl had claimed that the young marquis had viciously beaten and raped her. The Comte de Bresse had not admitted his son's guilt but had paid a sum of money to quiet the girl's father.

'What else has he done?' Paul asked. As he spoke, he reflected that with parents like the count and countess, their young son could easily have turned to the devil for guidance.

The count sighed. 'I realize, Colonel, that you have un-covered some of my son's youthful misdeeds. He also engaged in orgies with dissolute young men and women, though I'm not aware that he killed anyone. A few years ago, my wife and I threatened to have the king confine him to a royal prison. That improved his behavior, or at least made him much more cautious. He understood that his friend the Marquis de Sade was quite unhappy in the Bastille.

'Unfortunately, my son's valet, Denis Grimaud, a lowborn, bad subject, has lately gained far too much influence over him and led him again into reckless behavior. Grimaud has even managed to gain control of his money. In a recent message my son complained that Grimaud was stealing from him. I wrote back urging him to discharge the rogue.'

'We believe, Comte, that your son took your advice on the day before his disappearance. How do *you* think Grimaud might have reacted?'

'I see your point, Colonel. My son might not have gone off on a lark. Grimaud could have killed him and fled from Paris.'

'That's a plausible theory. Inspector Quidor has questioned Grimaud who remains in Paris. The inspector is also examining your son's financial records, creating an inventory of his assets, and trying to determine if a theft has taken place. We should soon have an answer.'

Anne and Paul were together in the coach, returning to Paris at night. Rain drummed on the roof. The horses's hooves rhythmically clattered on the paving stones. Anne stared cheerlessly out the window into the black void. At this moment she missed Georges. His simple, good-natured humour had a way of lifting her spirits.

But he had gone ahead on horseback. Back in Paris he would go to the morgue to oversee Lucie's autopsy, and then report the day's discoveries to Inspector Quidor.

Still nauseous in the aftermath of identifying Lucie's body, Anne felt worn out. The utter futility of the young woman's life and tawdry death deeply distressed her.

'What's on your mind, Anne?' Paul asked, his forehead creased with concern.

'In a word, crime. Men and women badly hurting each other for profit or pleasure. At the moment, I find it almost too painful to contemplate.'

He took her hand and caressed it.

After a minute or two of restful, healing quiet, Anne put on her best face and turned to Paul.

'After music and laughter, the most effective remedy for low spirits is to work. I'd rather fight crime than cry about it. We have unfinished business. For a start, Grimaud must be punished for enticing Lucie and for assisting in her death.'

'I agree,' Paul said. 'Then there's the marquis's disappearance. I assume that he's dead. My question is, who killed him?'

'We already suspect Grimaud,' Anne replied. 'But I see two other potential suspects.'

'I'll supply one of them,' Paul interjected, 'Grimaud's companion, Renée Gros.'

Anne nodded. 'Renée claims that they were together at home that night. But, in fact, she could have gone with him to the marquis's town house.'

'And the other suspect,' Paul added, 'is the marquis's female guest that night.'

'Who is she?' Anne asked rhetorically. 'And what has happened to her?'

For a moment it was quiet in the coach. Then Paul spoke tentatively. 'It's strange that Quidor and his agents cannot identify the woman. She has left no trace of her presence in the marquis's house. No one appears to have seen her. So, she's either dead, or she has strong reasons to remain hidden.'

'We need to discover those reasons, Paul. I feel certain that she's alive.'

Twelve

Murder

3 – 4 June

The next few days passed uneventfully. Hundreds of river folk had been alerted but thus far had not found the marquis. The Paris police were likewise unsuccessful. Then late in the afternoon on the following Tuesday, a servant called Anne to the provost's office downstairs where Paul and Georges were working. Inspector Quidor had arrived to report his progress in the investigation. Anne should join them. They gathered around the provost's conference table.

Quidor explained that while Anne, Paul, and Georges were searching for Lucie's body at the Bresse estate, his agents had discovered a rear exit from Renée's building, which the two suspects could have used without anyone observing them. But in the absence of the marquis's body, Quidor had decided not to hold them in prison. They were available for further questioning.

'Over the past few days, we've continued to search for Bresse, but to no avail. Still, there's a positive report from my agent, the expert on hair.' Quidor bowed to Anne. 'You were correct, madame, the hair on the hammer in the basement of the marquis's house matches the samples taken from his clothes.'

Paul asked, 'Did you discover irregularities in the marquis's financial books?'

'Not yet,' the inspector replied. 'An accountant is still examining the accounts. The marquis's system is quite complicated, deliberately so, thanks to Grimaud's management. Thus far we've learned that Bresse had very little money left in the bank. Grimaud had drawn out most of it, apparently with the marquis's unwitting approval. The house and its furnishings were rented. The marquis's assets included his expensive clothes, plus his paintings and sculpture, rings, pins, and other personal items of some value. His maid thinks that a gold ring is missing, as well as a few Louis d'or and smaller coins that the marquis usually kept in his purse. He might have had the money and the ring on his person when he disappeared. If not, then I'd say they were stolen and estimate the theft at about 500 livres, a sum that the marquis might lose at the toss of the dice, or an artisan might earn in a year.'

'The evidence that you've gathered points to robbery and murder, either by the valet or the female guest,' Paul remarked.

'Have you discovered any trace of her?' asked Anne.

'We still don't have a clue. At the Palais-Royal, my agents

questioned their contacts among those prostitutes who would risk going to a libertine's house. They were unaware of any missing acquaintances. The same was true at the brothels, whose inmates in any case weren't supposed to work outside.'

'That survey was incomplete,' Georges pointed out. 'It would be impossible to account for the thousands of prostitutes of Paris.'

'We don't have to account for all of them,' countered Quidor. 'Grimaud and Bresse are like male cats in rut. They prowl within a certain territory that they are familiar with. Bresse frequented only two or three different brothels in the Valois arcade. His valet solicited women mostly in the same arcade and rarely outside the Palais-Royal. I suspect that Bresse's female guest is in fact not missing, but most likely one of the women whom my agents questioned. She gave them a false alibi, lied to them. She probably drank the sleeping potion, at least half of it, but somehow survived that night.'

'I agree,' said Anne. 'Then she could have applied that hammer to the marquis's head.' Anne leaned back and said in a low voice, 'We should feel kindly disposed toward her, in view of what the marquis did to Lucie.'

The next day at noon, as clouds gathered and the scent of rain hung in the warm air, Anne and Paul were enjoying a cold fruit soup at home in the garden. Georges rushed toward them, breathless.

'Sorry to spoil your lunch,' he said, a grim expression on his face.

'What is it, Georges?' Paul asked, laying down his spoon.

'A body, sir.' Georges pulled up a chair. 'It's the marquis in breeches and shirtsleeves, but without ring or purse. There are wounds on his head that a hammer could have caused, as well as small cuts and bruises on his hands and face from tumbling in the river. Fishermen pulled him out near the Louvre. Quidor's agents have taken him to the morgue.'

'He came to a bad end,' Paul remarked.

'Few will grieve,' Anne added.

Paul nodded. 'Why should *anyone* care? Still, the law says it was wrong to kill him. The person who did it must be found.' He turned to Georges. 'We'll take the news to

Lieutenant General DeCrosne. He will be more upset than we are.'

At midafternoon, Saint-Martin and Georges arrived at DeCrosne's office in the Hôtel de Police and were immediately admitted.

'You told my clerk that the Marquis de Bresse's body has been found. Give me the details.' DeCrosne spoke quickly through tightly pressed lips.

Saint-Martin briefly described the body's discovery and its condition. Then he said, 'Bresse's assailant beat him to death with a hammer and threw his body into the river. His female companion of that evening is still missing. Her fate concerns us. She may have witnessed the crime and fled, unwilling to become involved. Or, the marquis's assailant may have killed her too, but her body has not yet been found.

'Since the marquis's disappearance, we have been able to search his home again. My wife has discovered his diary. It indicates that he habitually abused prostitutes beyond the bounds of the law, and was responsible for the death of Mademoiselle Lucie Gigot, a tenant of my aunt the Comtesse de Beaumont.' Saint-Martin handed DeCrosne a copy of the diary's relevant pages.

As the lieutenant general scanned the text, his face took on a look of surprise mixed with disbelief. He tapped the little book. 'If these pages are true, then he is guilty of reckless homicide. To use this as evidence, I would need independent confirmation of what it purports to say.'

Saint-Martin nodded gravely, then briefly described the search for Lucie from her disappearance to the discovery of her body at the Bresse estate. 'His attempt to hide her body confirms the diary's admission that he killed her. We are also seeking evidence that he may have killed other young women.'

During the colonel's presentation, DeCrosne grew increasingly perturbed, which he tried vainly to conceal. His voice took on an irritated tone. 'The marquis's criminal abuse of Lucie Gigot, coupled with his violent death, is fodder for gossip-mongers. That's regrettable! His mother, the Comtesse de Bresse, is related to the royal family. To prevent the scandal from growing worse, the case must be pursued with the utmost care. I have come to expect both skill and discretion from you, Colonel. So I'll put you in charge of the investigation of the marquis's death. Inspector Quidor and your adjutant Georges Charpentier shall assist you.'

'I'll do my best, sir. I appreciate your confidence.'

'Who is the chief suspect?'

'At present, Grimaud, the ex-valet. We think he may have stolen money from the marquis's account, and the marquis confronted him. Also, a ring and a few gold coins are missing.'

'Then the valet is your man,' DeCrosne remarked with a sigh. He appeared to have heard enough.

Paul signaled Georges and started toward the door, then turned back to DeCrosne with an afterthought. 'Our investigation will surely bring us to the Palais-Royal. May we assume your permission to enter the duke's jurisdiction?'

'Yes, of course. The duke and his men know that murder is the king's business.'

As they lingered outside the door to DeCrosne's office, Saint-Martin said to Georges, 'I propose we begin our investigation with the valet. Let's go downstairs to Inspector Quidor. He may have recently learned more about him.'

Quidor's clerk showed the visitors into an ante-room to the office and said that the inspectors were in conference elsewhere in the building but should soon be finished.

Saint-Martin agreed to be patient. Quidor was a busy man, one of only four inspectors who worked on serious criminal cases in the densely packed city of a half million imperfect souls. In these conferences the inspectors shared vital information and together resolved the more difficult problems. They also shared any rewards.

After a few minutes of waiting, Quidor appeared in the doorway, recognized his visitors, and beckoned them into his office. If possible, it was even more cluttered than usual. Stacks of paper and boxes of files covered every surface. Without apology he cleared three chairs and they sat down.

Saint-Martin began. 'What can you tell us about his ex-valet, our chief suspect?'

'I thought you would want to know. I pulled his file for you.'

Saint-Martin studied the file with Georges for a few minutes.

They learned that Grimaud was forty-one years old and a
native of Paris. His parents, both deceased, had been in
domestic service with a number of aristocratic families, the
father a steward, the mother a housekeeper. Prior to serving
the marquis, Grimaud was valet to an elderly count, for whom
he also served as a procurer. The count accused him of pilfering
money but dropped the charges when threatened with exposure of his own embezzlement of a relative's trust funds.

Quidor commented, 'In Grimaud's record, I find an incli-
nation to larceny but no acts of violence. Still there's always
the first time.'

'I agree,' remarked Saint-Martin. 'And Renée Gros could
also be involved in the crime, seeking revenge for the death
of her cousin. Grimaud would have copied the house keys.
He and Renée could sneak in and kill the marquis and his
female guest. The villains would then take the marquis's
purse and ring and throw the bodies into the river.'

Quidor raised a hand to object. 'Perhaps Bresse's female
guest killed the marquis while Grimaud and his companion
were in bed together, as they claimed.'

'That's enough conjecture,' ventured Georges. 'How shall
we proceed? Interrogate Grimaud again?'

'No, he would merely repeat his alibi,' Saint-Martin
replied. 'Our next step is to place one or more of our three
suspects at the scene of the crime.'

Thirteen
Old Comrades

5 June

The next day, the weather fair, Anne and Georges walked
to Michou's studio on Rue Traversine, to share what
they had learned about the marquis's murder. Michou and

Sylvie were preparing brushes, paint, and a canvas for use later in the morning. But they welcomed the visitors and invited them to coffee at a table in the studio.

'To what do we owe the pleasure of this visit?' Sylvie asked. She glanced at Georges in uniform. 'Official police business?'

'We have news of a crime,' Georges replied, 'but you may know it already. The body of the Marquis de Bresse has been found in the river.'

Sylvie replied, 'We learned about it last night at the Palais-Royal. Rumours were flying through the arcades. The most appealing one is that the irate father of an abused daughter had neutered him, then thrown him into the river. What really happened?'

'The police are keeping the details secret,' Anne replied, 'but I can tell you that he received blows to the head, and was almost certainly dead before going into the water. This is now a major murder investigation. The lieutenant general has placed Paul in charge.'

'Do the police have a suspect?' Michou signed.

'His former valet, Denis Grimaud,' Anne replied. 'Bresse had discovered him stealing money and intended to report him to the police.'

'Have they arrested him?' Michou asked.

'No, he's still working in the Valois arcade. His female companion called Renée has given him an alibi. We must find out if he, with or without help from her, had an opportunity to kill the marquis.'

'We know him – weak chin, bulging eyes,' said Sylvie. 'We'll watch him more closely.'

Confused, Michou asked Anne, 'Could you describe his companion?'

'An excitable, petite young prostitute. A bit strange in her ways. She's been called a firebrand.'

Michou nodded. 'Now I know who you mean. She's more like a servant than a companion. He's her pimp and protects her. She helps him find pretty women for rich gentlemen. Yes, I'll keep an eye on her.'

'I recall,' said Sylvie, 'that the marquis had a female guest the night he disappeared.'

'Yes, the police have not yet identified her.'

'Then we should also watch Berthe. I've seen her recently with Grimaud. Several months ago she arrived in Paris and now works in a brothel in the Valois arcade.'

'What's her family name, this Berthe?' Georges asked. The conversation about her had piqued his interest.

'Dupont. Berthe Dupont,' replied Sylvie. 'Like many young country women, Berthe started out in the Valois arcade's millinery shop, then moved to the brothel for more money.'

'Dupont,' murmured Georges. 'That name rings a bell.'

The conversation shifted to Lucie and the discovery of her body. Georges had agreed to pick it up at the morgue on Sunday, three days hence, and take it to the family. A funeral followed by burial would be held the same day, and Anne and Paul would attend. Michou would accompany them. She was more touched by the young woman's fate than Anne had expected.

The coffee arrived. A servant poured. Sweet biscuits were served. At a momentary break in the conversation Georges suddenly exclaimed, 'Dupont! Now I remember. Jean Dupont. We were at Minden together. He was blinded in the battle. Over the years, we lost touch. Berthe might be his daughter.' Georges frowned. 'If so, why is she in a brothel?'

'I'm intrigued,' Anne replied. 'I'll try to find out this morning.'

For an hour or so Anne searched for Berthe Dupont in the Valois arcade, but without success. Finally, she approached the brothel. At this late hour in the morning, only a few women were loitering at the entrance, and they were in conversation among themselves. No potential customers were in sight.

Anne surveyed the area for anyone who might know her. This was her second visit to the brothel, and she worried. She didn't want to create the impression that she worked in the place. That would feed the warped fantasy of malicious gossips. Anne recalled how the queen's innocent indiscretions had provoked obscene pamphlets and engravings that badly damaged her reputation.

A similar scandal involving Anne would be very embarrassing to Paul and hurtful to his career. At that point, she almost gave up the idea. Then she thought of bringing him or Georges along, but the madam would refuse to cooperate.

These concerns notwithstanding, Anne would not be deterred. She sensed that Berthe Dupont held a key to the mystery of Bresse's death and must be pursued even into a brothel. So with a deep feeling of uneasiness Anne climbed the stairs. The porter bowed to her with unaffected courtesy and showed her again into the parlour. The madam soon arrived, and they exchanged greetings.

'May I speak with Berthe?' Anne asked politely.

'Berthe will be out for the day,' replied the madam in an irritated, doubtful tone of voice. 'Her note said that her father was ill.'

Anne left a message asking Berthe to meet her in the nearby café the next morning at about eleven. The madam promised to deliver it.

On the way out Anne wondered about the madam's evident displeasure. She obviously suspected that the young woman had given a weak excuse and couldn't be depended upon. If she were to lose this job, could she realistically expect to find a better, less degrading one?

As Anne stepped into the arcade, she caught a glimpse of Denis Grimaud and Renée Gros in the crowd. They appeared to be arguing. That deserved close observation. As Anne had nothing else planned, she would follow them.

Denis Grimaud was in a foul mood. The past several days had not been kind to him. He had lost his position and his lodging with the Marquis de Bresse. The police had interrogated him twice. Clearly they regarded him as the prime suspect, first in the disappearance, then in the violent death of the marquis. Grimaud was sure that he was being followed, spied upon. To compound his problems he continued to lose in the gambling dens. Most of what he had stolen from the marquis had vanished. Finally, his companion Renée had changed. Ever since the marquis dismissed him and he moved in with her, she had been sullen, uncooperative, and contrary.

Now he tried to get Renée's attention – she had stopped to stare into the window of a café.

'Trying to see where the small silver spoons are kept?'

'What if I were,' she replied, and continued staring. 'That's none of your business.'

'I'm concerned that during the past week you haven't recruited a single young woman for me. What's going on?'

She turned away from the window and glared at him. 'I don't want to bring any more young women into this business and see them ruined. I often think about my cousin Yvonne, still missing. Whatever happened to her, Denis? Would you know?'

Grimaud started. Her questions had an accusatory tone, as if she held him responsible for her cousin's fate. Had Monsieur Bloch talked to her, perhaps revealed the circumstances of his daughter's disappearance and death? With the marquis gone, the old man might wonder who would pay his secret pension for keeping silent. Stupid bastard! He'll probably come to me.

Renée walked on, Grimaud followed after her. A few minutes later, she stopped at another shop, apparently just to provoke him.

'Don't be impertinent, Renée. I know nothing about Yvonne. If you refuse to cooperate, I'll think seriously about ending our relationship. You would be on your own.'

She ignored his threat.

He changed to a more conciliatory tone. 'I could be persuaded to charge you less for my services.' He paused. 'But in the meantime, I need ten livres this afternoon for the captain of the duke's guard.'

Renée looked straight ahead, avoiding his eyes. 'You'll have to get the money from someone else. I don't have even a copper coin.' She walked away from him. He had to trot to catch up.

'You're lying,' he said with heat. 'You've bedded several customers in the past few days and one or two this morning. But you haven't given me my share.'

'Your share? You forget that I pay rent and buy food for both of us.' She glared at him. 'By the way, that's a temporary arrangement. As of tomorrow, you must get your own room and begin to support yourself. It's not impossible for a bright man like you. Go find honest work, quit gambling.'

By this time, they had reached the millinery shop. 'Move on,' she said to him. 'I'm going to have a few words with the milliner, privately.'

'I'll have you treat me with greater respect, young lady. Remember, without my protection you couldn't survive a day in this hell.' That bit of harsh truth seemed to bring the tart to her senses. She kept her mouth shut, but still she didn't give him any money.

They parted. She entered the shop, probably to sell some stolen fabric. He kept on walking toward the duke's palace. It irked him to be even half civil to the little whore. He wished he could slap her brazen face. But he dared not touch her, for she knew too much. If she were to go to the police, she could cause him serious harm.

When he reached the captain's office in the palace guard-room, he had made up his mind. He would rid himself of Renée – very carefully.

'Grimaud! Good to see you.' Mockery resonated in the captain's voice. 'Shut the door.' The visitor obeyed. Seated at a battered writing table, the captain rudely motioned him to a chair.

The ex-valet and pimp swallowed his pride, gave a noncommittal shrug, and smiled to the officer, whom he detested but feared. For the captain was a cruel, hard-faced, self-important man with mean, black eyes – and great power over pimps and whores in the Palais-Royal.

'That will be ten livres,' the captain said in a low, soft voice, as if the walls were eagerly listening. He pushed a thick ledger across the table, then leaned back, staring balefully at Grimaud, like a cat watching a mouse.

Grimaud had regularly put the money in the book but today he couldn't. He felt sick in the pit of his stomach. The captain's jaw stiffened, his eyes narrowed. 'You realize, Grimaud, that I could put you in prison in Bicêtre any time I wished with or without a valid reason.'

'I'm temporarily in difficult financial straits, Captain. Would you accept a piece of useful information in lieu of payment of the ten livres?'

'I'm interested. Tell me more.'

'My tart, Renée, has organized the robbery of a café in the Valois arcade for tomorrow morning. While a group of prostitutes create a disturbance inside, she plans to steal several little silver coffee spoons.'

The captain sat up. 'They've pulled that trick before. If I

catch them, I'll delay your payment until next week.' The captain's gaze turned suspicious. 'But, tell me, Grimaud, why would you betray your whore to the police? I'm told that she still produces.'

'She's keeping money that she owes me. That's why I'm short. And her thieving ways will sooner or later cause me trouble. I'll find another woman who is easier to manage so that I can make my payments in a timely fashion.' He couldn't bring himself to admit the real reason, his bad luck with the dice. The captain would laugh in his face.

'Grimaud, you haven't the wits or the pluck of an honest pimp. Incredible! You expect us police to help you deal with a crazy woman half your size. Get out of here. I'll see you tomorrow near the café.'

Stung by the officer's insults, Grimaud left the guardhouse trying to convince himself that he had done the right thing. The captain and his guards would arrest Renée and any other whores within reach, turn them over to the Paris authorities who would send them in short order to the women's prison at the Salpêtrière. That was like burying her without having to kill her first.

He began to feel better, more confident. He strode into the garden. Yes, he had another woman in mind for Renée's place, called the Bitch, steadier, less moody than Renée. With her earnings, and a little luck, he'd soon recover financially and resume delivery of young country girls to rich gentlemen.

Suddenly, he became aware of being followed. He slipped behind a tree. Sure enough, a woman walked by looking for him. It was the colonel's wife. His heart sank. How much had she seen or heard? She might figure out his scheme.

Anne met Georges at a table outside Café de Foy. The air was warm, the sky blue. A perfect spring day. But she felt wretched. It was close to noon. He was waiting for her.

'Tell me what's happened. Is something wrong?' Georges gazed at Anne with concern.

A waiter arrived. They ordered lemonade.

When he left, Anne said, 'I've just made a fool of myself.'

'You're allowed to do that once in a while.'

'Thanks. I was following Grimaud. He caught me doing it, gave me a silly smile as I walked by.'

The waiter arrived with the drinks and left. They tasted the lemonade. Anne held up her glass. 'It's good, but not up to the standard of Nice.' During the recent winter months that Anne and Paul had spent in that Italian city on the sea, she had picked ripe lemons and made fresh juice nearly every day. Recalling that pleasure helped lift her spirit back to normal.

'Before he caught you, what did you learn?' Georges asked over the rim of his glass.

'For part of the way Grimaud walked with Renée in the Valois arcade. From time to time they stopped and were so absorbed arguing with each other that I could hide in the crowd quite close to them. I read their lips and heard bits of conversation. She refused to recruit more young women to share Yvonne's fate. He wanted money. She wouldn't give him any and left him outside the millinery shop.'

'That's interesting. Sounds like their relationship is breaking up. Could be dangerous for Grimaud. She might withdraw his alibi and say that she has no idea where he was on the night of Bresse's murder. What else?'

'After leaving her, Grimaud walked to the palace guardhouse. His expression was anxious. I didn't dare follow him in, so I don't know what he did there. When he came out, he looked preoccupied, worried. By the time he reached the garden, his expression had grown more confident. Any ideas?'

'From your description, I'd say that he went to the guardhouse on serious business and most likely talked to the captain. Grimaud serves the police as an informant and often delivers a piece of useful information. But his anxious appearance this time tells me that the object of the visit was himself, a problem in his relationship to the captain. Either the patronage Grimaud has enjoyed or the protection he has extended to Renée may be in jeopardy. Whichever is the case, I'm going to guess that Renée is in deep trouble.'

'Hmm,' murmured Anne. 'That could complicate our investigation of her role in the Bresse murder.'

Fourteen
An Incident in the Valois Arcade

6 June

L ate in the morning, Anne returned to the Palais-Royal. As she crossed the garden, she recalled yesterday's experience spying on Denis Grimaud and Renée. A troubled feeling crept into her mind, born of her distrust of the man. He had no scruples, consulted only his own advantage. Though exposed to reprisal, Renée had provoked him, perhaps unwisely. An odd little woman, she seemed lacking in common sense, courted misfortune.

Berthe Dupont was a very different sort of woman. Mature beyond her years, she seemed the victim of a singularly malevolent fate that blinded her father, snatched away her mother, and deprived her of any prospect of a decent livelihood. Had she received yesterday's message? Anne decided to stop at the brothel, taking what she now regarded as her customary precautions.

The brothel was being aired and cleaned and closed for business. The madam met Anne with less wariness than earlier. Yes, she was sure that Berthe had read the message. Then she had left the brothel, saying that she would return within an hour. The madam supposed that she went to a café nearby in the arcade where Berthe was occasionally allowed to drink coffee at this time of the day, a slack period before male patrons arrived in significant numbers.

The madam sniffed. 'Berthe likes to play the lady, though she can hardly afford to.'

As Anne approached the café, she noticed an empty tumbrel parked in front. A crowd had gathered near the café's entrance. Grimaud was among them. Suddenly, a guard wearing the duke's livery threw open the door and his comrades slowly emerged dragging several shrieking young women out of the café. The crowd cheered the guards, hurled insults at the women, 'Thieves, whores, away with them!'

'What's going on here?' Anne asked a bystander, though she could guess.

'These young tarts loiter outside the café and solicit gentlemen. Some even sneak inside, like today, create a distraction, and try to steal silverware. In the past the café's proprietor has warned them in vain, so he has complained to the duke. The guards will hand them over to the Paris police. In a week or two they'll go before the lieutenant general who will put them to work in the Salpêtrière for a couple of years.'

Anne shuddered. She had heard dreadful tales about the place. Located on the Left Bank near the royal gardens, it was a huge complex of buildings housing thousands of outcast women, the most miserable of the city's inhabitants: petty criminals and prostitutes, the indigent elderly, the insane. These young prostitutes already understood where they would be taken. They wept, struggled with the guards.

A waif of a girl – she looked hardly fifteen – broke loose from a guard. Anne gasped, the girl was Renée. The guard quickly caught her. She turned on him like a wild cat, bit his hand, kicked him in the groin. Doubled up in pain, he let her loose, and she dashed for the arcade where Grimaud was standing in front, watching the incident. She stretched out her arms to him, called for help. He backed away into the arcade, a cold, unfeeling expression on his face. The crowd closed ranks, rebuffed her.

Another guard seized her, tried to pull her back toward the tumbrel. She bit his arm, kicked his shins, and screamed obscenities at him. Finally, he lost patience and beat her with his fists. She fell, dazed, to the ground. With mounting rage, he gave her prostrate body a vicious kick.

He seemed about to kick her again, when Anne gathered her courage, approached the captain in charge, and spoke sternly to his face. 'Stop that guard or he will kill her. She's Inspector Quidor's witness in a murder case. If she dies, the Paris police will investigate. What will the duke think of that?'

The captain, a brutal, puffed-up man who had seemed bemused by the incident, suddenly became aware of the danger to his career. He shouted at the guard to stop. Other guards rushed to him, pulled him away, flushed, breathing heavily. They rudely picked up the girl and threw her into the tumbrel. She was unconscious and bleeding from the mouth.

The captain turned to Anne, a smirk on his face. 'If your inspector needs the little whore in the next few days, he'll have to look for her at the Châtelet. But I can't guarantee he'll find her.'

Anne acknowledged the information with a nod, then moved away, searching for Grimaud. He was nowhere to be seen.

A few moments later, two more guards emerged from the café, pulling Berthe Dupont after them. Anne felt a flash of anger at the rudeness of the guards, mixed with concern that she might lose a potentially important witness, or suspect, in the death of the Marquis de Bresse.

She returned to the captain of the guard, who now seemed thoroughly annoyed with her. 'Sir.' Anne spoke in a soft, deferential tone and pointed discreetly to Berthe. 'I was going to meet Mademoiselle Dupont in the café and discuss serious police business. She was not there to solicit men or to steal. Would you release her into my custody?' Anne showed him the identification papers that Paul had given her.

The captain examined the papers, glanced at Anne with grudging respect, mixed with suspicion. He ordered Berthe to be brought to him. 'Do you know this woman?' he asked her while pointing to Anne.

Anne prompted Berthe with an intense effort of her eyes.

'Yes,' Berthe replied confidently. 'She's Madame Cartier. We've been trying to meet to talk about a missing person.'

A quick-witted woman, Anne thought. The brothel madam had described Anne to Berthe and Anne's interest in her.

'Take her,' growled the captain to Anne. 'The tumbrel is full anyway. We've caught enough of these tarts to discourage the others.' He barked a command and his pathetic cortege moved off.

Anne and Berthe walked out into the garden and found a

shaded bench where they could talk. The signal cannon fired off a round, telling the noon hour.

'Thank you, Madame Cartier. You've just saved me from disaster.' Suddenly, her whole body began to tremble. She struggled for air. Pale, unable to continue speaking, she bent over, stared at the ground. Anne stroked her back, spoke soothing words until the trembling ceased. She straightened up, drew deep breaths. Anne patted her hand.

After a minute, she had recovered enough to say, 'I was in fact hoping to meet you this morning. What has happened to Lucie? My mistress told me that you found her.'

'Too late, unfortunately. The Marquis de Bresse, with a criminal lack of care, gave her an overdose of a drug that killed her. He and his valet tried to hide her body in a cave on his country estate. We found it there and will return it to her family for a proper burial.'

Berthe listened quietly, a subdued expression on her face, then she remarked, 'It could have happened to me – or to any one of the thousands of young women trying to earn a living this way. The public, especially the men who buy our favours, despise us. Many of them, like the marquis, consider us beyond the protection of the law and treat us cruelly. Rather than protect us, the police and the duke's guards demand bribes or arrest us, as you saw today.'

'Well, in a strange way, the marquis has paid for his sins. You may know that his body was found yesterday in the river.'

'Oh, really,' she exclaimed. 'This morning in the café, I heard a vague rumour to that effect. How had he died?'

'We believe his assailant killed him with a blow to the head.'

'Who might have done it?'

'We can only conjecture. The most likely suspect is his former valet, Denis Grimaud, discharged in disgrace from his master's service and living with Renée, the young woman whom the guard has just now beaten so brutally. The marquis had recently accused Grimaud of embezzlement, and the two men had quarreled. The marquis had a female guest that night. We're trying to learn her identity. She could help us solve the mystery of his death.'

Anne met Berthe's eye. 'By chance, would you know her?'

'It wasn't me,' she replied emphatically, 'in case you're wondering. Grimaud knew that I wanted to leave this kind of work and tried to persuade me to accept a position in the marquis's household. That was a risky business, so I declined. In fact I was home with my father.'

'Can you think of a woman who might have taken the risk and accepted Grimaud's offer?'

'Not really,' Berthe answered. 'I've come only recently to selling my favours and don't know many prostitutes outside of madam's brothel. My acquaintances aren't so desperate as to risk going to the marquis's house. But an experienced pimp like Grimaud could easily have found a willing prostitute either in the Valois arcade or in the streets just south of the central markets, close to the marquis's house on the Isle Saint-Louis.'

'Thank you,' said Anne. 'I'll pass your suggestion along to Inspector Quidor. His agents will make inquiries.'

The two women rose from the bench. Anne gazed sympathetically at her companion. 'If I may presume to ask, what turn of fate has brought you to this life?' She nodded in the direction of the brothel. 'It's not what I'd expect of you.'

'I'll take that as a compliment. My father is blind, able to earn very little money. My mother was a seamstress and supported us while I was growing up. As soon as I was able, I learned her trade. Then a year ago she died. At the same time, I could find no more work in Amiens. Father and I moved to Paris. I worked for a while in the millinery shop in the Valois arcade but didn't earn enough for father and me to live on. A seamstress earns even less. I also owed money to Madame Tessier. She demanded payment under threat of prison. I had no choice but to enter the brothel.'

'Does your father know?'

'I told him only recently.' They began to walk back toward the brothel. 'I've assured him that madam is fair, the house is well-kept, the other women are good companions. Most women doing this work are far less fortunate. My father still feels very badly, but he's not angry with me.'

As they were about to part, Anne asked, 'By the way, Berthe, is your father a Monsieur Jean Dupont, who served in the royal army thirty years ago and was wounded at the battle of Minden?'

Berthe looked astonished. 'Why, yes, I'm his daughter.'

'My friend, Georges Charpentier, was his comrade then. He recognized the name Dupont and asked me to inquire. Could we visit him?'

Berthe hesitated, her expression reluctant. 'Our rooms are very small and plain. We are ashamed to have visitors.'

'I believe you will find that Georges and I are interested in you and your father, not in the appearance of your rooms.'

'Then you are welcome to come tomorrow. I'm free in the morning.'

Behind those words Anne detected a distinct lack of enthusiasm.

Fifteen
The Beggar

7 June

A nne and Georges approached an old house on Rue Saint-Paul, near the church of the same name, no more than a five-minute walk to the marquis's house on the Isle Saint-Louis. Anne hadn't realized before how close Berthe Dupont lived to the marquis and the scene of his murder.

'Though I like the woman and sympathize with her situation,' Anne said, 'we must check her alibi. She and the marquis had a peculiar relationship. He seemed obsessed with her, and she seriously considered working for him, despite the risk.'

With a reluctant nod Georges conceded her point. 'But I'd hate to add any more grief to what my old comrade already bears.'

From across the street they surveyed the building. On the ground floor was a hairdresser's shop. Adjacent was a separate entrance to the stairway serving the upper three floors.

Georges rang the doorbell. The concierge opened, stared at him suspiciously – he was wearing a plain brown wool suit instead of his uniform. He told her their purpose, and she let them in – Berthe had alerted her to the visitors. They climbed up the stairs to the garret and knocked on the door.

Berthe met them with a polite bow and showed them in. Her father was standing, prepared to greet his visitors, a nervous smile on his lips. He was a well-built man with a healthy complexion and a full head of pepper-grey hair. The battle wound had not disfigured his broad, open face. His eyes appeared intact but lifeless. He could in fact distinguish light from dark, as well as large objects, but little more.

'Georges Charpentier, welcome to our home.' He extended a searching hand.

Georges took it, then embraced Dupont. They sat down to tea and sweet biscuits, an expense that even the poor felt they owed to guests. Berthe poured, served the biscuits, then sat next to her father. Beneath a calm surface she seemed tense, on guard. She folded her hands nervously. Anne sat back and observed while the two men recalled events of the war some thirty years earlier. They hadn't seen each other since.

'Jean saved my life at Minden,' said Georges, addressing the women. 'We were close comrades, stood in the line next to each other. We were moving forward when I tripped and fell. The air was full of smoke from the guns. We could hardly see an arm's length ahead. While I was lying there, suddenly a British soldier appeared, a huge, red-bearded Scot in red coat and tartan kilt. He raised his musket to bayonet me. His eyes narrowed, his teeth clenched in a wild, cruel grin. Before he could thrust, Jean shot him in the neck. His blood spurted all over me. I went into shock, couldn't move. Jean lifted me up, slapped my face until I revived, and we marched on.'

For a long silent moment the two men appeared to relive the battle, its acrid stench of gunpowder and the awful carnage. It seemed as clear and strong to them as if it had happened yesterday. A powerful emotion seized Dupont, and he couldn't speak.

Georges looked away, then said to Anne, 'The blast from a misfired musket later cost Jean his sight.'

Anne shifted the conversation to the discovery of the marquis's body. The atmosphere in the room cooled perceptibly. Berthe shifted in her chair, glanced at her father.

'I heard the news from my daughter,' said Jean Dupont. 'I can't say that I'm sorry. He hurt women for the pleasure of it. Good riddance.' He smiled wryly. 'Georges, I'll save you the trouble of asking, where *were* we that night?' He paused for a moment. 'I was here feeling depressed. Berthe stayed home with me.'

'All night?'

'Before retiring early, we walked along the river on the Quai d'Anjou for the fresh air and exercise.'

'That brought you close to the marquis's house. I'll ask Berthe, did you notice anything unusual on your walk?'

'No. The evening was warm and fair. Many people were out on the streets. It was still light outside, but we didn't recognize anyone. And we didn't loiter.'

Georges seemed satisfied with her answer. Anne shifted the conversation again. 'How do you spend your days, monsieur?'

'In the mornings for entertainment I visit a café in the Rue Saint-Antoine, not far from here. My acquaintances kindly read the newspapers to me. The rest of the day, I sometimes work in the neighbourhood. People feel sorry for me and give me odd jobs. I would like to earn enough so that Berthe would not feel obliged to support me.'

Anne detected pain in his voice.

On the way down the stairs, Anne said softly to Georges, 'I regret to have to ask you if the Duponts have told us the truth.'

'They are holding something back,' Georges replied, looking very glum. 'We must speak to the concierge. She should know them.'

In the entrance hall at the foot of the stairs, they knocked on a side door to the hairdresser's shop. The concierge appeared.

'We wish to speak to you privately, madame,' said Georges, showing his identification papers.

The concierge studied her visitors with experienced, wary eyes, then brought them into a small room with a concealed

window to the entrance hall. The room had a table and a
few chairs. Through an open door, Anne could peer into
the shop itself and see stalls, where clients were being
served. The concierge identified herself as the hairdresser's
wife.

She shut the doors and asked what they wanted.

'Tell us how you control people going to the upper floors.'

'The door to the street is always locked. From dawn to dusk,
when I am up and around, I open and close the door for visitors like yourselves. The persons living upstairs have keys to
the front and back doors and usually admit themselves.'

'You've just mentioned a back entrance.'

'Yes, it opens on to a courtyard where rubbish is collected.
From there an alley goes to the next street.'

'So your tenants can come and go as they like, any time
of day or night.'

'Yes, I know them all and trust them.'

'The blind man in the garret, how well does he move
around?'

'Remarkable man! He knows the neighbourhood like the
back of his hand. Uses a stout cane, more to protect himself
than to find his way. Goes out every day for bread and wine
or to do odd jobs.'

'And his daughter. What do you think of her?'

'Works at the Palais-Royal most afternoons and evenings.
Don't know what she does and I don't ask. She's always
pleasant to talk to. Good to her father. Clean and well-
behaved. She pays regularly, but of course she must. The
landlord is strict, will not tolerate delinquents.' She paused,
frowned. 'Come to think of it, she's a bit behind at the
moment. I'll have a word with her.'

'Here's a difficult question,' Georges said. 'Can you recall
what the father and his daughter did ten days ago when the
Marquis de Bresse disappeared?'

For a moment she reflected, stroking her chin. 'Actually,
I *can* recall that day. I noticed that the father didn't look
well. I asked him if I could help. "No, thank you", he replied,
"my daughter is home and taking care of me". Later, he felt
well enough for them to go for a walk. Then shortly after
their return, just before dusk, a boy came with a fancy, sealed
message for Mademoiselle Dupont. I climbed up to the garret

and delivered it to her personally. She glanced at the seal and frowned. I left her at the open door.

'A half hour later, while I was in the kitchen preparing supper, I heard the back door close. I glanced out the window and saw a tall young woman pass beneath the lamp in the courtyard. She was wearing a long cape and had pulled the hood over her head. I couldn't see her face but she must have been Mademoiselle Dupont, the only tall woman in the building.'

'Thank you, madame. You have been helpful.' Georges pressed a coin into her hand. 'We may speak to you again.'

At midafternoon, Paul asked Anne, 'Shall we have coffee in the garden? The weather is fair. I've heard from Quidor. We should discuss the Bresse case.'

'Yes,' Anne agreed. 'I'll fetch Georges.'

They sat around a table in the garden in the shade of a lime tree. Sparrows chirped overhead. The rose beds displayed a brilliant tapestry of pink and red, yellow and white. For a few minutes Anne, Paul, and Georges enjoyed the lovely early summer day while a servant poured the coffee, then left.

Paul stirred sugar into his cup, then began. 'Quidor stopped by the office just before noon. His agents had picked up Grimaud and brought him to the Châtelet for more interrogation. He gave Quidor the same story that he had told a week earlier. He had left the marquis's service early in the afternoon before the marquis's disappearance and had settled into Renée's room near the Louvre. He didn't know the mysterious female guest.'

'Did he still claim an alibi for the time when Bresse was killed?' Anne asked.

'Yes, he said that Renée would vouch for him.'

Anne frowned. 'Renée is almost certainly in too poor a condition to be questioned. The last I saw of her, yesterday, she was being hauled away from the Palais-Royal in a tumbrel, unconscious and bleeding.'

'That's unfortunate,' Georges remarked. 'Then we must delay confronting Grimaud again until we can question Renée and test his alibi.'

'We know where to find him,' Paul said. 'He remains in the Châtelet as a potential suspect in the marquis's death.'

'In the meantime,' Georges went on, 'we should investigate my old comrade Jean and especially his daughter. The marquis appeared to be interested in Berthe, and his valet attempted to entice her into their scheme for "entertainment". We discovered that Berthe and her father were loose with the truth. Their movements that night are obscure, their explanation inconsistent. I don't know why. They don't appear to have a motive to harm the marquis.'

'Will you confront them?' Paul asked.

'Not right away,' Georges replied. 'For this evening, I suggest that we retrace the route of the promenade they claim to have made that night. Though that was almost ten days ago, the street has long memories.'

Anne added, 'And we should explore the route between their room and the marquis's town house. Someone might recall seeing them on the evening of the marquis's death.'

'We?' Paul smiled. 'I have a mountain of work waiting on my desk.'

Georges smiled sympathetically, then finished his coffee. 'Perhaps Madame Cartier would enjoy an evening stroll on Rue Saint-Paul and the Isle Saint-Louis with a man old enough to be her father. Four eyes are better than two. And there's a deaf beggar on Pont Marie that I'd like her to question.'

'I take that as an invitation,' Anne remarked. 'What do you say, Paul?'

'Carpe diem. Enjoy the evening. I'll be in the office when you return.'

At dusk, Anne and Georges strolled past the Duponts' building on Rue Saint-Paul toward the river. It was Saturday evening, the end of the workweek, and the street was crowded with persons in search of pleasure. Anne realized that the crowd would have been thinner on the Thursday evening when Bresse was expecting his female guest, possibly Berthe.

At the river, they turned right on to Quai Saint-Paul. At Pont Marie, the bridge to the island, Georges stopped. 'See that beggar?'

At first it was difficult to see him. Almost the full length of the bridge was lined with busy shops and stalls on both sides of the roadway. Above them were piled dwellings helterskelter. The roadway was narrow and filled with traffic.

Anne finally noticed a small man, dressed in rags, seated on a box a few steps from a book stall. His face was composed in a pitiful expression of need. On his chest hung a crude sign: SOURD INVALIDE [deaf and infirm]. In front of him was an open sack for contributions. At his side was a cane. 'He's deaf, or pretends to be. An old injured soldier?'

'Possibly,' Georges replied, 'or a former metal worker from the noisy shops just west of here. I don't think his deafness is a pretense. That's why I particularly wanted you to be here. He may look like a hundred others of his tribe. I've studied many of them today in this area. But beneath the rags and dirt, this man is different. Watch him for a while.'

Anne pretended to inspect several stalls and small shops selling everything from fruits to pots and pans – all the while studying the beggar with sidelong glances. 'He's observing me, and everyone else on the bridge.'

'Correct. I've inquired about him. He's called Michel. No one seems to know his family name. He lives in a garret room a stone's throw from here, but he owns this spot and spends much of the day and night here. Two or three boys and girls work for him. Maids and other servants seem to give him information and receive instructions. And when he leaves to eat or sleep, he has a substitute to take his place. I'm guessing that he's some kind of police spy, engaged perhaps to observe the movements of certain magistrates of the Parlement who live on the island. They lead the opposition to the king's ministers. He could also be working for the fiscal authorities, trying to catch tax cheats or smugglers.'

'I see, Georges, the island's bridges are under watch night and day. Anyone going to the marquis's town house must pass under the sharp eyes of our deaf beggar and his associates.'

'He will shortly leave for supper at a nearby tavern. We shall join him.'

His supper was at nine o'clock in the evening. The tavern consisted of a large, simple, odd-shaped room with a low ceiling of exposed wooden beams and a tile floor. Men and women with empty jugs lined up at the bar for wine. Tables were half-occupied. The level of noise was tolerable.

Anne and Georges followed the beggar into the room. Leaning heavily on his cane, he limped to the rear and sat at an unoccupied, secluded table. The waiter seemed to know him. A few gestures were exchanged. In a minute or two the waiter reappeared with soup, bread, and wine.

Anne and Georges took a table as close to the beggar as they dared. They ordered the same as he. Soon after beginning to eat, he received a visitor, a man he knew, but not a friend. The visitor didn't order anything, nor was he cordial. The beggar stared intently at the visitor, reading his lips. They exchanged notes for a few minutes. This Michel was an unusual, literate beggar. The visitor passed a small package under the table. The beggar dug into his sack and passed a small package in a similar fashion to the visitor.

'The visitor looks and acts like a police agent or an official spymaster,' Georges remarked. 'His face is familiar but I can't place him.' The two men exchanged a few more notes, then the visitor left. The beggar returned to his supper. From time to time, he nodded to acquaintances, but didn't invite any of them to join him. Apparently they couldn't easily communicate with a deaf man, who was probably accustomed to eating alone. It might be difficult, Anne thought, to persuade him to open up.

When the beggar finished the soup and was lingering at the table over the remains of his bread and wine, Georges signaled Anne. It was time to approach the man.

'May we join you, sir?' Anne addressed him in the common sign language of the Parisian deaf community. The man started, his eyes opened wide. He clearly understood but was too surprised to respond. Anne gave him a kind, understanding smile. 'I'm sorry to disturb you at supper, but I have a few questions. Would you help me?'

The beggar collected his wits and gestured for them to sit down. 'Who are you?' he signed, his eyes cautious.

'I am Madame Cartier, wife of the Provost of the Royal Highway Patrol. This is Georges Charpentier, his adjutant. I've been engaged to find a young woman who disappeared over a month ago in this area. I've learned that she's dead. I want to find out what happened to her and who might be responsible for her death. Here's her picture.' Anne handed him Michou's sketch.

As he took it, he remarked softly, 'Since I lost my hearing as an adult, I can still speak and will do so for Monsieur Charpentier's benefit.' He turned his eyes to the sketch and he brightened. 'Pretty face. I've seen her. She gave me a copper coin. "For good luck", she said.' His smile vanished. 'She's dead, did you say? Then the coin brought her misfortune. I'm sorry.'

'Was Denis Grimaud with her?' asked Anne. The beggar would have often seen Grimaud going to and from the marquis's town house.

The beggar nodded.

'Can you remember seeing Grimaud the night of May twenty-eighth?'

The beggar responded with a wry smile. 'I see thousands of people cross the bridge twenty-four hours a day. And you expect me to remember a man crossing it in the dark of night ten days ago?'

Anne pulled a coin from her purse, laid it on the table, and met his eye.

He put the coin in his pocket. 'In fact, I do remember Grimaud on that occasion, and not because of your coin, though I thank you for it.' He studied Anne and Georges. 'Before we go any farther, I must make inquiries about you. I've got to be careful, or I might find myself in the river, like the Marquis de Bresse. I know the provost's residence and will contact you in a day or two. I might choose another place for our discussion.' He finished his wine, took his cane, and rose from the table. 'I must go back to work. Good night.'

Anne watched him limp out, then she turned to Georges. 'What do you make of him?'

'He's a spy for the government, an able one, despite his deafness. A mine of useful information. I hope he lives long enough to share it with us.'

Anne and Georges returned home about eleven o'clock. Paul's office was dark, but lights were on in the salon upstairs. Crossing the courtyard, they heard music coming through the open windows. 'That's Paul at the piano,' Anne said. As they entered the room, he glanced up. Anne gestured for him to continue. He smiled, hardly missed a note, and played to the end. They clapped. He rose from the instrument and bowed.

'A couple of hours ago, I finished work. After a light supper, I set to practicing the second movement of Mozart's new C-major concerto. Difficult but achingly beautiful. Calm, enchanting, it banished all my demons.' He folded the music, embraced Anne, clapped Georges on the shoulder, and waved them to chairs in front of the fireplace. For a moment, they gazed in silence at the glowing embers of a dying fire. Anne stole a glance at her husband and was pleased. He looked relaxed, harmonious.

'How was your evening's adventure?' he asked.

Georges responded, 'We met an unusual police spy on Pont Marie.' Georges reported on their encounter with Michel the Beggar. At the end, Georges nodded to Anne.

She added, 'The beggar remembered seeing Grimaud on the bridge on the night of the twenty-eighth. And he'll get back to us, hopefully, with more exact details.'

Paul glowed with satisfaction. 'Very promising! The beggar may prove that Grimaud lied to us. He *had* an opportunity to kill the marquis.'

Anne rose from her chair and pointed to a clock on the wall. 'But now it's nearly midnight, and time to retire. We must rise early.' Her voice faltered. 'For tomorrow we shall bury Lucie at Château Beaumont.'

Sixteen
A Country Burial

8 June

Anne and Paul rode silently side by side to Michou's studio. In little over three weeks, working from sketches, Michou had completed Lucie's small, intimate portrait in oil. It was her contribution to the young woman's commemoration at Château Beaumont.

Anne felt low in spirit. She hadn't slept well, unable to shake off a most distressing image of the corpse she saw in the marquis's trunk. That scene in the hidden cave, she feared, was forever planted in her mind. From time to time, it would rise up to torment her.

Even the weather on this early Sunday morning was depressing – grey, cool, and cloudy with the prospect soon of heavy rain. Streets were nearly empty, shops were closed. Anne glanced sideways at her husband. No solace there. His face had a grim, sad look, fixed on Lucie's burial today.

Dressed in black, Michou greeted them at the town house's entrance. 'I'll ride with you to the chateau and attend the funeral,' she signed to Anne. 'Through the painting I've come to know her better. I feel so sorry, as if she were my younger sister. In the years working in the Palais-Royal, I've known many poor Lucies. A few were murdered, most of them died young of disease or despair. If I had been more attractive, and a hearing person, I could easily have become a Lucie myself.'

In the studio upstairs, the portrait rested on an easel waiting for the visitors. They gathered in a semicircle around it. A solemn Michou removed the protective cloth and gestured to the picture of the young woman in all her beauty. Lustrous black hair framed her oval face, graced by a rich creamy complexion, a fine nose, and a determined chin. Her full lips gathered in a pout. Her large brown eyes, filled with troubled yearning, gazed past the viewer into an uncertain distance. With sad, loving care Michou had captured Lucie's half-conscious, vague aspirations, her childlike, petulant spirit.

Too moved to speak or sign, Anne hugged Michou. For several minutes, the group of friends gazed silently at the portrait. Then at Paul's signal, Michou wrapped it for the trip to Château Beaumont – she would carry it herself. They boarded the carriage and set off. Georges would meet them at the chateau. He had gone to the morgue to pick up Lucie's corpse.

They arrived at about one in the afternoon, on time for dinner. It was a modest meal, subdued, appropriate to the occasion. Until then, Anne hadn't given much thought to the funeral arrangements. During conversation at the table she was saddened and angered to learn that most of the villagers and their priest opposed any ceremony for the murdered prostitute. The priest held firmly against her burial in the village graveyard, which he called 'sacred ground'. According to church law, he argued, prostitutes, like actors and suicides, were public sinners and unworthy of Christian burial.

That rule was familiar to Anne. Three years ago in Paris, the body of her stepfather Antoine had been burned and his ashes scattered to the winds in the false belief that he had killed himself. He had in fact been murdered. With help from Paul and Georges, Anne had restored his reputation but still regretted that she couldn't give him a proper burial.

'The church is at least consistent,' Paul remarked with irony. 'It applies the rule to the great as well as the small.' He turned to his aunt. 'You must recall the controversy ten years ago over Voltaire's burial.'

'Yes, indeed,' she replied, addressing her words to Anne. 'There was a spectacular scandal. The great philosophe, a baptized Catholic but a lifelong, sharp critic of the church, was denied a church funeral. In the end, a friendly priest performed the rites for him privately.'

'What are you going to do for Lucie?' Anne asked the countess. 'Will you defy the villagers and their priest?'

'At another time,' she replied, 'I might have forced the issue and insisted on a proper service for Lucie in the village church. As countess and lord of this domain, I have a loud voice in its affairs. But the present mood of the people is so desperate, so contrary, that it would be unwise to provoke them. Instead, I have engaged a friend, a kindly retired priest, for the occasion.'

'The mood of the people – is it so desperate, even here?' asked Anne, wondering what it must be like in less enlightened places.

Marie nodded. 'Several village leaders, Lucie's father chief among them, speak out openly against me, as if *I* have ruined their crops and taken advantage of their misery. He claims I'm a freethinker, a libertine, and a bad influence on his daughters. I've had quite unpleasant conversations with him these past few weeks. I can't seem to change his mind.'

After dinner, they went to a small stone chapel on the estate. With its pillared front and classic proportions, it resembled a Roman temple. The countess's late husband had built it, shortly before his death a decade ago. The countess had buried him beneath its tile floor and, every year, had a memorial mass said for his soul.

For Lucie's burial, Georges had placed her casket, a plain wooden box, in the main aisle in front of the altar and covered it with a large black cloth, embroidered with a cross in silver. For the service, Lucie's mother and her sisters joined the countess, a few domestic servants, and the visitors. Lucie's father remained at home, hostile. Michou placed the young woman's portrait on her casket and stood nearby. Her mother approached it hesitantly, then stared at it. Tears poured from her eyes. She embraced Michou and thanked her.

The priest read aloud the service of Christian burial and preached a brief but pointed homily on a prodigal daughter finding a generous, forgiving welcome in the arms of her heavenly father. The portrait was removed. Servants carried the casket out of the chapel to the cemetery, the people following. With rain threatening, it was quickly lowered into a grave among the estate's deceased household servants.

Anne left the cemetery with Paul at her side. He took her hand. They exchanged silent, meaningful glances. This had been a dignified, appropriate conclusion to Lucie's sad story. Anne felt much relieved, her spirit released from anger.

By the time they reached the chateau, it had begun to rain. The funeral party of family and friends gathered in the salon for quiet conversation. A fine brandy was served. The portrait of Lucie was displayed again and admired.

The countess took Anne aside. 'Michou has told me that she would like to give the portrait to her mother. While she appreciates the offer, she's convinced that her husband would object. Indeed, he would destroy the painting if he could. So I've suggested that Michou loan the portrait to me. I'll hang it in my servants' dining room. Lucie's mother and sisters often eat there and can gaze at it.'

At home on Rue Saint-Honoré, rain was falling hard, tapping a steady beat on the windowsills. In the courtyard the lamps struggled against the evening gloom. Anne and Paul sat in the salon, their chairs turned toward the warmth of a glowing fire.

Paul poured Anne a liqueur and one for himself. She glanced up to him and expressed a thought that was pressing on her mind. 'Though Lucie is buried, I'm not through with my investigation. Her killer is dead, but his accomplice Denis Grimaud is still alive and may soon be set free.'

'Yes,' Paul agreed, then sipped from his glass. 'He'll be released from the Châtelet, when Quidor finishes questioning him concerning his master's death. The magistrates most likely will not charge him with complicity in Lucie's death. They are inclined to accept his claim that she went willingly with him to the marquis's house. After all, she was a working prostitute. The medical examiner at the morgue detected no broken bones or other evidence of a violent abduction.'

'But Grimaud enticed her to the house with false promises, I'm sure,' said Anne. 'And he must have known that the marquis intended to abuse her, as he had Claudette and other female "guests". He deserves to be punished.'

Playing the devil's advocate, Paul countered, 'Like the police, the magistrates assume that prostitutes deserve the abuse that they receive, short of death, of course. Even if magistrates were to agree that Grimaud contributed to Lucie's death, they would treat him lightly or perhaps strike a bargain with him. Should he agree to serve as an informer, his knowledge of the underworld could be useful to them. He's a wily rogue.'

'Nonetheless,' Anne insisted, 'if we could undermine his alibi and prove that he killed his master, he would face capital punishment. He couldn't easily bargain his way out of that. Justice would finally be served.'

Seventeen

A Special Agent Revealed

9 June

At noon, Anne was home in her garden reading a newspaper under the plane tree, informing herself about the country's current political crisis. It was hard to decide who was right, the royal government or the Parlement, when she knew so little about their controversy. Paul, who understood far better than she, was also undecided but claimed that a few facts were obvious. The government was rudderless, lacked a leader. The present king was a decent man but hopelessly indecisive and unsuited to govern. The Parlement offered no feasible plan of reform. Its call for an Estates-General was chiefly intended to preserve noble privileges.

Anne was pondering this matter when a servant announced that a young boy had come with a sealed message to be personally delivered to her. That must be from Michel the Beggar, she thought.

'He's waiting for you in the front parlour,' said the servant, a smile flickering on his lips.

Anne laid down her book and hurried to the parlour. The boy was a street urchin dressed in rags appropriate for a beggar's assistant. But there was intelligence and self respect beneath the layer of dirt on his face. Anne recalled seeing him with the beggar on the bridge.

'I'm supposed to wait for a reply,' he said with childlike authority, handing the message to her.

She broke the seal and read silently:

Meet me at the Jolie Veuve, this evening at dusk. It's
a tavern near the central markets. Ask the barman for
Michel. Michel the Beggar

Pen, ink, and paper were on a writing table in the parlour.
She replied briefly that she and Adjutant Charpentier would
be there, then sent the boy off. For a minute or two she
wondered about this strange beggar. How trustworthy was
he? Georges had said upon leaving this morning that he
would try to learn more about him.

From his bench in the garden of the Palais-Royal Georges
hailed Quidor who was lumbering toward him. Early in the
morning, Georges had inquired about Michel the Beggar.
Quidor had said that by noon he might have some useful
information. The little signal cannon had just fired off the
hour. Quidor was nearly on time.

The inspector eased himself on to the bench. 'I circulated
Michel's description among my colleagues in the criminal
investigation office. None of them knew him. They didn't
think he was working for the tax authorities, or he would
be at one of the city gates, near a bank, or in the central
markets.'

Georges whistled softly. 'We have to suppose that the lieutenant general has hired him and other spies in different
disguises to keep track of the island's rebellious members
of Parlement.'

Quidor agreed with a nod. 'My colleagues and I can't
think of any other troublemakers there who deserve the
beggar's attention.' He paused thoughtfully. 'Michel appears
to be rather new as a spy, resembles an actor I used to
know, Michel Fresnay. As a young man, he performed in
popular theatres on the Boulevard. Many years ago, he
disappeared, struck by a serious malady. That could account
for his deafness.'

'Inexperienced and deaf, Michel looks vulnerable to me,'
Georges remarked.

Quidor agreed. 'If those rich and powerful magistrates felt
threatened, they could set loose their servants on him and
his associates.'

'That wouldn't surprise me, Inspector. The situation is

very tense in the centre of Paris.' Just last month, Georges recalled, the government sent troops into the chambers of Parlement and arrested two leaders among the magistrates. That hadn't intimidated the others. They continued to block every move the government made to end its financial crisis, and insisted that the king call together the country's trad-itional legislature, the Estates-General, and submit to its authority. In such a conflict, small players like the beggar spy could easily be crushed.

'With his life at risk,' Georges mused aloud, 'how much information will the beggar share with us?'

Just before dusk, Anne and Georges entered the Jolie Veuve beneath the sign of a pretty widow. Georges had given Anne his latest conjecture about the beggar. They asked the barman for Michel and were pointed to a back room. To blend into the company Georges wore a plain brown suit. Anne had darkened her complexion and dressed as a male servant, a cap concealing her hair. Both were armed with small, hidden pistols. The area near the markets became dangerous after dark.

Georges gestured for Anne to knock. The door opened a crack.

Anne saw an anxious eye staring at her. It blinked at her disguise.

'Madame Cartier, come in.'

The door opened wider. She entered, followed by Georges. The beggar jumped back, his anxiety rapidly rising. Then he recognized Georges and relaxed.

After locking the door, the beggar said in a strained voice, 'One of my comrades disappeared a few hours ago and was just found dead in the river. I was tempted to skip this meeting. Probably been followed.'

With Anne signing for him, Georges tried to reassure the beggar. 'We'll see you home.'

He shook his head. 'The less I'm seen with you the better. You're too close to Baron Breteuil and the government. And so am I, in the eyes of those who would kill me. Still, I think we now understand each other, and within certain limits I'm allowed to help your investigation.'

Anne gave Georges a knowing look. Michel the Beggar

must indeed be working for Lieutenant General DeCrosne on a special assignment.

'I understand those limits,' Georges remarked, 'and will stay within them. Can you answer my earlier question – did you see the Marquis de Bresse's valet, Denis Grimaud, late on the night of May twenty-eighth or early in the morning of May twenty-ninth, cross the bridge to the Isle Saint-Louis?'

'Since you first asked the question, I have refreshed my memory. Yes, I saw him cross to the island at about midnight and return an hour later.'

'Are you sure?'

'Yes, the weather was warm and dry. My assistant took my place during the day. I watched at night. We take turns. Grimaud is one of the persons I'm paid to follow. His master's father is involved in Parlement's resistance to the king's ministers. The marquis himself meets with young men from the magistrates' families for seditious discussions. While procuring prostitutes, Grimaud also carries messages from the duke's partisans at the Palais-Royal to the rebellious magistrates on the island.

'Grimaud usually nods to me while crossing the bridge. This time, he tried to conceal his face. That intrigued me, so I followed him to the Bresse town house and observed him enter by the back way. I saw only the lower part of his face, chin and mouth. But I also recognized his gait.'

'Was a small woman with him?' Georges was thinking of Renée.

'I didn't see her. To escape notice she might have lagged behind him. If so, I would have missed her at the town house. I had no reason to wait for him, so I went back to the bridge. When he returned to the bridge, he again concealed his face. He was alone as far as I could tell.'

Georges's face began to glow with excitement. Grimaud was proving to be a more serious suspect than Berthe Dupont. He had opportunity as well as motive to kill his former master.

'Quidor and I must question Grimaud about this revelation at the Châtelet tomorrow morning.' Georges stirred as if ready to leave.

Anne raised her hand for him to wait. 'Shouldn't we ask if Michel might also have seen Berthe that same night?'

Georges frowned, then nodded with noticeable distaste. 'Yes, of course.'

Anne described Berthe and added, 'You would often see her in the morning, walking with her blind father. He uses a cane.'

'I know them well, among my most kind benefactors. Tall for a woman. She also crossed the bridge that night, a couple of hours earlier than Grimaud. I didn't follow her. No reason to. She's not on my list of suspicious characters and wasn't trying to hide. I don't recall her returning to the bridge – I nodded off a couple of times, late at night and early in the morning.'

Michel indicated that he wanted to leave. 'You go first,' he said to his visitors.

Anne and Georges exchanged glances, then rose from the table. 'You have been helpful, Michel. Thank you.' Anne signed with a smile, then followed Georges to the door. She turned with an afterthought and met the beggar's eye. 'We know you only as Michel the Beggar. Many years ago, would you have been Michel Fresnay, actor on the Boulevard?'

For a moment his eyes flashed with a mixture of sadness and pain. 'That was a different life.'

Once outside, Georges pulled Anne into a dark alleyway with a view of the tavern's entrance. 'We should follow Michel back to his room. As we passed through the tavern, I noticed a pair of ruffians duck out of sight. I'll bet they're waiting for him.'

She shuttered her lamp. A few minutes later, Michel stepped out, glancing anxiously up and down the dimly lighted, narrow street. With a quick sign of the cross for good luck, he walked briskly toward the river.

'There they are,' whispered Georges in Anne's ear, as the two suspicious men appeared in the doorway. Hesitantly Georges asked her, 'Are you willing to follow them?' The two men took off after the beggar.

Her heart pounding, she whispered, 'I'm willing. We must protect Michel.'

The street was crowded with people coming and going. The occasional streetlamps cast intermittent pools of light.

Michel's enemies would look for a dark and lonely stretch in order to attack. Anne couldn't see or hear them. For all she knew, they could be lurking in the next alley, ready to jump upon her and Georges instead of Michel.

Suddenly, she heard a commotion ahead, quite close. Georges took off, shouting as if he were a dozen watchmen. The ruffians fled, Georges heaving stones at them. To judge from a howl of pain, at least one of the stones hit its mark.

Michel's assailants had left him leaning against a wall. Anne unshuttered her lamp and inspected him. There was a bruise on the back of his head, but he was lucid and fully conscious.

'I didn't expect an escort, Madame Cartier, but I'm grateful. I should go back to simply begging. This spy business is more than I bargained for.'

The noise brought light to many windows, though no one dared to come out. Still, the street seemed safer. Georges approached Michel. 'We'll take you home.' He spoke with authority and took the man under the arm. He wobbled a little, but they set off at a fast pace.

When they reached Michel's building, Georges and Anne were prepared to say goodbye. But Michel signed to Anne. 'Would you two join me upstairs for a drink? We could continue our conversation.'

Anne translated the invitation to Georges and added, 'I'm willing.' She could foresee no danger, only an opportunity to advance the investigation. For a fraction of a second, Georges hesitated, then spoke for both of them, 'We accept with pleasure.'

Michel's residence was like no garret room Anne had ever seen. It was spacious and clean, the furnishings simple but comfortable and in good taste. One wall held a shelf of books, surrounded by engravings or prints. A writing table stood by a window. There was a sleeping alcove near the hearth in a small kitchen. The combination of begging and spying appeared to be profitable.

The host found a bottle of white wine and sat his guests around the table.

'How does your head feel?' signed Anne after they had lifted their glasses and toasted Michel's good fortune.

'It throbs, but not enough to complain about.' He emptied

his glass and poured another. Drowning his fears, Anne thought. By the time he finished the second glass, his eyes had glazed over and his signing had grown careless and free.

Anne saw an opportunity. With a gentle smile she signed, 'Would you tell us something about yourself, Michel?'

He didn't hesitate. 'I am indeed Michel Fresnay. My parents were actors in Paris, who trained me for the stage. For several years I acted in theatres on the Boulevard until I became seriously ill, nearly died, and lost my hearing.

'My parents and I moved to Angers. I worked at menial jobs in theatres, acting occasionally as a mime. My situation began to improve five years ago, when I met Charlotte Blouin, a student of the Abbé de l'Épée. She tutored me in signing and reading lips. Two years ago, my parents died and I moved here. Couldn't find work. Took up begging and did well.

'By chance I made the acquaintance of a police officer in Lieutenant General DeCrosne's office. He was looking for special agents to spy on the members of Parlement who were fighting with the king. After the officer and I had come to know each other better, I convinced him to employ me, an actor as well as a deaf beggar.'

Michel smiled mischievously at Anne. 'You spied on us at the tavern near the river. When I realized that you had seen us exchange packages, I was alarmed, but the officer reassured me that he knew you. It has been exciting and rewarding, until just recently, when the people I've spied on have begun to fight back. They've hired assassins posing as their grooms to ferret us out and kill us.

'As you already know, our work for the lieutenant general is kept secret even from the Paris police. In the Bresse case, since it involves the murder of a noble, the lieutenant general has allowed me to help you.'

'What more can you do for us?' Anne asked.

'I can inquire further among other secret agents into the movements of Denis Grimaud, Renée Gros, and Berthe Dupont at the time the marquis was killed. My comrades may add details to what we already know.'

He turned to Anne. 'Meet me on the bridge tomorrow afternoon.'

Eighteen
Elusive Truth

10 June

E arly in the morning, while Anne waited at home, Georges and Colonel Saint-Martin entered the tavern near the Louvre. Anne had been there a few days ago, visiting Renée, and had given them the address. They intended to search Grimaud's room for more evidence of his part in the death of the Marquis de Bresse. Michel the Beggar had undermined the ex-valet's alibi, had placed him at the scene of the crime and within the time that it most likely took place.

The bar was open and selling wine by the jugful to a long line of customers. Since the two officers were in uniform, they drew many nervous sideways glances. The barman flashed an anxious smile at them and dispensed the wine a little faster. A few minutes later he was free, and the colonel approached him.

'Sir, could you direct us to the room of a Monsieur Denis Grimaud?'

'He's is on the top floor, to the right. But you won't find him at home. The Paris police took him away three days ago.'

'I know. We've come to speak to his wife, Madame Grimaud.' The agents had reported that almost immediately after Renée was beaten and taken to prison, Grimaud had installed another woman in her room as his companion. Saint-Martin didn't know her name or much about her.

The barman sneered. 'I doubt that she's his wife. She's called the Bitch. Whatever she is, she's upstairs and moving about.'

Saint-Martin directed Georges to lead the way. They

climbed the rickety wooden stairs to the top-floor landing.
Georges knocked. A loud low voice asked who was there.

'The police,' Georges replied. The door opened a crack,
then wider, and the men walked in.

She was a large-boned woman, perhaps twenty-five, but
a hardened, ruthless expression made her look ten years older.
Barefooted, she wore only her shift with a scarf thrown
loosely over her shoulder. Saint-Martin's first reaction was
surprise that an enterprising pimp like Grimaud hadn't picked
a more attractive companion to replace Renée. But on closer
inspection, the Bitch displayed certain qualities that would
appeal to Grimaud's criminal instincts and his need for
gambling money: a quick intelligence; sharp, cunning eyes;
deft, swift moves; big, strong hands. A gifted cutpurse.

Saint-Martin glanced at her shoulder, exposed for a
moment, and saw a branded 'V' for *voleuse* [thief], before
she covered it. He imagined that a poor, abusive childhood,
followed by years in a royal prison, had schooled her for a
life of crime. She gestured carelessly to a wooden table and
they pulled up chairs around it.

'What have you done with Denis?' she asked, looking
doubtful.

'He's resting comfortably in a cell at the Châtelet while
we gather information. We'll interrogate him later this
morning. We have some questions for you.'

Her eyes narrowed as she assembled her defenses. 'I've
already told the police all I know.'

'A reliable witness saw Denis on the bridge to the Isle
Saint-Louis and followed him to the Marquis de Bresse's
town house at nearly midnight. He was inside for little more
than an hour. I believe he took certain articles that have
disappeared from the marquis's house. Will you tell me where
they are?'

'I think you're trying to trick me.' Her jaw had set firmly
and defiantly.

'As you wish, madame. Now we shall search your rooms.'

An expression of alarm flashed across her face. 'You can't
do that!' She jumped to her feet. Georges was quicker. He
caught her by the shoulders and pushed her down in her
chair.

'Hold her, Georges, for the first thing I'm going to inspect is the ring on her right hand.' Saint-Martin seized the hand and pulled a thick gold band off the ring finger. She strained against Georges's grip but he held her tight to the chair. 'That's mine!' she screamed. 'Put it back!'

Saint-Martin took the ring to a window and studied it. 'The Bresse coat of arms is inscribed on the inside. We'll ask your companion where he found it.' The colonel put it in his pocket.

'Now let's look for the marquis's purse. It was also reported missing.' Georges secured the woman's hands and feet to the chair, then searched the room. Within a few minutes, he found the purse hidden in a mattress. The Bresse coat of arms was inscribed on the fine leather. It jingled when he shook it.

Saint-Martin showed the purse to the Bitch and took out a handful of Louis d'or. 'I'll wager that you hid these gold pieces from Denis so that he wouldn't gamble them away.'

She glumly nodded.

'Now, tell me, when did he give them to you?'

'Four days ago. After Renée was arrested, he asked me to move into her room with him and be his companion. She wouldn't be coming home for a long time, if ever. I figured that he was in trouble, needed someone to watch out for him. That might be risky, I thought. So I asked him, "What can you offer?" He gave me the ring. "It's yours", he said. The purse was his. When the police took him away, I found the purse and hid it in the mattress. I suspected that he had stolen both the ring and the purse, but I kept them anyway.'

Saint-Martin added the purse to the ring in his pocket. 'Set her loose, Georges. We have what we came for. Now we are ready for Grimaud.'

Late in the morning, Georges and Colonel Saint-Martin made their way to a room in the Châtelet. Bailiffs brought in Grimaud and sat him at a table. He seemed typically cunning and self-assured.

Seated opposite, Saint-Martin began the interrogation in a casual tone. 'You have come to our attention too frequently during the past few weeks. First, we discovered that you were involved in the death of the prostitute Lucie Gigot. You also conspired with the Marquis de Bresse to conceal her death and burial. Now we believe that you also may have murdered your former master, the Marquis de Bresse.'

Grimaud smiled slightly, remained calm.

The colonel continued, 'Midafternoon on May twenty-eighth, the marquis discharged you for embezzling his money and threatened to report you to the police the next day. Witnesses at the Palais-Royal have told us that you appeared to be very angry. I see a clear motive for murder there.'

Saint-Martin had learned that the charge of embezzlement could not yet be proven. The marquis had properly authorized most of Grimaud's spending and bank withdrawals. But there were gaps in the record. Certain papers were missing that probably would incriminate him.

'No, Colonel, I did nothing illegal. The marquis had little understanding of his own financial affairs and spent heedlessly. When his creditors pressed him, he looked for a scapegoat and blamed me. True, I was angered but not to the point of killing him. I'm not that foolish, for I would be an obvious suspect.'

'You're whistling in the wind,' Saint-Martin rejoined. 'You feared that the police would take the marquis's side and throw you in prison. You couldn't return the money. Most of it was lost in gambling dens.'

Beads of perspiration began to form on Grimaud's brow.

Saint-Martin pressed on. 'Furthermore, your alibi for that night doesn't stand up. In a previous interrogation you claimed you were with Renée Gros during the crucial hours. But she has testified that she couldn't account for you while she was asleep. Even more damning is that a credible witness observed you entering the marquis's house by the back way at about midnight and leaving an hour or so later. What did you do during that time?'

Grimaud hesitated, searched Saint-Martin's eyes, then Georges's, for a sign that they might be bluffing. Finally, he sighed. 'I thought you wouldn't believe me if I told the truth. Frankly, I went to the marquis's house because I had grown concerned about what he might do to his female guest, a certain woman with whom I had been associated.'

'And who was that?' Georges asked.

'Berthe Dupont. The marquis had approached her at the Palais-Royal. She rebuffed him. But that only increased his desire. He ordered me to persuade her to come, promised her much money, a secure position in his household. She was sorely tempted and refused reluctantly. That night I wondered if he had finally prevailed upon her with an offer she couldn't refuse. His obsession had become unnatural, extreme, even for him. I feared that he might seriously harm her. People would think that I was partly responsible for what happened.'

'Your concern is touching,' Saint-Martin remarked with a strong hint of irony.

Grimaud appeared not to notice. 'So I stole into the house through the back way. The ground floor was empty, quiet. As usual, the servants had been sent out. I went upstairs to the dining room. The dishes were still on the table, the meal had been partly eaten. I hurried through the rest of the house. It was empty. I saw no sign of struggle or violence. I concluded that the marquis and his guest must have gone to a secret nest somewhere, so I returned home. That's the truth.'

Saint-Martin glared at the man. 'When I interrogated your friend the Bitch this morning, I noticed a gold band on her ring finger. While my adjutant held her down, I removed the band and discovered the marquis's coat of arms etched inside. I then searched your room and found a fine, tooled leather purse with several Louis d'or inside. On the outside, again, was the marquis's coat of arms.' Saint-Martin turned to Georges, off to one side taking notes. 'What do you think of that, Monsieur Charpentier?'

'Well, sir, I conclude that Monsieur Grimaud saw those things while searching the house and helped himself. He may also have removed certain incriminating financial papers.'

Grimaud sighed, then said defensively, 'He owed me a month's wages. But I swear that I never saw him that night, much less killed him.'

Saint-Martin signaled the bailiffs. 'Take the prisoner back to his cell.' They began to escort Grimaud out. Before they could leave the room, Saint-Martin stopped them and addressed the prisoner. 'By the way, Grimaud, were you alone as you searched the house that night?'

He hesitated for a fraction, then said, 'Yes, I was alone.'

'No more questions now,' said the colonel and waved the bailiffs and their prisoner off.

For a few more minutes Saint-Martin and Georges lingered in the interrogation room.

'I could have challenged Grimaud's claim that he had been alone. I'm sure he had a companion, most likely Renée. But I'd rather question her first.'

Georges looked doubtful. 'The police appear to have lost her. One of Quidor's agents checked at the Châtelet and she's not there. Worse yet, thanks to the beating from the duke's guards, she might not be *able* to answer you.'

'We'll have to find her somehow. In the meantime, Georges, we both are nearly convinced that the marquis's female guest was Berthe Dupont. Contrary to what she told us about spending the night with her father, she did in fact leave home and cross the bridge to the island.'

Despite efforts to control his feelings, Georges began to look apprehensive.

Saint-Martin continued, 'We must hear her explanation of what really happened in the marquis's town house.'

Nineteen
Berthe's Story

10 June

After a bite to eat in the garden of the Palais-Royal, Saint-Martin and Georges walked to the Valois arcade. Berthe Dupont would be near the entrance to the brothel, discreetly soliciting suitable customers. Georges pointed to a red gown in the crowd that thronged the shadowed arcade. 'There she is,' he said. They drew quite close to her before she recognized them. The forced smile on her face vanished, replaced by a mixture of apprehension and resignation.

'I expected you to come for me,' she said. 'We can't talk here.' The crowd pressed upon them. Many stopped and stared. The sight of two blue-coated police officers talking with a prostitute in a red dress aroused a great deal of curiosity. Berthe's eyes pleaded with Saint-Martin. She murmured, 'Madam would be much embarrassed, and angry with me, if we were to enter the brothel together.'

Saint-Martin smiled gently, tipped his hat to Berthe, and said softly, 'Come to my aunt's town house on Rue Traversine in a half hour. It's a short walk. My adjutant and I will be waiting.'

Berthe murmured, 'I'll be there. Thank you.' She seemed greatly relieved. So did his adjutant, Saint-Martin noticed.

Saint-Martin turned to his adjutant as they climbed the stairs of the town house. 'I may have need of Michou. We must see if she's in her studio upstairs.' On the second floor the door to the studio was closed. Saint-Martin opened it slightly and peeked in.

A beautiful, dark-haired young girl, perhaps ten years old, dressed in a lovely white silk gown, was sitting for her portrait. Her rich, fashionable, indulgent-looking mother sat to one side with Sylvie, who interpreted for her and Michou.

Saint-Martin backed away and closed the door. 'We'll meet Michou when she's free.'

A quarter hour later, he and Georges were waiting in the downstairs parlour when a servant announced that Berthe had arrived.

'Show her in,' Saint-Martin ordered. Georges moved to one side to take notes.

The colonel received her courteously, showed her to a chair, and began a casual conversation. This was his first opportunity to study her closely. She was an attractive young woman, tall, large-boned, and erect, simple and direct in speech and manners. What struck him now was the sad resignation in her wide, golden-brown eyes. Endowed with a strong sense of her own worth, she was now mired in a desperate situation. Poverty forced her into prostitution. Obliged to perform degrading work, she was exposed to constant insult and contempt, with no hope of redemption in sight.

'According to my adjutant, Monsieur Charpentier,' he waved

in Georges's direction, 'your father said that you were at home with him on the night of the twenty-eighth and twenty-ninth of May, when the Marquis de Bresse was killed. Is that correct?'

She moistened her lips. 'Yes, he did say that.'

'And you did not contradict him, did you?'

'That's true,' she replied. 'Should I?'

'Perhaps he didn't know that you left the house at dusk on that fatal night and shortly afterward crossed the bridge to the Isle Saint-Louis. Two credible witnesses separately observed you.'

She glanced at Georges, flushed, and averted her eyes. For a long moment the room was unnaturally silent. She looked up. Her eyes began to tear. The colonel offered her a kerchief. She took it with a quick, slight smile and dabbed at her eyes.

'This is almost more than I can bear. I've not only ruined my own life, I've also made my father look like a liar.'

'Tell me what happened.'

Berthe cast her eyes down, sighed, then began to explain that late that afternoon the Marquis de Bresse sent her a sealed message, stating that he held her in the highest regard. Would she be willing to serve as his housekeeper and take over duties formerly performed by Monsieur Denis Grimaud? He was just that afternoon discharged for financial crimes. Berthe quoted from memory:

> I have full confidence in your intelligence and your char-
> acter. I realize that your father's tragic misfortune has
> forced you into your present occupation. I consider your
> loyalty to him a badge of honour. I would be most pleased
> to have you in my service.

'In closing, he offered me generous wages and accommodations. My inexperience was not a problem, rather an asset, since I would not be entering into the position with the bad habits that Grimaud had. The marquis said that he preferred to train me himself.'

'So you took him at his word,' remarked Saint-Martin, unable to conceal his skepticism.

'In hindsight, of course, I was truly foolish to believe him. But I was desperate. I told myself, maybe he wasn't as evil as people said. I read the message again. He had a way with words and knew how to exploit my situation. I had fallen behind in the rent. The brothel madam complained that my customers found me stiff and aloof. Unless I soon changed, she would have to turn me out. What was I to do?'

'Did your father know about the marquis's invitation?'

'No, I put him to sleep and sneaked out the back way. I didn't want anyone to know until I was sure I had the position and it was as good as the marquis had promised. Also, if the brothel madam learned somehow that I was going to the marquis, she would throw me out.'

'What happened when you met the marquis?'

'I was surprised that he came to the door in shirtsleeves and breeches. But he was gracious and charming, showed me around the house. I asked him why there were no servants. He replied that he was a lenient master. They had finished their work early and were free for the evening. His explanation quieted my concern – his manner was still courteous and amiable.

'Supper would be informal, he said. He led me into a small dining room. We lit candles and laid out a light supper that the cook had prepared. In good spirits, he served it himself to show me how he wanted it done. By this time, the man had quite bewitched me. Like the devil himself, he knew precisely my weaknesses and how to use them. And I drank more wine than I should have.

'When we had cleared the table, he poured a sweet wine for us. At the time, I didn't take note of the fact that he had turned his back to me when he filled the glasses. Within a few minutes I began to feel hot. My nerves were tingling and my head felt numb. I could hardly think. It was as if I were out of my body, watching myself at a great distance.

'He noticed my condition, helped me from the chair, said I needed to walk about. We went upstairs, with me leaning on his arm, into a strange room. By this time, my eyes were focusing badly, but I think he pointed to pictures of nude men and women. He pushed aside a cabinet, lifted a trapdoor, and said we would visit his secret treasure room.

'Down the stairs we went, struggling and stumbling. He held a lantern with one hand and me with the other. At the bottom of the stairs he opened a door, shoved me into a dark room, and lit several lanterns. It was a room without windows. On the stone walls hung whips, ropes and chains, a sword, and various strange instruments. Hooks were fixed into the wooden ceiling. A large straw pallet lay on the floor.'

Saint-Martin glanced at Georges. They nodded to each other. From their previous visit to the house they recalled the basement rooms, including this one.

'My knees buckling, my mind numb,' Berthe continued, 'I was hardly able to move. With a ghastly leer on his face, he took off most of my clothes and pushed me down on the pallet. He clamped his hands around my neck and slowly began to choke me. "I'm going to kill you," he said softly, then added, "but not right now." Those are the last words that I heard, and I passed out.'

'What happened next?'

'I was unconscious for maybe an hour. When I woke up, the lanterns were still lit. I was lying on the pallet in my shift. I felt nauseous. My head ached. For a few minutes I lay still. Nothing stirred. I got up on my bare feet and looked around. Then I saw him, in shirtsleeves and breeches, sitting against the wall, his head bowed. I sensed he was dead. I looked closely. There were large bloody bruises on his left temple. A bloody hammer lay near his body.

'I must have killed him while I was unconscious. How was that possible? Perhaps under the drug's influence I functioned without being aware of what I was doing, like a sleepwalker.

'Panic set in. The police would accuse me of murder and I'd be tortured, then burned on the Place de Grève. I had noticed the large drain in the middle of the room. I lifted the grate and saw a tunnel below. I figured it led to the river. I pushed his body into the tunnel, dragged it to the river, and dumped it in.'

'Did you notice a gold band on his finger?'

'He was wearing it when he met me at the door. I didn't notice it at supper when he served me. I suppose he took it off while he was showing me through the house.'

'After you threw him in the river, what did you do?'

'I glanced at my hands. They were bloody from having dragged him. My shift was bloody too. I washed my hands in the river and returned to the room. My gown and shoes were tossed into a corner. I rolled the bloody shift into a bundle, dressed, and walked home. The next day, I washed the blood out of the shift. My father slept through all of this, and I never told him.'

She paused, smoothed her gown, then searched Saint-Martin's face. 'Do you believe me? It's an incredible story. Sometimes I ask myself, how much of it is fantasy, how much is true?'

'Frankly, mademoiselle, I don't understand how you could have beaten the marquis with a hammer and not have been aware of what you were doing. I've heard of sleepwalking, or somnambulism, but persons afflicted with the disease are not known to be violent. Perhaps certain drugs might induce violent, unconscious, and involuntary reactions. I'd be surprised if a magistrate would accept such a theory.'

Georges spoke up. 'If you did strike the marquis, you could argue self-defense. He had drugged you and said that he was going to kill you.'

She looked at him doubtfully. 'Would a magistrate believe me? I had gone freely to the marquis's home, aware of his reputation for abusing prostitutes. Furthermore, he left no mark of violence on my body. And, of course, no one observed us.'

Saint-Martin stroked his chin and reflected. 'You have a point there. Self-defense might be difficult to prove. I would have to say that you are a suspect in the marquis's death. But you can take comfort in the fact that you aren't the only one. Denis Grimaud is another. You are free to leave. We shall speak again so remain available to us in Paris.'

Steps were heard in the entrance hall outside the parlour. Saint-Martin nodded to Georges, who opened the door. Michou and Sylvie were escorting the young girl and her mother to the courtyard. Upon their return to the hall, they met Berthe leaving the parlour.

Saint-Martin introduced them to each other, adding that Mademoiselle Dupont was the daughter of Georges's old comrade in arms.

Michou's eye fixed on Berthe's face, fascinated by something that she perceived there. Saint-Martin encouraged her with a nod, then drew the others into a brief conversation. Michou stepped to the side and appeared to mentally sketch the woman's features.

After Berthe's departure, Michou pulled a small sketch-book from her pocket, sat down at a table, and began to enter her impressions. The others left her alone.

Saint-Martin asked Sylvie about the young girl's portrait upstairs in the studio.

'Michou's technique is rapidly improving. This portrait will be worthy of Madame Vigée le Brun,' she said, then added wryly, 'but much less expensive.' She inclined her head in puzzlement. 'Why have you encouraged Michou to sketch Mademoiselle Dupont?'

'She's a suspect in a murder case. A good picture of her might prove useful.'

After ten minutes, Michou joined them and handed the sketch to Saint-Martin. 'I've studied her before in the Valois arcade,' she signed, and Sylvie translated. 'I see her as a misfit, unhappy, angry. Shouldn't be in a brothel, hates it. Has too much self-respect.'

Michou continued to sign, but Sylvie hesitated before translating.

'What did she sign?' the colonel asked, curious.

'Berthe is also big and strong. If a man were to cheat or abuse her, she might hurt him badly.'

Saint-Martin thought of Berthe pulling the marquis's dead body to the drain in the basement floor, casting it into the tunnel, and dragging it to the river. He met Michou's eye and signed, 'I agree.'

Rain threatened that afternoon. Anne hurried through busy streets with the graceless step and the rude manners of lower-class Parisians. Posing as a poor scullery maid, she wore an ill-fitting, patched grey dress. A white bonnet concealed much of her face. At heart still an actress, she enjoyed playing various roles.

Today she had to disguise herself for Michel's sake. Mindful of last night's violent incident, she expected him to be more anxious than ever. His enemies were probably spying on him and would be alarmed if they were to recognize him in the company of a police colonel's wife.

He was sitting on his box on the bridge to the island, posing in his usual attitude of supplication. As she approached him, she signed her question, 'Are your enemies watching you?

Could you leave your post and meet me?' She threw a small coin in his sack.

He looked up and recognized her but without changing in the least his beggar's piteous expression.

'Yes,' he signed in reply. 'Two of them are loitering on the bridge. But they are bored and not paying close attention to me. I'll meet you in the island's church of Saint-Louis in twenty minutes.'

She was there with time to spare. He hobbled into the church and went directly to an empty chapel, crossed himself, and knelt down laboriously on a prayer stool. Anne understood that she should join him. She knelt on a prayer stool facing him, and crossed herself as well. They were positioned to sign to each other and read lips. Observers would hear nothing and would conclude that these two kneeling figures were simply deep in their devotions.

To begin, Anne inquired about his head injury from the previous night.

It was causing him considerable pain, he replied. He was now afraid to spy at night. 'As I promised, I asked other special agents surveying the island, if they could add to what I told you about Grimaud's movements that night. Since he was also on their list of persons to watch, one of the comrades had recorded the exact time of his departure from the marquis's house, five minutes after one o'clock in the morning. I had recorded his entry into the house at five minutes before midnight. Grimaud was in the house for an hour and ten minutes.'

'Did your comrade observe Renée Gros that night?' Anne asked.

'I know who you mean, you inquired about her before at the Jolie Veuve. My comrade had seen a small person leaving the marquis's back door a few minutes after Grimaud left. She was wearing a long cloak. A hood covered her head and concealed her face. It wasn't possible to make a positive identification.'

'You've been helpful, Michel. No doubt the small person was Renée. Since she and Denis chose to travel in disguise apart from each other, it appears that they were intent on crime.'

By the time Anne reached home, rain was falling. Dark, heavy clouds covered the city. She and Paul sat comfortably in his office, enjoying tea while they exchanged news.

'Unfortunately,' said Paul, 'no one can tell us when Berthe left the marquis's house.' He then reported on his interrogation of Berthe and compared her version of that fatal night with Grimaud's.

'Had Grimaud gone to the house, while Berthe and the marquis were still there?' Paul asked. 'Or had Berthe already killed the marquis, thrown him into the river, and left?'

Anne sipped her tea, reflecting, then replied, 'Let's suppose Berthe and the marquis *were* still in the basement. Grimaud would certainly have found them. That's where the marquis usually took women whom he intended to abuse.'

'According to Berthe,' Paul continued, 'she was unconscious for a while. At that time, the marquis and his ex-valet could have confronted each other. Grimaud might have pleaded for the marquis not to report him to the police. The marquis would have refused and ordered him out of the house. Enraged, Grimaud could have seized the hammer and struck the marquis, then left Berthe still unconscious to serve as a scapegoat.'

'A plausible conjecture,' Anne granted.

'In the meantime, what was Renée doing?'

'Thieving most likely,' Anne replied. 'This afternoon I learned from Michel that she furtively left the marquis's house a few minutes after Grimaud.'

'Then she, like Grimaud, had the opportunity for a much more serious crime,' Paul mused.

Anne added, 'But we won't know what she did until we find her. And that won't be easy.'

'You are right, as usual, my dear.' Paul winked, then drained his cup. 'I've contacted Quidor. For the past few days, one of his men has searched in vain for Renée in the Châtelet, where she should have been held for a magistrate's hearing, accused of thievery as well as prostitution.'

'It's four days since the police arrested her,' Anne recalled. 'Something must have gone wrong.'

Paul nodded. 'Quidor believes that the Paris police have omitted the usual judicial procedures – the Châtelet is over-crowded. They may have put her temporarily in the Salpêtrière's prison unit, where prostitutes are confined.'

'Or,' Anne suggested, 'since her arrest was violent and she might have been seriously injured, they could have brought her to the hospital's infirmary.'

'Right again.' Paul smiled and met Anne's eye. 'Quidor has asked for your help. He wants you to search for her at the Salpêtrière.'

'Really?' Anne exclaimed. 'What a bizarre idea! How can I, a simple woman, find Renée among the thousands of unfortunate inmates in that hideous place? That's a job for his agents. They get paid for that kind of work.'

Paul waved her objection aside. 'You know Renée, Quidor's agents don't. He also believes that the search requires a shrewdness and tact that he's discovered in you. His agents would feel hopelessly lost in a badly managed institution like the Salpêtrière, with its thousands of elderly, insane, or criminal women. The administration and the inmates would receive you with much less suspicion and fear than they would his agents.'

Anne struggled to overcome her reluctance. It came mainly from the profound revulsion she felt at even visiting such a place. Its sights and sounds and smells were so disgusting. On the other hand, she didn't like to be governed by her feelings. Paul clearly thought she was up to the job. And in her mind she was inclined to agree. Finally, she convinced herself. She could search the Salpêtrière for Renée as well as any of the inspector's agents.

She said to Paul, 'I realize that I can save that old fox Quidor much expense and bother. But I also appreciate his confidence in me and welcome the opportunity to be helpful.'

Twenty
A Women's Prison

11 June

After breakfast, Anne, Sylvie, and Paul met in his office for final preparations. Last night, Anne had briefly described the challenges to finding the missing Renée and had invited Sylvie to take part. She could serve as a companion. She had shown a lively interest. Like Anne herself, Sylvie now seemed eager to go. At the least, it would be an adventure and stimulate their wits.

Anne turned to Sylvie. 'You have had time to reflect. Are you sure that you would like to join me? But I must warn you, if half of what they say about the Salpêtrière is true, you will see truly shocking scenes.'

Sylvie raised her chin, spoke in a firm voice. 'I want to go with you, Madame Cartier.'

'Good.' Anne turned to her husband. 'Paul, if we find her, what exactly do you want us to do?'

Paul thought for a moment, then replied, 'Determine if she is able and willing to undergo interrogation. If not, then find out what steps we must take to make her ready.'

Anne understood that under the best of circumstances Renée would be a reluctant, difficult witness, very shy of a uniformed police officer. Anne and Sylvie would have a daunting task to convince her to cooperate.

Thus far, Sylvie had said little but had listened attentively, a question gathering on her furrowed brow. 'I've heard that the officials in charge at the Salpêtrière generally discourage visiting the hospital or the prison. Will they allow us to enter?'

'They will try to keep you out,' Paul replied. 'Unfortunately, conditions there are shameful and embarrass the authorities. But there's a way to get around them. A regulation of Parlement requires hospitals and prisons to allow charitable visits. A few years ago, after the authorities tried to block him, the famous British prison reformer, John Howard, made use of that law to gain access to the Paris prisons. So can you.'

Paul searched through the papers on his table. 'Here's a copy of Parlement's regulation.' He handed it to Anne. 'And these might also prove useful.' He gave her and Sylvie letters of recommendation from the Baron de Breteuil and Lieutenant General DeCrosne. 'And finally, you will need money to bribe the guards and the officials.' He pushed a purse across the table to Anne.

Anne shook it. The coins clinked. 'I believe we are ready to go. Two servants are waiting outside with food and clothing for the indigent sick.'

As she rose to leave, she glanced at Sylvie. The young

woman's eyes were bright and eager. It had pleased her to be asked, and she had readily accepted. Her aristocratic training had instilled in her a sense of noblesse oblige. Even after she had given up her privileged status, she still felt personally obliged to help the less fortunate.

But Anne was concerned about Sylvie. Only a year and a half ago, Captain Fitzroy had assaulted her, causing severe emotional trauma. Her recovery was slow and fragile – jeopardized by malicious ridicule from certain aristocratic acquaintances. She perceived the ridicule as a kind of ostracism. Driven to despair, she had attempted suicide. But Paul and Georges had saved her in the last second. From this painful experience she had felt compassion for poor sick people, prostitutes, the insane and other social outcasts.

'Sylvie,' Anne gently asked again, 'are you sure that you're ready to do this? It's one thing to hear about these mentally broken, stinking, dreadfully ugly women. It's another thing altogether to confront them in the flesh.'

'I feel much stronger than before. My godfather the Baron de Breteuil thinks I'm well enough and has encouraged my desire to relieve the needs of others. He's an enlightened man, and claims that the practice of benevolence will strengthen my character, help me overcome my bouts of depression.'

Still uneasy, Anne clasped the young woman's hands and said, 'Then let's be on our way.'

Rain pelted the carriage on the way to the women's hospital, the Salpêtrière. Inside, Anne and Sylvie discussed the forthcoming visit.

Sylvie remarked, 'I know who Renée is but very little about her. Could you tell me more?'

'Of course,' Anne replied, then briefly described the sordid life of the young prostitute, a struggle for survival almost from infancy to the present moment.

Sylvie listened thoughtfully and asked a few questions. At the conclusion, she observed, 'Until now, I wasn't fully aware of Renée's mental problem – though people often said that she was odd. It's remarkable that she's still alive. But why has she become so important? Is it because she has been Denis Grimaud's companion and might have played a role in the murder of the Marquis de Bresse?'

'Yes,' Anne replied. 'We believe that Renée was in the marquis's house the night of his murder.' Anne described the beggar Michel's revelations yesterday. 'She was seen leaving the building. If pressed, she might admit having gone to the house with Grimaud. He would have told her that he intended to retrieve his back pay and to persuade the marquis not to go to the police.'

'In that case,' Sylvie said with a touch of irony, 'Renée might wonder why Grimaud would negotiate such matters with the marquis in the middle of the night. I think it likely that she realized from the start that Grimaud intended to rob the marquis at a time when the servants were gone and the marquis was occupied with his female guest.'

'Yes,' Anne granted. 'Renée could serve as a lookout and receive a share of the stolen goods.'

'Since Renée was a petty thief as well as a prostitute,' Sylvie continued, 'she wouldn't object to the robbery. But she could be concerned that Grimaud might also kill the marquis to prevent him from reporting the embezzlement to the police.'

'Why should that matter to her?' Anne asked.

'The blame for Bresse's death would fall on the female guest.'

'So?'

'According to your account of Renée's life, she is known for her loyalty to other prostitutes. I think she wouldn't allow one to be falsely accused of murder.'

'On the other hand,' Anne objected, 'Renée passionately wanted to avenge Yvonne's death at Bresse's hand.'

'That's true,' Sylvie granted. 'Renée might be pleased if Grimaud unwittingly became the avenger and took the blame.'

Anne agreed. 'Renée surely never liked him. As her pimp and companion, he exploited her, and recently, I believe, he betrayed her to the captain of the guard.'

'As much as she might wish to punish him, how could she report his crime?' Sylvie asked. 'Renée was in the house as a thief. She would have to compromise herself and spend the rest of her life in prison.'

Anne shook her head. 'I doubt that Renée hated Grimaud that much.'

*   *   *

At midmorning, during a break in the rain, the carriage approached the women's hospital entrance and discharged its passengers. The two servants with the gifts accompanied Anne and Sylvie to the hospital's iron gate. Anne and Sylvie inspected each other's appearance. They had learned that the staff of the hospital were almost all women, from the director down to the guards. Knowing that women pay attention to what other women wear, Anne and Sylvie had chosen simple but well-tailored, light silk dresses, blue for Anne, pink for Sylvie. Plain enough to avoid unwelcome attention, and not *so* plain as to cause them to be mistaken for a pair of prisoners, their costumes would help to earn respect from the administration and the guards.

For a few moments the visitors stared through the gate at the hospital's architecture, astonished. A tall, domed chapel dominated a complex of several buildings, courtyards, and gardens on a grand, unified plan. To Anne the contrast of the Salpêtrière's outward magnificence with the misery inside was deeply distressing.

Unable to suppress her feelings, she turned to Sylvie and remarked, 'A small, sick Renée is probably trapped among the thousands of inmates of this monstrous place. We must now find her.'

At the gate two guards confronted them and refused to open. 'No visitors,' said the older of them, a slow-witted hulk of a man.

Anne showed him the copy of Parlement's regulation and her other papers. He fumbled with them, squinted at them. Anne realized that he couldn't read, so she quickly added, 'We aren't ordinary visitors. We're bringing food and clothing to the prisoners in the *Maison de Force*, the prison. The magistrates of the high court say we're allowed to enter.' She pointed to Parlement's seal on the copy.

'I don't know anything about this,' complained the hulk. He fluttered the copy, then glanced at his comrade, who grimaced, shrugged.

The guard handed the copy and the papers back to Anne. 'You'll have to go to the administration office.' He pointed to a distant building and let them pass.

In the office no one had heard of Renée or knew where she was. Anne also gained the impression that no one appeared to care.

'Did you say she was arrested five days ago?' asked a clerk, who had fingered through a box of cards for recent arrivals. 'The police should have taken her to the Châtelet for a hearing. It could be two weeks or more before she would come to us.'

'The Paris police officer who took the prostitutes from the duke's guards claims that he brought them to the Châtelet. We've checked at the Châtelet and the other prisons in the city. They had not received Renée. Perhaps they didn't have space so they sent her here.'

Anne gave the clerk the names of a few other prostitutes who had been arrested with Renée.

'I don't have their cards, either,' said the exasperated clerk. 'I suppose that they haven't been processed yet. Go to the women's prison building and inquire.' She gave them directions, and off they went.

The prison was a grim brick and stone building, consisting of the ground floor plus two storeys and a mansard. Anne and Sylvie left their servants to wait with the gifts in a small entrance hall while they entered through a barred gate. A pair of harridans gave them a cursory search, then escorted them into an office. There they repeated their request to another clerk, who was as hapless as the administrator.

'I have no record of her,' said the clerk, throwing up her hands.

'May I see the warden, please?' asked Anne, growing irritated. The prison's administration seemed inept.

'She's not seeing visitors today,' replied the clerk, glancing toward a handsome, thickly varnished door.

Anne waved a hand at the door. 'Tell her that this visit concerns an investigation authorized by the Lieutenant General of Police Thiroux DeCrosne into the murder of the Marquis de Bresse.'

For a moment the clerk hesitated, then went to the door, noticeably trembling. Her knock provoked a distant, gruff response, rather like a bark. She entered, was inside for a minute, and came out white-faced.

'You may see the warden,' said the clerk weakly.

Leaving Sylvie with the clerk, Anne walked into the office, expecting to face a tiger of a woman. In fact, seated behind a large writing table was a person who looked more like a reptile. She was Anne's age, and much smaller than Anne had guessed from the voice, except in one particular, her head. It was large, out of proportion to her small, thin body. She wore a black silk gown, on her head a black bonnet. Her large, dark, glittering eyes searched Anne indifferently down a long, thin nose. Her wide, thin, purple lips pressed together in a firm straight line. Framed by the black bonnet, her sallow face took on a ghoulish, demonic aspect.

At first sight, Anne shuddered involuntarily, but she had resolved to be calm and forthright and quickly mastered her distaste.

The warden let Anne stand facing her and remarked, 'I'm aware of an investigation into the Bresse murder. I didn't realize that a woman was leading it.' Her lips shifted into a crooked ironic smile.

Anne smiled politely in return. 'The officer in charge, my husband, Colonel Paul de Saint-Martin, has sent me here to find Renée Gros, a young female prostitute whom he believes may have witnessed the crime. I have previously met the woman and would recognize her.'

Anne briefly described Renée and added that she was injured during her arrest. 'My husband thinks I can assess her condition as well as manage her irascible, violent temperament. I hope to dispose her to cooperate with the investigation.'

Anne handed the warden the letters of recommendation and closely watched her read them. Her masked expression revealed little of her mind. As she handed the papers back to Anne, she remarked, 'The lieutenant general thinks well of your abilities. But how do you propose to find your Renée? My clerk tells me that we have no record of her. It seems that the police came with dozens of prostitutes, as well as many other felons, and just dumped them in our entrance hall. Overwhelmed, the clerk on duty processed them hastily, didn't get all their names, just shoved them into the main hall, then left for the day. We quickly confined them and will eventually find out who they are. But right now we can't help you.'

'May my companion and I go into the main hall? We might recognize one or more of the prostitutes from the Palais-Royal who could tell us what has happened to Renée.'

The warden glanced at her large gold watch. 'Most of the prisoners are at work in the shops or fields. You would need a guard to show you the way, and I can ill afford to lend one to you. We are very short-handed. You can't wander through the prison alone. It's too dangerous. We have women who would kill for the fine gown you are wearing.'

'I understand the difficulty of managing a prison,' Anne granted easily, but she was not about to be put off. 'Hence I came prepared to pay a reasonable sum for the extra service that a guard could provide.'

The warden sighed. 'It's probably better that *you* hunt for the girl than that the lieutenant general send a clumsy, blundering inspector.' She rang for the clerk. 'Find Sister Claire for me.'

Sister Claire beckoned Anne and Sylvie. 'Follow me.' She unlocked and unbarred a heavy door and stepped into the large hall. 'Stay close to me,' she ordered. 'You look for the girl, I'll watch out for trouble.'

The guard was a young woman. The warden had said she was a soldier's widow and had worked at the prison for a year. She was tall, lean, and broad-shouldered, an amazon dressed in a nun's black habit, a cord girding her waist. From the cord hung a club. She walked with a man's gait, her whole body alert, her cool grey eyes surveying the hall.

'Is she really a nun?' signed Sylvie to Anne. 'They call her Sister.'

Anne shrugged, puzzled. Raised in Protestant England, she had no contact with nuns. During the last two years, living in France, she had occasionally seen them from a distance. They hadn't looked like this one.

Sister Claire turned to Sylvie. 'You're right. I'm not a nun. I just dress like one. All of us who work here are called Sister. We live together under rules like nuns but we can leave if we wish. And, by the way, a few of us have learned to sign a little. It can be useful when prying visitors inspect us.'

The hall was a plain bare room, filled with beds only inches apart. A few inmates were cleaning the floors and windows and doing other chores under the watchful eye of a guard. Neither Anne nor Sylvie recognized a familiar face.

In the workshop Sister Claire again turned to Sylvie. 'The more trustworthy inmates live in the hall and work here. We keep the more dangerous ones chained in cells below.'

The women were carding and spinning wool, dyeing fabrics,

sewing cloth. 'We don't trust them with knives or scissors,'
Claire remarked in passing. She never smiled, always looked
sternly at the prisoners, who seemed thoroughly cowed.

After scrutinizing them, Anne didn't recognize any familiar
faces.

'Where are the most recent arrivals?' she asked. The inmates
she had seen thus far appeared to belong to a select group,
accustomed to the prison and its routine. Renée could not be
among them. Sister Claire was deliberately showing the prison
at its best side.

The guard hesitated momentarily, then said, 'I'll take you
there.' She led them across a courtyard to a long, low stone
building. 'They're in here.' She unlocked another heavy door
and stepped in cautiously, instinctively touching her club. Anne
and Sylvie followed her, absorbing her tension. The room was
lighted only by a few high, barred windows, unglazed but
insufficient to ventilate the room on a warm day. The stench
was nearly overwhelming. It took a while for Anne's eyes to
adjust to the dim light.

The prisoners were chained to straw-covered planks, some
lying, others sitting up, side by side. Several were naked. A
narrow aisle extended from one end of the room to the other.
A few prisoners taunted or cursed Claire. But when she drew
her club, the room became silent. On previous occasions she
had obviously used the weapon to good effect.

'We try to clean out the room once a day, and feed and
exercise the women. But it always smells like this.'

'How long do they stay here?' asked Sylvie.

'Perhaps two weeks or a month. Until places open up, either
in the hall or in the cells. Look them over. Be quick about it.
I can't control them for long. They'll soon begin screaming
and spitting and pounding on the planks.'

Anne and Sylvie followed Claire up and down the aisle.
Suddenly, Anne recognized a familiar face and nudged the
guard. 'That one! She worked in the Valois arcade and must
know Renée.' Anne pointed to a woman sitting on a plank,
naked to the waist, staring at her.

Claire fixed her eyes on the woman, then signed to Anne,
'Let's go. I'll get the keys to her shackles and another guard
and fetch the prisoner, clean her, dress her up a bit. You can
meet her in the parlour.'

The parlour was a small plain room with a barred window to the hallway for a guard to see and hear whatever happened inside. After some twenty minutes, Sister Claire appeared with the prisoner, now clothed and washed, hands tied at the wrists. Claire was about to shackle her to a ring on the floor when Anne objected. 'That won't be necessary.'

Claire frowned, then walked to the door. 'I'll be watching at the window.'

Anne, Sylvie, and the prisoner sat around the table. The prisoner was sullen, suspicious, not the least grateful. Anne signed to Sylvie, 'Let the prisoner get the grudge off her chest.' So they waited quietly for a minute or two.

'I've seen you before,' the prisoner said, staring at Anne. 'You were there in the Valois arcade with the captain of the duke's guard that day when they arrested us. You saved Berthe Dupont. But you let the rest of us go to hell.'

'I merely chanced to meet the captain and had little personal influence over him. At least I saved Renée Gros from being kicked to death.'

The prisoner sneered. 'So what do you want from me?'

'I couldn't help you then, but I might be able to help you now. If you cooperate.'

'Can you get me out of here?' The prisoner sounded doubtful.

'That depends mainly on you. For a start, I can give you some food and clothing. Now let me tell you what I want.'

The prisoner leaned back, cocked her head. 'Go ahead.'

Anne met her eye. 'What has happened to Renée?'

'They took her away.'

'Why?'

'She screamed without stopping. Out of her mind.' The prisoner suddenly glanced at Sister Claire at the barred window, listening, a frown on her face.

'Where did they put her?'

The prisoner began to tremble. 'I don't know.'

Anne pressed on. 'Where is she?'

'I've said too much,' said the prisoner so softly that Anne could barely hear her.

'Well, thank you. I'll arrange to get food and clothes to you.' Anne signaled the guard. The visit was over.

* * *

'Out of her mind,' Anne murmured to Sylvie. 'Can you guess where Renée is now?'

'Among the insane,' Sylvie replied. 'And I think our guard knew it all along. That's a part of the prison they don't want us to see.'

Sister Claire had removed the prisoner. Now she reappeared. 'Was the prisoner helpful?'

'Yes, unwittingly,' Anne replied. 'I would like you to take us to the ward for the insane.'

The guard's eyes darkened, narrowed. 'You don't want to go there.'

'So, I'm correct. That's where Renée is kept. And you knew it all the while that you gave us a tour of the prison.'

The guard flushed at the accusation. Whether with embarrassment or anger, it was hard to tell. She didn't defend herself. Just stood there staring at Anne.

Angered, Anne persisted. 'Why did you deceive us?'

'Your Renée can be of no use to you. She'll never bear witness in the Bresse case. Her mind is completely gone, or in the devil's hands.'

'Take us to her. We shall judge for ourselves.' Anne glanced at Sylvie. Her face was taut, nearly white, but she nodded vigorously.

Twenty-One
Out of the Depths

11 June

Sister Claire led Anne and Sylvie to a long, two-storey brick and stone building behind the prison. In the distance Anne saw inmates working in large gardens and orchards. Two guards stood at the building's entrance, closed by an iron gate. At a word from Claire, one of the guards with a ring of keys on his belt opened the gate and joined them.

They walked into a small, enclosed courtyard. Though the rain had stopped, low, dark clouds scudded overhead. The midday air was warm and moist, the paving stones still wet. A few inmates walked aimlessly about, splashing through puddles, talking to themselves. One of them caught sight of the visitors and shuffled toward them. Sister Claire waved her off with a brusque gesture.

'I assume,' said Anne, 'that these are the healthier ones.'

The guard nodded. 'They live in another world, but they're harmless.'

'Do they receive any treatment?'

'We clean, clothe, and feed them, prevent them from injuring themselves or others, and pray for them. Nothing more can be done. This is their fate, punishment for their sins or the sins of their parents.'

'I understand that scientists are doing experiments—' Anne had overheard Paul and Comtesse Marie speak about new methods of care that might cure mental illness or greatly miti-gate its symptoms.

Claire cut her off. 'Like the Austrian Doctor Mesmer and his idea of animal magnetism? A godless quack. And the rest of so-called enlightened scientists are no better. They awake false hopes and do more harm than good.' She pointed to a door and said with a sneer, 'Hold your nose. We'll pass through one of the main halls on the way to your prostitute.'

Anne had noticed Sister Claire growing more rigid and hostile, the closer she came to the insane. She seemed to profoundly detest them. Anne wondered how she could ever give them humane care.

The guard from the gate unlocked the door and led them into a large hall, poorly illuminated through high, barred windows. The odor of urine and other human waste was over-powering. Anne nearly gagged. Dozens of inmates were lolling about, chattering, screaming, drooling. Others were staring blankly at the walls, lying on the floor. Many wore shackles on their legs, a few were chained to the walls. All of them were clad in rags, hair unkempt. Their facial expressions ranged from empty to utterly grotesque.

'We've determined that these, like the ones you saw outside, are harmless, merely disgusting.'

'Where do they sleep and eat?'

'In this hall. We serve food there.' She pointed to a long table against the far wall. 'They sleep on the floor.' She gestured to straw mattresses piled up against the other walls. 'We have a similar hall at the opposite end of the building.'

Anne glanced sideways at Sylvie. She was struggling bravely, throat taut, lips pressed tightly together. Halfway through the hall, a toothless old woman suddenly lurched toward Sylvie, bony arms outstretched for an embrace. Sylvie clung to Anne's arm, a look of horror on her face.

In an instant Sister Claire drew her club and struck the old woman a glancing blow on the shoulder. She yelped like a wounded animal and slunk back, whimpering piteously.

Anne detected the flicker of a smile on the sister's face.

'Hurry,' she ordered her companions. 'We're attracting their attention. Some of them think your pretty friend Sylvie is their daughter. They'll mob her.'

At the exit, the gate guard unlocked the door and led them into a narrow corridor and down a flight of stairs to the basement level. To the left and right of a long hallway were tiny cells behind locked doors with small, unglazed, barred windows. The air in the basement was clammy and smelled of heavy mold.

As they walked briskly down the hallway, Anne glanced into a cell. Three women were chained to the walls in a jumble of body parts. Other cells were equally deplorable.

Sister Claire stopped in front of a door, peered through the window, and motioned for Anne to come closer. A naked Renée lay in the fetal position on the straw-strewn floor. She was chained by the waist to the wall. Her arms were bound to her body, her feet were shackled.

'She's quiet now, and exhausted. If she hears us, she'll begin to scream. If we didn't restrain her, she would scratch and bite anyone who came near, or she'd throw herself against the walls and beat herself.'

Anne beckoned Sylvie. 'Take a look,' she whispered.

The young woman peeked through the opening, shuddered,

withdrew. 'Why?' she asked softly, her voice echoing her inner distress.

'We'll discuss this matter later outside,' Anne replied, then indicated to Sister Claire that she wanted to enter the cell.

'No! We can't allow that. She will hurt you and I'll be blamed.'

Anne addressed the gate guard standing nearby. 'You are witness that I take full personal responsibility for entering the cell. Please unlock the door.' Anne turned to Sister Claire. 'Renée is bound and chained. The worst she can do is spit. I can handle that.'

The gate guard glanced at Claire. She grudgingly nodded. The guard unlocked the door and Anne stepped in. Sylvie followed her.

Anne thought that the noise from the lock and the creaking door would arouse the prisoner. But she didn't stir. Anne knelt down, drew close to her, felt the pulse at her neck. It was very weak and irregular. Her breathing was shallow, her eyes half-open but sightless. Her body was covered with welts and bruises.

Anne pointed out the wounds to Sister Claire. 'These were caused by a strap and a club, not by throwing oneself against a wall.' She rose to her feet and confronted Claire.

'Examine her, Sister.'

Claire knelt down, took the prisoner's pulse, studied her for a few moments. 'She's very weak, doesn't drink, hasn't eaten in five days. In another day or two, she'll probably die.' The sister's voice lacked any emotion or concern.

Anger surged through Anne's body. She wanted to throw herself upon the sister and beat her. But she checked herself, stepped back, and drew a deep breath.

'Then we agree,' Anne said through clenched teeth. 'Renée is close to death. This is an outrage. She's a major witness in the Bresse murder case. If she dies here of obvious, flagrant abuse and neglect, I shall inform the lieutenant general, and I guarantee that he will be irate. She must be unchained and carried immediately to the infirmary.'

Sister Claire rallied, stung by Anne's criticism. 'She was bruised when we got her and still wild, a maniac. I had to

subdue her. She spat on me and bit me. Hard. Look.' Claire
pulled up a sleeve to show the ugly marks of teeth that had
broken the skin. The bitten area was still black and blue.
'You're unfair! How in God's name can a few guards like
myself keep order here among thousands of demented,
criminal, and furious women.' Claire seemed genuinely
distraught.

Anne chose to avoid a pointless quarrel. 'The authorities
will have to sort out the responsibility for this situation. You
did what you're trained to do. But I want this woman to get
proper care right now. She cannot be allowed to die.' She
ordered the gate guard to fetch a stretcher and blankets. 'Sylvie
will help the guard carry the woman. She's anyway as light
as a feather. You and I, Claire, will hurry ahead to the infirmary to make arrangements to receive Renée. I expect resistance there.'

Grim-faced, Claire nodded.

The infirmary was a new addition to the Salpêtrière, which
previously had sent its sick inmates to the Hôtel-Dieu in the
city's centre, the main hospital for medical care. The infirmary's resident medical doctor was at dinner in the administration building. None of his servants dared to disturb him.
But Claire knew the sister in charge and described the situation to her.

'Are you bringing us a mad, violent prostitute and without
warning?' The sister appeared incredulous. 'Near death, you
say. Be merciful for God's sake. Let her die. Besides, every
bed is taken. Where shall we put her? What can we possibly
do for her?'

Anne spoke gently to calm the sister. 'This is a very special
case. Renée may have witnessed the murder of the Marquis
de Bresse and must recover the ability to give testimony. She
needs emergency treatment here for a day or two until we can
move her to a more suitable place in one of the city's hospitals, or elsewhere.'

The sister frowned, grumbled under her breath, shook her
head.

Anne tried to mollify her. 'I would like to report to the lieutenant general and to the Baron de Breteuil that together we
have saved their witness. I'm sure they will offer you tokens

of their appreciation. I have also brought along baskets of food and clothing for the sick woman and that should lessen the burden on you. Finally, I can pay something toward the inconvenience she will cause you.'

That lit a light in the sister's eye. She grumbled some more, then shrugged. 'I'll see what I can do.'

Minutes later, Anne heard a commotion at the entrance. She and the sisters hurried there to see Sylvie arguing with a servant. Halfway through the door were two guards carrying Renée on a stretcher, wrapped in blankets.

The sister in charge intervened and gave orders to the guards. Renée was carried to a small, secure room and placed in bed. At Sylvie's suggestion, a warm bath and liquid nourishment were ordered for her. Sylvie also fetched her two waiting servants who came with their baskets of food and clothing. Anne directed it to the sister in charge.

Sylvie's initiative surprised and pleased Anne. The young woman had overcome her fears and now displayed courage and good judgment. Her measures for Renée made sense. At a free moment, Anne asked her to explain.

'When I was recovering at Château Beaumont from my attempt at suicide, the Comtesse Marie prescribed a regime of baths, nourishing food, exercise, and engaging work. In a short while, I felt much better. Then recently I read an article by Doctor Philippe Pinel who argues for a similar regime for many of the mentally ill. It might help Renée. Shall we contact him?'

Anne agreed. 'But in the meantime, we'll have to move her out of the infirmary and into a more permanent place for her treatment. One of our servants and I should stay here with her, perhaps even overnight, until I'm sure that she will be well cared for. I'd like you and the other servant to return home and report to Paul what we've done. He will have to persuade the lieutenant general to transfer Renée from this prison to a place and a regime suitable for her health. Pass on to Paul your suggestion about Doctor Pinel.'

Sylvie and the servant had hardly left when the infirmary's resident doctor returned from dinner. That was sooner than Anne had expected. Apparently a servant had been sent to alert him. He accosted Anne as she was bathing Renée, who was still unconscious.

'What in God's name do you think you're doing here?' he shouted. 'Leave the hospital premises immediately or I'll have the guards arrest you. That little whore will go back to the cell where she belongs.'

The doctor was a small, self-important, irascible, middle-aged man. His eyes squinted, his droopy cheeks shook with indignation. That he would be displeased was predictable, but the vigor of his reaction suggested to Anne that he had probably received a misleading report.

Anne beckoned her servant, who was standing nearby, open-mouthed with alarm. 'Finish bathing Renée, while I speak with the doctor.' Then turning to him, she said quietly, 'You may not have been told that I'm here on a mission from Lieutenant General DeCrosne. Shall we go to your office? I'll explain what I'm doing.'

Her reference to the lieutenant general confused the doctor. He hesitated for a moment, then muttered, 'Follow me.'

His office was cluttered with anatomical charts and models. Shelves of books with Latin titles covered the walls. Curious-looking specimens in glass bottles were displayed on a counter. He sat down behind his writing table, intending to let her stand. She smiled to herself, pulled up a chair, sat down, and faced him. Then without ceremony she handed him her official papers.

At first his expression was dismissive, but as he read on, he grew more respectful. 'You should have told me that you are the wife of Colonel Paul de Saint-Martin. Had I known, I would have tempered my remarks.' Though he tried, he could not keep a tone of reproach from his voice.

Anne gave him a forgiving smile, then offered him the same explanation of her mission as she had given to the sister in charge.

As Anne spoke, the doctor's expression changed from petulant resistance to grudging acceptance. When she finished, he sighed, then said, 'The patient can remain in the room until you are able to move her. That should be soon. I shall examine her now.'

Anne grew anxious that he might reach an erroneous diagnosis and prescribe a harmful cure, so little confidence did she have in him. She followed him to Renée's bedside, prepared to do battle if necessary.

The bath was completed and the patient appeared to be

reviving. 'I'm thirsty,' she said feebly and half-opened her eyes. The servant raised her to drink. She grimaced with pain. They lowered her and gave her water through a tube. She closed her eyes.

After examining her, the doctor said, 'Some of her ribs are broken.'

Anne nodded. 'A guard kicked her side.'

'Keep her still, if you can. With time and care her body will heal. Her mind is another matter. There's not much more that I can do.' He prescribed ointments for her bruises and a binding for her chest, then left to see his other patients.

Anne and the servant applied the ointments and bound Renée's chest. Through the evening and into the night they took turns resting on a pallet and watching the patient. At times she was restless but she was too weak to become a problem. She calmed down when Anne stroked her head or gave her water. The doctor's words hung in Anne's memory and prompted her to wonder what could be done for the woman's mind.

Late that afternoon, Colonel Saint-Martin was at work in his office when Sylvie walked in.

'We found Renée,' she exclaimed. 'She needs care immediately.'

Saint-Martin called Georges, and they gathered around the office conference table. Sylvie described how she and Anne had discovered Renée at Salpêtrière, beaten, starved, and near death.

'Conditions in the prison are scandalous,' she concluded. 'So Anne has moved Renée into the infirmary, over the objections of a reluctant resident medical doctor and his staff. Anne will stay with the patient overnight, but tomorrow we must find another place for her.'

Saint-Martin stroked his chin, reflected on the situation. He would need the lieutenant general's authorization to remove Renée from prison. That could possibly be done tomorrow morning. A hospital had to be found that could offer a healthier environment than the prison and was acceptable to the lieutenant general. That reservation largely ruled out the Hôtel-Dieu, the city's primary medical institution. It was no less dangerous to health than the Salpêtrière, according to a prominent medical expert, Doctor Tenon, who had recently investigated the city's hospitals.

'May I make a suggestion, Paul?' Sylvie had followed his thinking.

'Yes, of course.'

'Take her to Aunt Marie's town house. The breakfast room is rarely used. It overlooks the back garden and is quiet and restful. It is also close to the kitchen, a source of hot water for laundry and baths.'

'That's a good suggestion, Sylvie. Aunt Marie wants to put the house to good use.' He paused, a question rising in his mind. 'Who would give care to Renée there? She would be too much work for you and Michou. And I don't think we could trust the young servants who are presently looking after the house. They already have enough to do.'

Georges had been listening thoughtfully. Now he broke into the conversation. 'I can think of a person who knows Renée and is well qualified to take her on.'

'And who might that be?' asked Paul.

'Berthe Dupont.' Georges leaned forward, his expression earnest. 'She's both intelligent and kind, has cared for her blind father, and has gotten along well with Renée when they worked in the Valois arcade. She's also strong enough to restrain her if necessary. She needs honest work.'

Paul nodded. 'But she can't supply the expert treatment of Renée's mental condition that's required, if she's to become a credible witness.'

Sylvie asked, 'Could we persuade Doctor Pinel to treat Renée? If he's willing, he could direct Berthe.'

'Possibly. I'll contact him. I'll also send messages to Aunt Marie and to Lieutenant General DeCrosne.' He turned to Georges. 'Find out if Berthe Dupont would be interested. There could also be a place for her father in our scheme, assisting his daughter.'

Saint-Martin exchanged guarded smiles with his companions at the table. The investigation had taken a hopeful turn.

Twenty-Two
Homeless

12 June

The air was cool and fresh, the sounds of the city still just a faint rumble. The early morning sun broke through the clouds and sent long shadows slanting across the garden. Georges found Colonel Saint-Martin in his shirtsleeves, bent over his rose bushes, inhaling their scent. To judge from the gentle, rapt smile on his face, the bushes appeared to talk to him.

Georges indulged his superior this odd behavior. It seemed a healthy antidote to the evil and the stress that he had to confront daily. Unlike many men in high office, he took his duties seriously. So much so that even shortly after a long winter vacation, he was already showing signs of wear and tear.

'Sorry to disturb you, sir. I've just learned by messenger that Grimaud was released from the Châtelet late yesterday. Magistrates from the Parlement interceded for him, men to whom he had supplied female companions. It appears that he had also provided useful information, frustrating police attempts to spy on them.'

'I regret that he's free. That complicates our work. It was convenient to keep him in prison. But he'll stay in Paris. We can pick him up when we wish.'

Georges put on his hat. 'Well, sir, I'm off to visit my old comrade, Jean Dupont.' Georges's tone was matter-of-fact, though his feelings were in turmoil.

'This is also a good time to find his daughter at home,' remarked Saint-Martin. For a moment, he turned his attention back to the roses. His expression was enigmatic.

'Yes, that happens to be true,' Georges granted. 'Early yesterday afternoon in the Palais-Royal, I noticed that Berthe Dupont wasn't at her usual spot in front of the brothel. Women working in the area couldn't say where she was. Later in the day, I inquired again. I got the same response. I concluded that she had stayed home to care for her father. But, after sleeping on the matter last night, I'm concerned that something bad might have happened. I'd better find out.'

'Right, Georges. We'll meet later in the day. This morning, Sylvie and I have an appointment with the Lieutenant General DeCrosne and Doctor Pinel at the Hôtel de Police. I've informed DeCrosne that Sylvie and Anne found our missing Renée in the mental ward at the Salpêtrière. She's in a poor condition. We must determine what to do with her. The lieutenant general will be skeptical. Why should he invest any of the scanty resources of a bankrupt government to cure a badly damaged little prostitute?'

Georges's search for Berthe began again at the brothel in the Valois arcade. Since he came in uniform, the madam gave him a frosty reception. Bad for business, she claimed. Scares away customers.

'Where is Berthe Dupont?' he asked rather too abruptly.

'Gone,' she replied as sullenly as she dared.

'Why?'

Madam explained that Berthe's aloof and rigid manner had displeased the house's patrons, and she was getting worse rather than better. 'My girls have to at least pretend they enjoy what they're doing. I had to turn her out. She didn't tell me what she would do or where she would go.'

Georges then questioned other women working in the arcade. A few recognized her from Michou's sketch. They agreed that she left the brothel and the arcade without speaking to anyone. She seemed to be in tears. Georges asked himself, had she fled from the city, contrary to orders? As a suspect, she was supposed to remain available for questioning.

Georges approached the Duponts' house on Rue Saint-Paul with mounting anxiety. The door was open. The concierge was in the entrance hall sweeping the floor.

Georges greeted her. 'Are the Duponts at home?'

'No.' She gave him a sour look. 'They left last night. Hadn't paid rent for this month. The landlord ordered them out and took their furniture. Wasn't worth much.'

'Where did they go?'

'They didn't say. Don't suppose they knew. Walked north toward the markets. A pitiful sight, she leading him by the hand.'

Meanwhile, Colonel Saint-Martin and Sylvie had walked to the Hôtel de Police and met Doctor Pinel in the lieutenant general's antechamber. Though they both knew Pinel by reputation, this was their first meeting face to face. By messenger last night, he had agreed to examine Renée and possibly treat her.

While they conversed, waiting for DeCrosne, Saint-Martin discreetly studied Pinel. Dressed in a plain black silk suit, he was a modest, mild-mannered, even shy man, of conservative taste. Yet he was proficient both in mathematics and in medicine, and he inspired confidence and respect. Well-read in the works of John Locke and Jean-Jacques Rousseau, he shared their belief in man's natural goodness and society's primary influence on human development. That belief was the philosophical basis of his approach to treating mental illness.

During their conversation, Sylvie seemed to struggle inwardly and appeared tense. Finally, she caught Pinel's eye and spoke in a low, hesitant voice, 'Sir, my visit yesterday to the mental ward at the Salpêtrière, as well as my own attempt at suicide, have made me wonder why certain men and women become mentally ill while others don't.'

The doctor's eyes grew troubled at her reference to suicide. He leaned toward her with concern and reflected for a moment. Then he replied, 'I've traced much mental illness to excessive stresses on a person's brain, such as childhood abuse, poverty, extraordinary misfortune, a disorderly life, cruel personal relationships and the like.'

Saint-Martin glanced sideways at Sylvie. She nodded where the list fitted her, surely recalling Captain Fitzroy's assault, an extraordinary and cruel misfortune, aggravated by the ridicule of her social peers. The injury to her spirit seemed deep and lasting.

Sylvie persisted, 'If I break my arm, you can set the bone and nature will heal it. But how can you reach into a damaged mind and treat it?'

Pinel bowed to her. 'I like your analogy, mademoiselle. By words and gestures, I reach into the mind.'

He paused, as if to allow Sylvie to digest what he was saying. His eyes focused kindly on her, a slight smile on his lips.

He continued. 'Through trial and error, I have learned to listen patiently, attentively, so that the sick persons feel encouraged to speak freely. With artful questions I can then help them gain self-understanding. That's the basis for any mental improvement. I also prescribe warm baths, nourishing food, music, exercise, and meaningful, engaging work in a pleasant environment. Such measures help nature to recover the proper use of its faculties.'

Sylvie nodded in full agreement and remarked, 'You can hardly imagine, Doctor, the shocking condition in which we found Renée yesterday – beaten, neglected, near death. I have heard that you oppose the use of isolation, shackles and clubs in treating the mentally ill.'

'Correct, mademoiselle. I condemn what was done to the young woman. Such traditional methods are immoral, contrary to reason, based on the false belief that our nature is inherently flawed, prone to evil, and can only be corrected by the grace of God and the fear of punishment.'

Pinel had begun to speak with more passion than he deemed appropriate. He drew a deep breath, smiled slightly in self-reproach, then continued. 'In practice, the traditional methods make mental illness worse and punish a patient for failing to improve. Take the case of Renée. Even though she's a prostitute, I consider her to be sick, rather than a sinner. Rooted in dreadful childhood abuse and abandonment, her mania and melancholy are a mental disorder over which she has had little control.'

Saint-Martin agreed with Pinel thus far. But, naturally cautious, Saint-Martin wondered to what extent the doctor's method could heal Renée. 'Can her illness ever be *fully* reversed?' he asked. 'Or will some damage always remain?'

'Perceptive questions, Colonel. I contend that the human mind is not a mechanical device, like a clock, that can be turned back to its original state. Mental disease will leave a mark on the mind, as when fire has attacked a tree. Nonetheless, given a healthy environment and kindly, rational care, her mind will heal much of its own mental illness, mitigate its symptoms, and enable the young woman to live comfortably with the remaining scars.'

Saint-Martin was encouraged. Renée could probably be brought to witness in the Bresse case. He stole a solicitous glance at Sylvie. She was smiling as she thanked the doctor for his views. Saint-Martin breathed a quiet sigh of relief. She seemed at peace with herself, untroubled by her mental scars.

After a few more minutes of conversation, the visitors were called into DeCrosne's office. Though it was not yet noon, lines of fatigue creased his face. But he gave them a polite welcome and seated them comfortably in the spacious, airy, and well-ordered room. A clerk was present to take notes. DeCrosne sat at his writing table facing his visitors, scanned last night's message from Saint-Martin, and went immediately to the point.

'Colonel, why should we be so concerned about the physical and mental health of a wild young prostitute? After all, the state's resources are limited, now more than ever. I can imagine far more deserving poor, young, decent women with a much better claim upon our assistance.' The expression on his face was distinctly skeptical.

'That's a reasonable question, sir,' Saint-Martin replied. 'Renée was the companion of Denis Grimaud, the chief suspect in the murder of the Marquis de Bresse. We have reason to believe that she may have witnessed the crime or have learned about it from Grimaud. My adjutant and I found the marquis's ring and his purse in her room. Unfortunately, we can't question her. She resisted the duke's guards when they attempted to arrest her for prostitution and theft in the Palais-Royal. They severely beat her, breaking her ribs, then took her away.' Saint-Martin gestured to Sylvie to continue.

'For five days the Paris police couldn't say where she was. Finally, Madame Cartier and I found her alone in a cell in the mental ward of the women's hospital, the Salpêtrière, unconscious and nearly dead. She also seems to have sunk into a manic-melancholic state of mind. Temporarily, we moved her to the prison infirmary, where madame continues to nurse her.'

'Why don't you leave her there?' asked DeCrosne impatiently. 'Can't the prison doctor treat her? We recently erected the infirmary and hired him full-time to care for the inmates.'

'If she is to have *proper* treatment,' Saint-Martin replied, 'she must be moved. The prison doctor has hundreds of other patients and has neither the time nor the energy to treat the young woman's physical condition. In addition, her mental illness is far beyond his competence. She cannot give convincing evidence unless she is of sound mind. That's why I've asked Doctor Pinel to join us.'

DeCrosne shook his head. 'Before we proceed further, allow me to say that I'm aware of the shortcomings of our General Hospital, including the Salpêtrière. The Baron de Breteuil and I have many ideas for reform, but alas no money. Still, let us hear from Doctor Pinel.' He turned to the doctor. 'How would you go about making our patient a credible witness?'

Pinel reflected for a moment. 'Since I haven't seen her, my opinion is based only on what I've been told. She does appear to suffer from mania and melancholy. But up to the time of her arrest and imprisonment, she functioned rather well in her sordid environment. That's encouraging. However, her appalling experience since then may have significantly worsened her mental illness. If she were to remain in prison, you would learn nothing of value from her. If I am to improve, if not completely cure, her condition, she must be moved to a better site for treatment.'

DeCrosne frowned, stroked his chin for a long moment. 'What expenses would be involved?'

Pinel replied, 'I would have to put her in a congenial but secure environment. A pair of sisters would be needed to care for her. I would treat her without charge as an intriguing case.'

DeCrosne turned to Saint-Martin. 'Could we place her in the Hospital of Sainte-Pélagie? It's devoted to sheltering fallen women. I believe they have a few secure rooms.'

Saint-Martin shook his head. 'At least initially, I would rather take her to the town house of my aunt, the Comtesse de Beaumont, on Rue Traversine. A room can easily be made secure. It offers a nearly ideal environment for Doctor Pinel's approach to healing mental illness. The patient's recovery would be quicker there than elsewhere, the cost less.'

Saint-Martin then deferred to Pinel.

'I have visited the countess, so I know the house,' said the doctor. 'I could work with the patient there.'

'And I know a woman,' added Saint-Martin, 'who could care for Renée at a reasonable cost.' He had in mind strong, intelligent Berthe, who knew Renée and could deal with her erratic behavior. That Berthe was one of two serious suspects in the murder of the Marquis de Bresse did not disturb Saint-Martin. If she killed the marquis, she most likely acted in self-defense. Granted, a magistrate might balk at the idea of her innocence. But he would be better disposed if she were no longer a prostitute but a capable nursing sister.

Sylvie spoke up, 'My friend Michou and I live there and would like to help.'

'Enough! I'm persuaded,' said DeCrosne, allowing himself a thin smile. 'Colonel, please make those arrangements. I want the patient moved this afternoon and her treatment begun immediately. She must be brought to her senses and give testimony as quickly as possible.'

Saint-Martin tilted his head, glanced at the doctor with a question in his eye.

Pinel replied with a gentle smile. 'I'm confident, Colonel. It's quite amazing what kind, humane, and reasonable care can do.'

Twenty-Three
Prospect of Hope

12 June

As the sun set, Georges hurried through the central markets trying to find a certain stall that sold vegetables. His hopes had risen. He had received a lead to the whereabouts of Jean and Berthe Dupont. It was now near closing time. Stalls were shutting down left and right. He squeezed by carts loaded with leftover produce blocking his way. Berthe might leave her stall at any minute and disappear again into the vast belly of the city.

Georges had spent most of the morning trying to find her. When it was nearly noon, Georges thought of Michel the deaf beggar. He might have seen her. He was perched as usual on the bridge to Isle Saint-Louis, pleading for alms, even as he observed everyone passing by.

Yes, he told Georges in his odd voice, she had come to him yesterday, given him a small coin, and asked if he knew of any job that she could do. 'She must have noticed that I seemed familiar with domestic servants on the island and wondered if they had told me of a household that might need a new maid. I said I couldn't help her. Frankly, there were no openings in the households or places of business that I was familiar with. Moreover, with my limited resources, I couldn't hire her as a spy, nor could I afford to give her charity.'

He smiled wryly, his eyes heavy with sadness. 'She probably had given me her last coin. I offered to return it. She shook her head and started to leave. I called out, "Wait, there are usually opportunities for day labour at the central markets. Hard work, poorly paid, but it might tide you over this rough patch." I think you might find her there.'

So, for the rest of the day, Georges had searched through the markets until they were about to close, showing the sketch in vain to anyone who would look at it.

Now, he had a bit of luck. A sharp-eyed merchant had recognized Berthe from the sketch. She had approached him in the morning looking for work. He couldn't use her, but he had directed her to a nearby vegetable stall that was shorthanded.

When Georges first spotted her, she was moving produce from the front of the stall to the back, preparing to close for the day. For several minutes, Georges observed her from hiding. She was wearing her red dress, now somewhat tattered. She appeared very tired and hungry. Georges wondered if she had slept last night. Her employer, a thick-bodied, weather-beaten peasant woman, busy with customers, paid little attention to Berthe, occasionally barking a command over her shoulder.

As they closed the shutters on the stall, the two women began a conversation. It grew heated. Their voices rose. Georges moved close enough to overhear. The peasant woman refused to pay Berthe for the day's work, claiming that she had eaten the equivalent of the money in produce. Fists clenched, Berthe appeared at the point of striking the woman.

Alarmed, since Berthe would be charged with assault, Georges decided to intervene; a risky move. He was in uniform but had no authority in the market. Nonetheless, he strode up to the women. 'What's going on here?' he asked sternly, giving Berthe a guarded wink.

When he had heard their stories, he asked the peasant woman, 'Name the produce that she has eaten.'

The question took the woman by surprise. She fumbled for words, then came up with: 'Leek.'

Georges beckoned Berthe. 'Let me smell your breath.'

Embarrassed, she nonetheless complied.

Georges turned on the peasant woman. 'Madame, you know the smell of leek as well as I. This woman has not eaten leek – nor anything else today, to judge from the look of her. Now give her the wages you agreed upon or I'll have the market police take you in for serious interrogation. They would question how you run your stall. Who knows what they might discover and fine you?'

The peasant woman grumbled in dialect, most likely uttering potent curses. Finally, she reached into her purse and counted out coins into Berthe's hands.

'Are you satisfied, madame?' Georges asked Berthe.

'Yes, thank you.'

'Then I'll escort you safely out of the markets. They can be dangerous after closing, when many women like you leave with money in their pockets.' Georges had noticed a hard, cunning glint in the peasant woman's eyes. Either she or a confederate might indeed knock Berthe on the head and steal her day's wages.

Georges and Berthe walked silently through the markets, she leading the way to the great merchants' church of Saint-Eustache, he with his hand gripping the hilt of his sabre.

'Father and I share a room behind the church,' she said.

When he was sure that they hadn't been followed, he beck-oned her into one of the church's empty chapels.

'I've been looking all day for you,' he said. 'Later we're going to have a serious conversation. But first we shall buy food. I'm sure neither you nor your father has eaten today.'

Berthe nodded, then began to sway. Georges thought she would faint. He caught her under the arms and set her on a bench. 'Rest for a few minutes.'

When she had recovered her strength, Georges took her to a small, decent tavern across from the church's main entrance, ordered a hearty vegetable soup for both of them, and one to take out to her father.

The food was quickly served and soon revived her.

'Thank you again,' she said softly, though they sat in a secluded corner and could not be overheard. 'Since early morning, that peasant woman harassed me mercilessly. When you intervened, I had come to the point of exploding. You saved me from certain prison.' She bowed her head, dejected. 'I feel like I'm trapped in quicksand. The more I struggle, the deeper I sink.'

'I can offer you a ray of hope,' Georges began. 'Colonel Saint-Martin needs someone like you to care for a very sick young woman whom you know, Renée Gros.' He went on to describe what had happened to her at the women's hospital and how Madame Cartier and her friend Sylvie de Chanteclerc had found her in poor physical and mental con-dition. 'We believe her testimony could help us solve the Bresse case. Doctor Pinel is willing to treat her at the house on Rue Traversine, but he needs a strong, intelligent, caring woman to assist him.'

'Why me? I have no training in such work.'

'Doctor Pinel will direct you. Besides, you have an advan-tage – you know Renée and the circumstances of her life. She trusts you as much as anyone. You've also cared for your father. Even Lieutenant General DeCrosne is persuaded that you are suited for the work. Michou, Sylvie, and, yes, your father will assist you in the daily chores of caring for this very sick, probably difficult patient. In return, you and your father will receive room and board and small stipends. At the least, the job will last a few weeks, until Renée recovers a sufficient degree of mental health to testify in our investigation. In the meantime, you can continue searching for a more permanent arrangement.'

'Monsieur, I'm so depressed now that I feel unable to make another decision, even when the prospects are so promising.' She covered her face with her hands and began sobbing.

Georges allowed her a few minutes of grief, then sat next to her, put his arm around her. 'Allow me, Berthe, to decide for you. This is your only option. We shall go now with the food to your father, my old comrade. When he has eaten, I'll take both of you to the house on Rue Traversine. Renée should be there already. We shall go right to work.'

She breathed out a deep rush of air, pulled a kerchief from her bodice, and patted her eyes. 'I'll trust you, monsieur.' She jingled the coins in her purse. 'This isn't enough for another day's rent, not to mention food.'

Georges helped her up, paid the barman, and they went out into the night.

The Duponts, father and daughter, were living in a garret room under the roof of an old, decrepit building in the shadow of Saint-Eustache. Their room was little more than a closet with a window. Fortunately for them, the weather was mild, since the room lacked heat. Two thin straw pallets lay on the floor. Jean Dupont sat on the only chair. From his dejected expression it was clear that he now was fully aware of their desperate situation.

'Must I beg in the street and risk being swept up by the police and put into the Bicêtre among thieves and madmen?'

'I think not,' Georges replied. 'Berthe and I have discussed an alternative. But first you should eat supper.'

While the old soldier ate the soup, Georges described the work involved in caring for Renée Gros at Rue Traversine.

When the meal was finished, Dupont remarked, 'Berthe can be useful there, but what can a blind man do?'

'Don't fret, Jean. There's work for you, too. Help in the laundry and the garden, wash dishes, clean floors. There's a stable off the courtyard. The porter will ask you to feed and brush the horses. I'm sure there'll be more to do when we've established a routine for looking after the sick young woman.'

Dupont grew thoughtful. He reached for his daughter's hand. 'We'll do our best, Georges. We're grateful for the opportunity.'

'Then let's go,' said Georges. He paused for a moment at the door and shook his head. 'It's amazing, if you think of it, what we are going to do for little Renée, a street waif, a cast-off bit of humanity. We'll treat her like a queen because we think she has a secret story to tell, how an evil rake of a nobleman was killed.'

Berthe turned to him with a puzzled expression. 'Why would *she* have such a story?'

Georges replied, 'Witnesses have placed her with Grimaud at the marquis's house when the murder most likely took place. We wonder, did he speak to her later about what he had done? Or did she witness or even take part in the crime?'

For a moment Berthe seemed lost in thought, puzzled, then she whispered to Georges, 'Renée might have seen me.' She glanced toward her father and brought a finger to her lips. 'He doesn't know that I was there, and was nearly killed.'

Georges agreed to her wish with a simple nod. But the very thought of her dying had given him a moment of consternation.

Night had fallen when they reached the countess's town house. Yes, the porter said, Madame Cartier had arrived with the sick young woman early in the evening. At the front door, Sylvie greeted them, told Berthe and her father there was food in the kitchen if they were hungry, and showed them to their rooms on the ground floor at the rear of the house.

'Where's the patient?' Georges asked, when Sylvie returned.

'Madame Cartier and Doctor Pinel are with her in the garden room. Follow me.'

She scratched lightly on the door. Madame Cartier opened, raised a finger to her lips, and whispered, 'Renée's sleeping. The ride from the Salpêtrière was very painful to her broken ribs.'

Georges remembered Renée from occasional contact in the Palais-Royal, a wild, lively young woman in perpetual motion. Now he stared at her in bed. The contrast could hardly be greater. The figure before him seemed dead, her face grey and gaunt, her mouth half-open. Will she ever utter a helpful word? he asked himself.

Doctor Pinel was standing next to the bed, thoughtfully observing the patient. As Georges drew near, the doctor looked up, beckoned Georges to leave the room with him.

'Have you brought the new sister?' he asked. 'I'd like to meet her.'

'She's very tired, worked a full day in the central markets, but I'll fetch her.'

'I'll just have a few words with her now and start training her tomorrow.'

A few minutes later, Georges returned with a flustered Berthe.

The doctor put her at ease, even while he studied her. For perhaps ten minutes they exchanged views about the patient, then the doctor bade Berthe good night.

When she had left the room, Pinel said to Georges, 'A promising sister, this Mademoiselle Dupont. Strong, sensitive, and intelligent. Good choice, Charpentier. I'll see you in the morning.'

Twenty-Four
A Cure?

13 – 27 June

Nature came alive in the garden outside the room's open windows. Bird songs roused Anne sleeping lightly on a pallet on the floor. She did a quick toilette, and joined Sylvie at Renée's bedside. Together they checked the patient. Her pulse was stronger, her breathing had improved. Anne had taken turns with Sylvie watching the patient and sleeping in her room.

Renée needed constant observation. The exhausting ride from the women's prison could have caused serious complications in such a weak person. She awoke once during the night to relieve herself and drink water through the tube. Otherwise she slept fitfully, moaning because of pain from her broken ribs.

'I'm rested and can look after her,' Anne told Sylvie.

Sylvie gave her a tired smile. 'Then I'll retire to my room upstairs.'

At breakfast time, Renée awoke again, dazed and uncomprehending. Anne washed her face and hands with warm water, then fed her bread soaked in a mixture of milk and egg.

At midmorning Doctor Pinel arrived and examined the patient.

'She's young and resilient,' he said to Anne. 'I detect physical improvement already. Keep her warm, give her liquids, comfort her. She can have small doses of laudanum to ease the pain. I'll speak now with Mademoiselle Dupont. She should soon take over your duties.'

An hour later he returned with Berthe. She appeared rested but a little anxious about her new task. 'The two of you may now give the patient a warm bath,' the doctor said. 'I'll return later in the day.'

After the bath and when the patient was sleeping quietly, Berthe appeared to have something on her mind. Anne encouraged her to speak.

'Yesterday in the market I reached the end of my rope. From the minute that she hired me, that peasant woman drove me mercilessly, without respite. Made me do the work of two women. At the market's closing, I felt that I was at the edge of hell, about to battle vainly with the devil for my day's wages. Then Monsieur Charpentier came out of nowhere and saved me and my father. I have to pinch myself. This doesn't seem real.'

Anne smiled. 'Charpentier is a man of many talents, and a great heart.' She paused to savour memories of Georges's kindness to her. When they first met over two years ago, he had acknowledged her intelligence, supported her belief that her stepfather's violent death was murder rather than suicide, and involved her in the subsequent investigation. Since then he had treated her like a promising apprentice, taught her how to pick locks, follow a suspect, search his room, record an interrogation, and the like. His good humour had often lifted her spirits.

Anne's thoughts turned to the patient lying prostrate on the bed. 'Doctor Pinel seems pleased that you know Renée. That should speed her recovery. Tell me about her.'

Berthe glanced at the sleeping woman and lowered her voice. 'I didn't know her mother, a prostitute on Rue Pelican near the central markets. I heard that she died when Renée was still an infant. She grew up with little guidance or help from anyone. Somehow she learned to give as well as take. Shrewd, slow to trust, she's a loyal friend. If betrayed, she can be a fierce enemy. Began selling herself when she was hardly more than a child.'

'Have you noticed her mental disorder?'

'Yes, ever since I came to Paris,' Berthe replied. 'I'm told that she has always been a little odd. Doctor Pinel says she suffers from a combination of mania and melancholy. In hindsight that explains her hysteria, her occasional ranting and gesticulating over issues that the rest of us would shrug off. After a manic episode she would fall into depression and sulk for a day or two. None of us could cheer her up. But I never thought that she was insane. She usually managed to please her customers – better than I could.'

There was a scratching at the door. 'That's my father,' Berthe said. 'Probably has a question. He's studying the plan of the house, has already learned to fetch the charcoal for the stove and to prepare the bath water.'

Berthe opened the door. Monsieur Dupont stood there smiling. 'I'm going to wash the kitchen floor. One of the young maids will get me started.'

'I'll know where to find you,' Berthe remarked and sent him off.

Anne felt relieved that Berthe and her father had adjusted so quickly to their new roles. 'I'll leave you now with Renée and go home to my husband. I must rest for an hour. Later we'll talk more about Renée.'

At noon, after her rest, Anne went to Paul's office and found him absorbed in a pile of papers. As she entered, he looked up, smiled, signed a document, and laid down his pen. 'How's Renée?' he asked, as Anne pulled up a chair.

'Improving.' Anne gave him a brief report. 'I left her in Berthe's hands.' Even as she said those words, an unbeckoned thought leaped to her mind. She stared at Paul.

The same idea had come to him. 'Berthe is a possible suspect in the marquis's death. Renée is a possible witness of that death. Up to now, we've always assumed that Renée might have seen Grimaud kill the marquis while Berthe lay there unconscious.'

Anne picked up the thread of his thought. 'But let's suppose that Berthe did in fact kill the marquis and now suspects that Renée observed the deed. How would Berthe feel toward her patient?'

Paul smiled. 'She would want her to recover and testify that she acted in self-defense.'

'Frankly,' Anne agreed, 'I can't imagine any other reason why Berthe would have killed him. Despite her poverty, she's not a thief. And she didn't steal anything that night, though she had the opportunity.'

'Yes, I think we can safely continue to employ her.'

Anne smoothed her gown and rose to leave. Suddenly, an afterthought occurred to her. 'Renée and Berthe both have strong reasons for harming Grimaud.'

Paul appeared puzzled.

'Let's suppose that Berthe did in fact kill Bresse. I believe that she despises Grimaud sufficiently to shift the blame to him, rather than plead self-defense. And Renée's attitude is similar. I observed her carefully while the duke's guards were arresting the prostitutes. When she fled to Grimaud in the arcade and he abandoned her, she must have felt betrayed, resentful. She might therefore gladly collude with Berthe in putting the guilt for Bresse's death on to Grimaud's shoulders, even if he were innocent.'

Paul pondered the idea. 'Conjecture, of course, but I must admit that it's plausible. I'll keep it in mind when I interrogate these suspects again.'

That afternoon and for the next several days, Doctor Pinel visited in the afternoon, examined the patient, spent an hour with Berthe, her father, and Sylvie – the patient's principal caregivers. They were learning the symptoms and probable causes of mania and melancholy, as well as the most effective treatments. Pinel entrusted Berthe and Sylvie with a notebook and taught them to make careful observations of changes in the patient's condition.

After a few days of Pinel's regime, she could sit up and walk about the room. The laudanum helped ease the pain from her ribs. Salves and other treatments reduced the swelling from her bruises. But she hardly spoke, seemed confused and depressed. The doctor asked her kindly how she felt and where it hurt. She replied, almost like a child, pointing to her ribs, to her bruises, whimpering a few words.

By the end of a week, she was still in pain but was eating almost normally, gazing out the window, taking small steps in the garden. But she was becoming restless. One day, to distract her, Anne introduced three kittens into the room. The cook's cat had recently produced a litter. While Renée was standing by the window, watching the kittens gambol on the floor, one of them detached herself from the others and planted herself between Renée's feet.

'She's chosen you,' Anne remarked. 'You can have her.'

The kitten was a charming mixture of many breeds, mostly a short-haired tiger with a white spot on the tip of her tail and bits of calico in her fur. She was very playful, leaping upon shadows on the floor, nosing into an old slipper.

'I love her,' said Renée, picking up the kitten and petting her. 'I'll call her Princess.'

A few days later, Renée seemed restless again, a sullen expression on her face.

'Where am I?' she asked Anne, who had come for what was now a daily visit. The young woman sat up in bed, with a suspicious, cunning look in her eyes. Having observed her progress, Anne wasn't surprised.

'You are in the town house of the Comtesse Marie de Beaumont,' Anne replied and awaited quietly the next question.

For a moment Renée was silent, her brow furrowed with the effort of thinking. 'Why am I here?'

'To recover your health, Renée. I found you in prison, chained to the wall, beaten, barely alive, so I brought you here. The countess who owns this house is my friend and has agreed to lend you this room. Berthe Dupont and Doctor Pinel offered to treat you.'

'Can I leave?' she asked. Her voice had an angry edge.

'The doctor says you have greatly improved but are still too weak. Your broken ribs have not yet healed.'

This exchange appeared to tire Renée. She nodded non-committally and slipped down under the covers.

On the way out of the house, Anne met Berthe to whom she related the conversation.

'Be watchful,' Anne warned. 'She may attempt to escape. You must restrain her. Be careful of her ribs.'

Late that night, Berthe ended a visit with Renée and announced that she was going to retire. They had played a game of dominoes. Renée already knew the game, but this was the first time that they had played together. They used a set of yellowed ivory tiles belonging to the Comtesse de Beaumont. Madame Cartier had found them in a fine leather-covered box, hidden away for years. Quite proficient, Renée played all her tiles first, demonstrating that she had recovered her mental agility. Berthe also noticed that the young woman seemed distracted, as if she were plotting moves other than those of the game.

Thus forewarned, Berthe only pretended to go to bed. She blew out her candle and waited in the dark. A few minutes after the house quieted down, Berthe heard noises in the adjacent garden room, then the squeak of a door opening, the meow of a kitten. She allowed Renée to make her way to the front door before sneaking after her and lighting her candle.

'Aren't you taking too great a risk, mademoiselle, going out so late at night?' Berthe drew close, smiling, but using her height and bulk to intimidate the small, young woman. 'It's raining outside. Listen.' The faint patter of raindrops could be heard through the door.

'I'm tired of being shut up here,' Renée replied petulantly. 'I want to go home to my own room by the Louvre. You can't stop me.' Her eyes had grown bright, her chin jutted out defiantly. She clutched the kitten to her breast.

Berthe inserted herself between Renée and the door and spoke gently. 'I understand that you're restless. It's hard to be sick for such a long time. But you couldn't walk to the end of the block before you'd collapse. Your ribs would ache like you can't ever imagine. I'd have to pick you up off the street like a wet rag, pat you dry, and put you to bed.'

The young woman was tiring and breathed heavily. As she

started to sway, Berthe swept her up and set off for the bedroom. Renée cradled the kitten in her arms and leaned her head against Berthe's chest.

'First, we'll make you strong,' said Berthe as she covered the young woman. 'Then, if you like, we'll take you home. When that time comes, you will probably want to talk to Madame Cartier and Doctor Pinel. They will help you figure out what to do with the rest of your life.' Berthe stroked the young woman's forehead. 'Good night, Renée. Sleep well.'

Twenty-Five
Eye Witness

28 June

'I believe this is the best time to question Renée,' Anne told Paul. 'Her body is still weak, but her mind is clear.' They were seated in his office, Anne reporting the latest development. 'Last night,' Anne continued, 'Berthe foiled the young woman's attempt to escape from the town house. A second attempt, when Renée has grown stronger, might succeed. The opportunity to question her would be lost.'

'Then we must act.' He reached into the drawer of his writing table and brought out Bresse's ring and his purse of gold coins. 'We'll confront her with this evidence of her presence with Grimaud in the marquis's house on the night of his murder.'

They hastened to the town house with Georges. He and Sylvie would serve as witnesses in case Renée could be persuaded to give testimony. Success was by no means certain. Her moods shifted from joy – especially while playing with her kitten – to despondency when the pain from her side grew severe and the laudanum didn't seem to help.

Anne and Sylvie entered the garden room apprehensive of Renée's mood. But they were soon relieved to see that this morning she appeared to be comfortable and in good spirits, sitting at a table by the garden window. Princess had curled up in her lap and was purring. The visitors took chairs facing her. Paul and Georges had remained outside. Since her beating, Renée had grown ill at ease with men, especially those in uniform. Berthe was away shopping.

Anne began. 'Renée, I believe now is the time to have a serious conversation. It's been a month since the Marquis de Bresse was killed. The king's magistrates need to know who did it and why. My husband, Colonel Paul de Saint-Martin, is charged with finding the answers. I believe that you can help him.'

The young woman frowned. 'What do I know about the marquis's death?'

Anne leaned forward and spoke in carefully measured words. 'You and Denis Grimaud were observed at the back door of the marquis's house on the night he was murdered.' Anne laid the ring and the purse on the table between them. 'You recognize them, don't you? Notice the marquis's marks.' Anne held up the ring, then the purse, and pointed out the marquis's coat of arms on each of them.

Renée's eyes widened. 'Where did you find them?'

'My husband and his adjutant visited your room near the Louvre and discovered a woman called the Bitch living there with Denis Grimaud. The woman was wearing the ring. The purse was hidden in a mattress.'

For a long moment, Renée simply stared at the items before her, as if she couldn't believe her eyes. Then she pointed to the ring and exploded. 'The bastard! That ring was mine. I found it on the marquis's writing table. I never wore it outside my room. Otherwise the police would learn of it and accuse me of stealing it, unless a jealous whore saw it first and knocked me on the head and stole it.'

Anne had correctly sensed a serious breach between Renée and Grimaud. He had abandoned her in the Valois arcade when the guards beat her. Why should she protect him? And he had added insult to injury by immediately choosing a new companion and giving her the gold ring.

'So Grimaud brought the Bitch into my room. And gave

her my ring.' Renée grew red in the face, her eyes blazed with fury. She dropped the kitten to the floor. It scooted away in fright. Renée appeared about to have a manic fit that would prevent her from testifying. Anne offered her a cup of water. The gesture seemed to calm the young woman. She took the cup and drank slowly, her eyes now focused inwardly. Finally, with a nod to Anne she returned the cup. Her lips tightened. She spoke slowly in a low, taut voice. 'Let me tell you what really happened that night at the marquis's house.'

Anne sent Sylvie to fetch Paul and Georges. They had to hear what Renée was about to say.

Renée scarcely gave the men a glance as they entered the room. Her mind seemed fully transported back to the night of May twenty-eighth to twenty-ninth.

'Yes,' she said, 'we went to the marquis's house that night. Denis claimed that Bresse had unfairly dismissed him and owed him back wages. He intended to steal as much loose money as he could find. He would also take away certain financial papers that revealed his embezzlement of the marquis's funds. The best time to carry out the plan was when the servants were away and the marquis was busy with his female guest. Denis had copied the house keys. He brought me along to watch out for trouble and give him a warning. So, while Denis went upstairs to the study, I searched for the marquis. Soon, I heard him going down to his basement "treasure room".

'I hurried into a ground-floor storeroom. Grimaud had told me about peepholes that he had drilled through the floor into the room below. He used to watch the marquis playing with his victims. By the time I found the holes, he had stripped to his shirt and breeches. Mademoiselle Dupont was lying on her back on a pallet, barely conscious, wearing only her shift. Her clothes were piled to the side. The marquis bent over her, seized her by the neck, and began to choke her. But he hesitated, then loosened his grip and stepped back. He stood there, rubbing his chin, as if he were thinking. A minute later, he left the room, to relieve himself in the water closet or to work in his laboratory.

'I ran upstairs to the study and told Grimaud what was

going on in the basement. He had found the marquis's purse and several important papers and was ready to go back to my room. The ring lay on the writing table. "I want to see for myself what the marquis is doing," he said to me as he left the study, and added, "Meet me inside at the rear door."

'I put the ring in my pocket, waited a minute, and went back to the storeroom. Grimaud wasn't there. I looked through the peepholes. He had gone down to the basement and was standing by the door leading to the water closet and the laboratory. It looked as if he were trying to hide. He had his back to the wall and a hammer in his hand.

'When the marquis entered the room, Grimaud hit him twice on the head with the hammer. The first blow stunned him, the second dropped him to the floor. Grimaud pulled him to the wall and sat him up. With the hammer still in his hand, he walked over to where Mademoiselle Dupont lay. For about a minute he looked down at her, glancing once or twice at the hammer. I thought that he was about to kill her. Instead, he bent over to make sure that she was unconscious and hadn't witnessed his deed. I sensed that he was about to leave, so I rushed to the back door.

'When he joined me a few minutes later, I asked what had happened. He replied, "Nothing. For all I know, the marquis is still in the water closet." Grimaud left first, I followed a few minutes later. I've never told him what I saw. He would have killed me.'

While Renée spoke, Georges took notes. Now he sat at the table preparing a deposition. When he finished, he read it to Renée. She nodded that it was correct, and he gave it to her to sign. Since she was illiterate, she made a mark and Anne and Sylvie witnessed it. Her ordeal over, Renée collapsed in her chair, exhausted, clutching her injured side, her face contorted with pain. Anne and Sylvie eased her out of the chair and into bed.

'You spoke well,' Anne said to her. 'Now perhaps justice will be done. Rest easy.' Anne gave her a sip of the laudanum, wiped her brow, spoke comforting words. Gradually, her breathing returned to normal and she fell asleep.

Georges walked through the entrance hall, about to leave the town house. There was a spring in his step. Renée's account of Bresse's death had greatly encouraged him. He had received orders from the colonel to apprehend Grimaud and put him in the Châtelet for interrogation tomorrow. What would he say, now that his alibi was gone and an eyewitness had accused him?

At the door Georges met Berthe coming in with a basket of groceries on her arm. For a moment they gazed fondly at each other. Then he led her into the front parlour. She immediately became apprehensive.

He gave her a reassuring smile. 'A short while ago, Renée signed this statement. Would you read it to determine that it's accurate as it pertains to you.' He handed her a copy. They sat down facing each other.

As she read it, her facial expression changed from apprehension to guarded relief. 'If she's telling the truth, I had no part in Bresse's death.'

'Why would she lie?' Georges asked, puzzled. 'The statement puts Renée herself at risk of a charge of theft. After all, she illegally entered the marquis's town house and stole his ring. In this country poor women have been branded *voleuse* and have spent a hard life in prison for crimes no worse than hers.'

Berthe shrugged. 'She would lie if it meant more to her than telling the truth. That's her nature.'

Georges felt uneasy about the direction of this conversation. 'You know her better than any of us. What has prompted her to make this statement?' He gestured to the copy in Berthe's hand.

'Renée is a passionate woman,' Berthe replied. 'For years Grimaud exploited her and, finally, betrayed her to the duke's guards. She also blamed him for her cousin's disappearance.' Berthe pointed to the copy. 'So this could be Renée's revenge. Grimaud might in fact be innocent of the marquis's death. Or guilty, I'm not sure.'

For a long moment Berthe searched Georges's eyes. 'I'm afraid I've muddied the water and distressed you. In no way do I wish to plead for Grimaud, a despicable man. But, sad to say, Renée is a clever, problematic witness.'

'My distress . . .' Georges waved it away. 'I thank you for this insight into Renée's mind. Her motives need closer scrutiny.' Georges rose from the chair. 'Nonetheless, when

I interrogate Grimaud tomorrow, I'll confront him with her story. His reaction might help us determine whether she has told us the truth.'

Anne and Paul took a walk in the garden behind the house, each quietly mulling over Renée's story. To Anne's mind it rang true. But she realized that Paul might have a different impression. As the officer in charge of the investigation, he had to present a final report that would satisfy a magistrate, in this case, the lieutenant general. With a sidelong glance Anne studied her husband. Lines of doubt creased his forehead.

Anne was the first to speak. 'What do you think, Paul?'

He reflected for a long moment before replying. 'Renée gave us a remarkable performance, truly an eyewitness account. So detailed and intense, it almost convinced me. But what gave me pause is the suspicion that she might have designed her story to conceal her own role in Bresse's death.'

'Really! What can you mean, Paul?'

'Just for the sake of discussion, Anne, imagine yourself as Renée, peering through the peepholes at the scene unfolding in the room below. For you Bresse is evil incarnate. He has killed your cousin Yvonne and perhaps many other young women. For months you have single-mindedly plotted revenge. Tonight you have gained free access to his house. In the person of Berthe, helpless on the pallet, you see your dear cousin Yvonne in mortal danger. The hated Bresse bends over her, clutches her neck, begins to choke her. Now a unique opportunity presents itself. He leaves the room but you know he will return.'

Paul met Anne's eye. 'What would seize Renée's mind at that point and banish every other consideration?'

'Rage.' Anne felt it welling up within her.

'Absolutely,' Paul agreed. 'Again, if you were Renée, and Bresse left the room, what would you do? Run to Grimaud, tell him to come and take a look – Grimaud, a man you detest and intend to punish, an accomplice in Yvonne's murder?'

'No,' Anne replied. 'I would rush to the basement room, pick up a hammer, and crush the marquis's skull.'

Paul nodded. 'Then you would dash upstairs to Grimaud and trick him into believing that the marquis was about to leave the basement. You and he had better flee from the house.'

This conjecture raised a question in Anne's mind. 'Why would Renée leave Berthe behind, likely to be blamed for Bresse's death?'

'Renée would be so intensely focused on revenge that she simply wouldn't consider Berthe's predicament. Anyway, Renée would be pressed for time. Berthe was unconscious and too heavy for Renée to move. Berthe would have to fend for herself.'

Their walk had taken them to the far end of the garden. They turned and gazed back at the house, at the room where Renée lay, a weak, pitiful creature. Anne turned to Paul. 'Although I don't want to, I could imagine Renée observing still another scenario.'

'Yes?' He motioned for them to start walking back to the house.

'When the marquis began to choke Berthe, he in fact revived her. While he was out of the room, she rose from the straw pallet, picked up the hammer, and struck him when he returned. Convinced that no magistrate would believe that she acted in self-defense, she has claimed that she remained unconscious, hoping that Bresse's body would not be found, or that Grimaud would be blamed for his death.'

'A plausible alternative,' Paul granted. 'And if that's what Renée saw, she would gladly divert the blame to Grimaud and let Berthe go free. Either way, Renée would have her revenge for Yvonne's death. Grimaud would be convicted, then executed on the Place de Grève. She most likely planned to be there in front and watch.'

At this point, Anne found herself confused, and nearly overwhelmed by conflicting emotions: on the one hand, fondness, even admiration, for the two prostitutes, now suspected murderers. On the other, revulsion and contempt for their victims, and a sense that justice was done to them.

'What shall we do, Paul? It would be terribly wrong if either Renée or Berthe were convicted of the marquis's murder and executed. It would also be wrong for Grimaud to be severely punished for a crime that he didn't commit.'

'You're right, Anne. Unfortunately, our magistrate, the Lieutenant General DeCrosne, will be strongly influenced by the fact that both Renée and Berthe are prostitutes. In most respects, he is an enlightened and humane man. But he has only contempt for prostitutes: he sends them by the hundreds to the Salpêtrière with little if any compunction. As matters stand now, he would see no reason to lessen the guilt of either Berthe or Renée. The former went to the marquis's house freely; the latter arrived as a thief and has also been erratic and violent.'

Their walk through the garden ended at the house's back door. Paul held it open for Anne. 'Take heart,' he said. 'Tomorrow, Georges and I shall interrogate Grimaud at the Châtelet. We may discover that our dire conjectures were all wrong. Renée may have told the truth after all.'

Twenty-Six
Confession

29 June

In the early morning quiet of his office Georges leaned over a sheet of paper bearing the seal of Comte Savarin, royal archivist and expert on code. For weeks Georges had been trying to construct a pattern of Bresse's murderous movements. From the diary that Anne had discovered in the marquis's study Georges had drawn up a list of female guests. Many were hard to trace since Bresse had usually identified them only by pet names or code.

A month ago, Georges had sent the list to Comte Savarin at Versailles. Savarin was a busy man – the Foreign Office had needed his services, so his work on the list was delayed and his report arrived only yesterday.

Among the marquis's listed guests, Savarin had found

Yvonne Bloch and Lucie Gigot, both already known. But he had also solved the difficult code for Antoinette Minard and Josephine Bourget, together with the dates when they 'entertained' the marquis and other bits of information. These were the two missing young women whom Sylvie and Michou had earlier linked to Grimaud and the millinery shop.

Now Georges had strong circumstantial reasons to believe that the marquis had murdered four young prostitutes. However, thus far, only one body, Lucie's, had been recovered. It was time to find the other three.

Georges reached for his hat, brushed his blue coat, and strapped on his sword. He would confront Denis Grimaud in the Café Odéon. For two days the man had evaded Georges.

Grimaud saw him coming into the café and tried to slip out the back door. But he ran into a pair of French guards whom Georges had stationed there. They held him until Georges could catch up.

'I've nothing more to say, Charpentier.' His voice had a whining tone. 'Why do you harass me?'

Georges ignored him and turned to the guards. 'Take him to the Châtelet. Colonel Saint-Martin and I shall question him shortly. Remain nearby. You might be able to help us later.'

Within half an hour Grimaud sat opposite Georges at a table in an interrogation room, Colonel Saint-Martin and the French guards stood off to the side, observing.

Georges adopted an unsmiling demeanor. In a level voice he named the three young women and the dates when they went missing, excluding Lucie Gigot. 'You took each of them to the marquis. Afterward, they were never seen again. Where did you bury them?'

'I don't know what you mean.'

'In the marquis's diary we have figured out his code. In the case of each woman he wrote: "And Grimaud will take her away." I'm reasonably sure that you didn't dump them in the river. They would have surfaced eventually. I've checked the morgue. No sign of them. So where did you put them?'

Beads of perspiration began to appear on Grimaud's brow.

'The marquis meant only that I would escort the young women back to the Palais-Royal.'

Georges bristled, brought his fist down hard on the table. 'You've got to do better than that. Do you think I'm stupid! The women never returned to the Palais-Royal. You told their acquaintances, like Renée, that they went back to their villages in the country.'

He leaned over the table to within inches of Grimaud's face. 'If you continue to lie to me, I'll persuade the magistrates that you were the marquis's willing accomplice, helped him torture and kill those women. You'll end up burning on the Place de Grève.'

'And what if I tell you?' Grimaud asked weakly.

'The magistrates will relent and send you to scrape barnacles and break rock at the Brest naval prison for the rest of your life. No guarantee.' Georges backed off, smiled a little. 'The naval prison isn't as bad as I just made it sound. A clever fellow like you would find ways to make life easier. It's certainly better than burning.'

Grimaud glanced up at the two French guards. They stared at him, stone-faced, without pity. He turned toward the colonel and received a similar response. Grimaud sighed. 'I'll take you there.'

'They're buried in a vault beneath the stable,' Grimaud admitted. He had led the policemen back to Bresse's town house and into the basement. The vault was cleverly concealed. With Grimaud's directions, the two guards opened a wall and revealed a small chamber. 'There are his victims,' Grimaud said. Three lead-lined boxes were laid one on top of the other, each with a name inscribed. Yvonne Bloch, Antoinette Minard, and Josephine Bourget.

'Why did he keep them in the house?' Saint-Martin asked.

'At first, this seemed the safest place. He didn't want the bodies to be discovered and increase the risk of prosecution. But with the fourth body, Lucie's, he changed his mind. He had become aware that Michel the Beggar and other spies were watching his house. It might also be searched. So he planned to eventually move all the bodies to the cave on the Bresse estate.'

The men fell silent for a moment, rendered mute by the

enormity of the evil they witnessed. Georges often felt a deep numbing sensation in the presence of malicious death, magnified as in this case by the fact that the victims were poor, outcast women, led to their deaths by false promises of a better life.

One of the guards broke the silence. 'Sir, shall we take the boxes to the morgue at the Châtelet?'

Georges nodded. 'We'll identify them there. But not right now. We have unfinished business here.'

Georges, Saint-Martin, and the guards escorted Grimaud into Bresse's so-called treasure room. The pallet and the hammer were still on the floor.

'Monsieur Grimaud, you are familiar with this room, are you not?' Georges stared at the man. 'Tell us how the marquis used it.'

'Among other pleasures, he abused or, as he would say, played with prostitutes here.'

Georges pointed toward the ceiling. 'And you watched him through the peepholes, isn't that true?'

Grimaud nodded, with a surprised expression.

'Then tell us how he killed Yvonne and the other two women, after he had "played" with them.'

'He strangled them.'

'Was he wild, out of his mind, enraged?'

'No, he seemed perfectly calm.'

'Why didn't you stop him, or at least report to the police what he had done?'

He paused, brow furrowed, searching for an answer. Finally, he replied, 'My master did what he pleased, as if the law didn't apply to him. He told me the women were just prostitutes and nobody – even the police – really cared about them. I wasn't so sure, so I saved several women, when I sensed that he planned to kill them, like Claudette, who works in a tavern by the central markets.'

Georges continued, 'Tell us what happened here on the night of May twenty-eighth to twenty-ninth.' The police had kept secret the circumstances of the marquis's murder. Berthe was instructed not to mention her experience to anyone.

'When you last questioned me, three weeks ago, I told

you that I had searched through the house and hadn't seen
either the marquis or his female guest.'

'And you also said that you were alone.' Georges glared
at him. 'Do you still stand by your statement?'

'Yes.'

'We found your former companion, Renée Gros, at death's
door. She has recovered sufficiently to tell us today a story
about the night of May twenty-eighth to twenty-ninth quite
different from yours.'

Grimaud seemed shocked, though he tried to conceal it.
He managed to say, 'But she's a liar and can't be trusted.'

'That may be true,' Georges granted, 'but she mentioned
facts that only an eyewitness could know, for example, the
identity of Bresse's female guest. Renée also accurately
described the room and everything in it, including the murder
weapon. While you were in the study stealing Bresse's money,
Renée was watching him prepare to assault that guest. Renée
rushed upstairs and told you what was happening. You told
her to go to the back door while you went to see for yourself. Instead of leaving, she sneaked to the peepholes in the
storage room and watched you kill the marquis. Her description of your blows correspond exactly to the wounds we
found on his body.' Georges paused for a moment, fixed
Grimaud with his eyes. 'What do you have to say now?'

The ex-valet appeared stunned, speechless. His lips trembled with fear and confusion. 'That's not what happened,'
he finally stammered. 'Renée came to me in the study and
said that we must leave in a great hurry. Bresse had finished
"playing" with the guest and would soon come upstairs. I
gathered a few papers and the purse, she grabbed the ring.

'We walked home separately. Spies were everywhere.
Back in her room I asked who the guest was. Renée replied
that she didn't recognize her and gave me only a vague
description. At that time, I had no reason to doubt her. But
after Bresse's body was discovered, I tried again to talk to
her about the case. She refused, became quarrelsome and
stopped working with me. Two days later, the police arrested
her and I haven't seen her since.'

Colonel Saint-Martin took Georges aside and spoke softly.
'I want you and the French guards to bring the marquis's
victims to the morgue for identification. Take Grimaud with

you and put him in a cell at the Châtelet. Get a written, signed deposition from him. Then bring it to my office. I believe that we may have a problem that we didn't sufficiently anticipate.'

Early in the afternoon, Anne had returned home from a visit with Renée and was resting in her room. A servant called her to Paul's office. She found Georges and Paul at the conference table with a chair for her. Georges slumped in his chair, looking tired and disgruntled, Paul seemed even more serious than usual in his office. When Anne had taken her place, Paul briefly described the Grimaud interrogation and nodded to his adjutant.

Georges sat up, cleared his throat. 'The morgue will identify Bresse's victims in a day or two, since the bodies are well preserved. But there's no reason to doubt the names on the boxes. Yvonne Bloch is one of them.' He reached into his portfolio, pulled out a paper, and handed it to Paul. 'Here's Grimaud's deposition. It might be true.'

Paul scanned it and passed it to Anne. 'I'd like your opinion,' he said evenly.

She read it with mounting concern and returned it to Paul with a sigh.

'We're in trouble,' Anne said. 'Renée's story of the night of May twenty-eighth to twenty-ninth is still clear in my mind. Grimaud's version is distressingly different. Each seems plausible but hides a self-serving motive. Renée wanted to take revenge on Bresse and to punish Grimaud. He wanted to prevent Bresse from charging him with embezzlement. Both Renée and Grimaud were at the site illegally and could have killed the marquis.'

She glanced at her companions. 'How shall we get to the truth?'

'I'll reply with another question,' said Paul. 'Who had the stronger reasons for killing Bresse?'

Georges responded. 'Prior to searching Bresse's study that night, Grimaud would have killed to avoid arrest and imprisonment for embezzlement. But while in the marquis's study, he stole the incriminating records. His motive for killing Bresse greatly weakened. Furthermore, Grimaud's record is free of violence. He enjoys watching it, but he's a voyeur rather than a perpetrator. If he were at the peep-holes watching Bresse assaulting Berthe, he wouldn't inter-vene, much less kill Bresse.

'In contrast, Renée's desire for revenge against Bresse remained strong. Given the opportunity that she had that night, she might gladly kill him. And she does have at least a slim record of violence.'

Paul agreed, 'Grimaud is a vile human being, but he's perhaps innocent of killing Bresse. We must find a way to persuade Renée to tell the simple truth, even though it might have dire consequences for her.'

Late that afternoon, Berthe and Renée sat at the table by the window, again playing dominoes. The kitten Princess frolicked at Renée's feet with a ball of yarn. The cook served the two women hot chocolate, a drink that Renée had learned to enjoy. As a freelance prostitute, it had been too expen-sive for her. She sipped from her cup, her eyes smiling at Berthe over the rim. Berthe sensed her patient's growing affection and higher level of trust.

An hour ago, Madame Cartier had raised with Berthe the possibility that Renée's testimony was flawed. She, rather than Grimaud, might have killed Bresse. Her motive: revenge for his assaulting her cousin months ago. She implicated Grimaud to punish him for aiding the marquis.

'Berthe,' Anne had said, 'you have become the person closest to Renée. Could you draw the truth from her?'

None of this came as a surprise to Berthe. 'I shall try, madame.'

The game finished with Renée the winner. She drank the rest of her chocolate and sank back in the chair with a sigh of contentment. Berthe judged that the moment was right.

After they put away the tiles in the box, Berthe began with an affectionate smile. 'Renée, for some time since getting to know you better, I've wanted to tell you how grateful I am that you saved my life there in Bresse's base-ment. That was a generous, courageous act. He would surely have killed me. And, if he had caught you, he would have killed you, too.' Berthe could speak with perfect conviction and utter sincerity. What Bresse might otherwise have done made her shiver even now.

'How do you know it was me? You were unconscious.' Suspicion mixed with puzzlement in her eyes.

'Oh, that's easy. It had to be either you or Grimaud, the only two persons in the building who could have done it. Grimaud would never lift a finger to help me. Frankly, I think he's a coward as well as a thief. He didn't help you either, did he, when the police caught you in the Valois arcade.' Berthe paused for a moment. Renée was struggling, uncertain how to react to what she was hearing. Berthe added, 'How could you know when to come to my aid?'

Renée seemed to slip back in time, grew engaged again in the scene. 'I was in the storeroom above you, looking through peepholes. The marquis started to choke you. I felt helpless. Then he left the room. I ran to the basement, my heart in my throat. He might return before I was ready. I picked up the hammer and hid by the door. A few moments later, he came through and I hit him. Twice. Yes, he would have killed you like he killed Yvonne.'

'And as he would have killed other young women, had you not stopped him. By the way, the colonel and his men have found Yvonne's body. She's at the morgue.'

Renée's eyes began to tear. She sniffled, 'I must give her a proper burial – her father won't. But I'm sick and haven't any money.'

'I'm sure that Madame Cartier and the colonel will help you.'

'They might be angry with me.' Renée dried her eyes. 'I misled them. I said that Grimaud killed the marquis.'

'They are quite sure that he didn't. Once he had found the financial papers, he no longer feared the marquis and didn't need to kill him.'

'Still, I'd better tell the colonel the truth.' She paused for a long moment. 'But I don't want to go to prison. Never again.' Her fists clenched, a terrible grimace seized her face. 'I'll kill myself first.'

Berthe shuddered.

Anne paced the floor of the parlour, calming her agitated mind. She glanced at Berthe. 'Yes, I agree. Renée meant what she said. She would indeed kill herself rather than go to prison.' Berthe had given Anne an account of Renée's confession and her threat. Then Anne had prepared a written version and Renée had put her mark to it. Anne and Berthe countersigned.

'Will the police arrest her anyway?' Berthe asked Anne. 'She did steal a gold ring. Poor men and women have been severely whipped for crimes less than that.' Berthe's voice broke with emotion. 'If that happened, I would feel devastated.'

'I can speak for my husband. He will do his utmost to protect her.' Still, Anne fully realized that Lieutenant General DeCrosne and the Parlement of Paris would have the last word in this case. Anne could not promise that they would do the right thing.

Twenty-Seven
Justifiable Homicide

2 July

Three days later, while crossing Place Vendôme on their way to the Hôtel de Police, Saint-Martin discussed with Georges their final report to the lieutenant general concerning the death of the Marquis de Bresse.

'Are you worried, sir?' Georges raised the question that pressed on Saint-Martin's mind. 'The lieutenant general might claim that Berthe and Renée, abetted by a corrupt ex-valet, killed the marquis in the course of a robbery, then concocted a fantastic story about one prostitute saving the other from his depraved attempt to kill her.'

'Yes, that's what he's likely to think. And I *am* worried,' replied Saint-Martin. 'Our case depends greatly on Renée's credibility, which I'm sure DeCrosne will be loath to accept. In general, he takes a jaundiced view of prostitutes. Like beggars, they are human refuse that must be purged from the city. Most of them are inveterate liars, diseased, petty criminals. Once a month, he condemns them by the cartload to the Salpêtrière – I believe about eight hundred last year. Or he exiles them from Paris.'

Saint-Martin paused, glanced sideways at his adjutant. Georges had fallen into an unusually heavy silence. He had been offended by the lieutenant general's indiscriminate contempt for prostitutes. One of them, Berthe, had won Georges's heart. Her sordid occupation – a sacrifice of self for her father – had only increased his respect for her. For a moment Saint-Martin wondered if he should caution Georges not to challenge DeCrosne, if he were to make an injurious remark about Berthe.

When they reached the lieutenant general's office, he received them immediately. 'What do you have for me, Colonel?' He merely nodded to Georges.

'The final report on the Bresse case, sir.' He drew a bundle of papers from his portfolio and handed them to his superior.

'Give me the gist of it, now, Colonel. I'll consider the details later.'

Saint-Martin delivered a brief account of the fatal night in Bresse's town house, then concluded: 'By attacking Mademoiselle Berthe Dupont, the marquis provoked his own death. Mademoiselle Gros came to her defense and killed him in what I consider justifiable homicide.'

DeCrosne frowned doubtfully. 'Tell me more about their struggle.'

'The incident took place in a small basement room where Bresse sometimes staged cockfights and other animal cruelties, and also tormented prostitutes. His valet Denis Grimaud used to watch through hidden peepholes, which he had drilled through the floor of a storeroom above. On this occasion, Bresse drugged Mademoiselle Dupont and dragged her to the basement room. Through the peepholes Mademoiselle Renée Gros observed him threaten to strangle Mademoiselle Dupont. Fortunately, he interrupted his assault in order to visit the water closet. While he was gone, Mademoiselle Gros ran to the room and seized a hammer. When he returned, she hit him on the head.

'An hour or so later, when Mademoiselle Dupont regained consciousness, she determined that the marquis was dead.

Fearing that she would be blamed, she threw his body in the river. Until very recently, she was unaware that anyone else was in the house at the time. So she didn't know who had saved her. In the meantime, Mademoiselle Gros and the ex-valet had fled from the house. The latter didn't know for several days that his companion had killed the marquis. That's the short of it.'

DeCrosne inclined his head at a skeptical angle. 'Colonel, you have described what Mademoiselle Gros did as "justifiable homicide", a desperate measure that was necessary in order to save Mademoiselle Dupont's life. The facts, however, contradict your argument. Mademoiselle Gros entered the house illegally, unbeknown to the marquis and ignorant of his intentions. As she watched through the peepholes, why should she assume that the marquis meant to kill Mademoiselle Dupont? His choking gesture might have been merely in fun. Don't prostitutes expect rough play from gentlemen and receive money for their bruises and moments of terror?'

With a nod Saint-Martin acknowledged the force of that argument. 'That is perhaps often the practice. But this case is different—'

Irritated and skeptical, DeCrosne impatiently cut off Saint-Martin. 'I'm convinced that your little prostitute exaggerated the danger to her fellow prostitute and heedlessly took the life of a young nobleman from one of the kingdom's most ancient and distinguished families. Couldn't she have tried to distract the marquis, persuade him into a less threatening course, raise an alarm?' DeCrosne paused, glanced at the colonel, then answered his own question. 'In view of her recent encounter with the duke's guards in the Valois arcade, I conclude that she's inclined to rash judgments and violent reactions.'

Saint-Martin shook his head. 'In this case, Mademoiselle Gros's judgment was quick, rather than rash. She had little time to decide and had good reason to fear for the unconscious woman's life. The marquis's behavior seemed homicidal, consistent with a pattern he had displayed over the past year. She justifiably believed that he had killed her cousin Yvonne Bloch several months earlier under similar circumstances, and she rightly suspected him of the deaths of Lucie Gigot and other young acquaintances.' The colonel paused for emphasis. 'My adjutant has confirmed Mademoiselle Gros's opinion.' Saint-Martin gestured for Georges to continue.

The lieutenant general's aristocratic prejudice and his present skeptical manner appeared to intimidate Georges. His neck was taut, his eyes glistened with heightened awareness. Nonetheless, he spoke with a clear and forceful voice. 'With help from Inspector Quidor, Comte Savarin, and dozens of the marquis's acquaintances, I have uncovered his true, murderous character. In the past year, he killed at least four young women, including Yvonne Bloch, Mademoiselle Gros's cousin. We have identified their bodies. All were poor young country women, enticed like Berthe Dupont with offers of work as maids in his house. According to a medical examiner, the three women buried in his basement had been strangled. They are now at the morgue. As you know, the fourth, Lucie Gigot, died of a poison, accidentally. We believe that Bresse would otherwise have strangled her like the others.'

Saint-Martin added, 'Some observers might conclude from Bresse's actions that he was insane. But the entries in his diary reflect the mind of a cold, calculating killer. Prostitutes who survived his cruelty support our conclusion, such as the woman called Claudette. Finally, we offer the testimony of his valet, Denis Grimaud, who observed all four deaths and helped dispose of the bodies.' The colonel paused for effect, then stated, 'Bresse knew that murder, even of prostitutes, was against the law, but he did it anyway for the pleasure.'

'Three, possibly four murders!' DeCrosne shifted uncomfortably in his chair, averted his eyes. For a long moment he was silent. The corners of his mouth twitched nervously. Finally, he cleared his throat and said softly, 'I didn't realize that he was so depraved. A most regrettable mistake. I thought I knew him. Two years ago, his parents brought him to my attention, said he was keeping bad company, gambling heavily, and dissipating his fortune. His orgies in the house on the Isle Saint-Louis were disgracing the family. Would I commit him to a royal prison? they asked, having in mind Bresse's friend and mentor, the Marquis de Sade.

A few years earlier, my predecessor in this office, Lieutenant General Lenoir, had sent Sade to the Bastille.

'But Bresse was still young and not as deeply steeped in vice as Sade. Besides, the Baron de Breteuil and I agreed with you, Colonel, that the king's power of arbitrary arrest by *lettres de cachet* should be used rarely and then only for very pressing reasons of state. So I told the Bresse family that they could and should take their wayward son in hand. And, as you now know, I put him under surveillance.'

'A sensible solution,' Saint-Martin ventured to say. 'Subsequently, Bresse at least pretended to mend his ways, even while living a vicious secret life.'

DeCrosne grew reflective, his eyes focused on an inner truth. 'In hindsight, of course, I should have committed him.' He sighed, then glanced with a pained expression toward Saint-Martin and Georges.

They all understood that had he imprisoned Bresse, when asked, the four young women might still be alive.

'Gentlemen, I thank you for the care and skill of this investigation. Your conclusion of "justifiable homicide" has merit. The case will go to the Parlement for a final decision. In the present crisis, who knows what they will do.'

They bowed and left him with his thoughts.

Twenty-Eight
In the Lap of the Gods

4 – 25 July

At the town house on Rue Traversine, Anne and Comtesse Marie welcomed Doctor Pinel, who had come with a carriage to take Renée and her kitten to his private clinic. Occupied with estate business, Marie had been out of touch with the Bresse case since the burial of Lucie several weeks ago. Now she had a free moment and wanted to catch up. They spoke with Pinel in the front parlour.

'Is the young woman fit to be moved, Doctor?' Marie asked. 'She could stay here a while longer if you wish.'

'Thank you, Comtesse,' the doctor replied. 'I examined her yesterday. Her ribs have healed enough that she can be comfortably moved. Her mental illness can now be more conveniently treated at my clinic. I've engaged Mademoiselle Berthe Dupont, my trusted assistant for the past three weeks, to continue to care for the sick young woman and to take on a few other patients. I've also found work for her father, Jean Dupont.'

They said farewell to Renée in the courtyard. She replied with a grateful smile. The doctor put her and the kitten in the carriage and climbed in after them. Berthe and her father sat outside. Off they went in a clatter of hooves.

'It seems so quiet here now,' Anne said, as they entered the front hall and the door shut behind them.

'I'm pleased that you put the house to such good use,' Marie remarked. 'Tell me more about Renée's part in the Bresse murder.'

Anne explained how the young woman came to be in the marquis's house and why she killed him. 'The lieutenant general decided that the stolen ring should not become an issue. It was returned to the marquis's parents, together with his purse and its gold coins. They buried him privately on the estate.'

'For a week,' remarked Marie, 'fashionable society has been aghast and talked of nothing but the marquis's monstrous deeds, clear evidence of a diseased mind.'

Anne smiled wryly. 'Common folk have lower expectations of young aristocratic men and are merely titillated by a prostitute killing an aristocrat in defense of another prostitute.'

'The scandal in all its variant forms will soon die down,' opined Marie. 'The worsening conflict between the government and the parlements, the failed harvest, the growing malaise among artisans and other urban workers will drive the Marquis de Bresse from the public's mind.'

The two women inspected the garden room where Renée had convalesced.

The countess picked up a ball of yarn left by the kitten.

'Tell me more about the progress that the young woman has made.'

'Her moods continue to swing between nervous excitement and melancholy depression. But the peaks and the depths are less pronounced. She occupies her days with repairing clothes and knitting – she's clever with her fingers.'

'Does she yearn for her former life?'

'I think she does. She complains of missing the bustle, the exotic sights, sounds, and smells of the Palais-Royal, the company of other prostitutes and outcasts.'

'Then I can imagine that the broken ribs are a blessing.'

'Yes, for their pain helps persuade her to accept her confinement.'

'That's true. But she must nonetheless be a restless, difficult patient. How did you occupy her mind for the past week?'

'The kitten distracted her, as did cards and dominoes with Berthe. Michou taught her how to draw and to paint, which she seems to enjoy. Sylvie read stories to her. She especially appreciated the fables of La Fontaine, as did Jean Dupont, who often listened. And I put on an occasional puppet show or a juggling act. To all these events the cook, the young maids, Berthe, and the porter were invited and usually attended. Renée relished being the centre of attention.'

Marie reflected for a moment. 'It isn't reasonable is it, to expect Doctor Pinel to provide so much individual, personal attention to the young woman for the rest of her life? At some point she will be on her own, forced to rely on her own resources.' Marie met Anne's eye. 'Will she fall back to her old ways?'

'That would truly be a great pity,' Anne replied. She had often thought of that possibility with a mixture of sadness and dread. Even now she shivered as she replied, 'Because of her cruel past going back to infancy, the odds against her ever achieving full mental health are enormous. Her recovery is fragile. But Dr. Pinel's own interest requires that she not fail. His reputation is at stake. He will do all that he can to place her in the best possible situation, some kind of protected environment.'

Marie sighed, 'I feel just a little more hopeful.'

* * *

Late in the afternoon three weeks later, Paul came home from a meeting with the lieutenant general. He and Anne sat down to tea in the salon overlooking the courtyard.

'Grimaud has just been sentenced to life in the naval prison at Brest,' Paul announced with a smile.

'I'm pleasantly surprised.' Anne was expecting to hear a much lighter sentence. 'I had thought that he was going to the men's prison at Bicêtre. At Brest he will receive the harsh punishment that he deserves. He was the person most responsible for putting Lucie into the marquis's hands, knowing that he would abuse her.'

'You're right, of course,' Paul agreed wholeheartedly. 'The court convicted him of stealing the marquis's purse of gold Louis d'or and of embezzling the marquis's funds. Quidor had found the stolen financial records. The court also condemned him for corrupting Bresse, a weak, susceptible young man, and aiding and abetting his crimes.'

'So the magistrates tried to shift blame away from one of their own class.' Anne shook her head in disgust, paused, then asked, 'Was Renée brought into the proceedings?'

'The magistrates read her deposition in the most favourable light,' Paul replied, 'and accepted her claim to have acted in defence of Berthe. They credited both women for the reformation of their lives, reclaimed from the devil, redeemed by enlightened philanthropists, "friends of man".'

That line of thought led Anne to the desperate social and economic situation of poor young women, like Lucie, Berthe and Renée. Thanks to the efforts of Paul, Georges, and herself, two prostitutes had been rescued. But at least four had recently suffered violent deaths, hundreds were dragged annually into prisons where conditions were appalling, and thousands were mired in brothels and other degrading circumstances and exposed to disease and violence.

While her mind was still struggling with this issue, her eyes were drawn to the striding figure of Georges crossing the courtyard toward the gate to the street.

Paul followed her gaze. 'Where's he going?'

'To Doctor Pinel's clinic,' Anne replied. 'Berthe has invited him to dinner. Under her supervision, Renée is learning how to cook. Seems to enjoy preparing a meal.'

'Georges and Berthe make an odd couple,' Paul remarked, then added, 'the difference in their ages is troubling.'

'True,' Anne replied. 'Georges is old enough to be her uncle. However, she is older than her years. Poverty and misfortune have bruised her, have made her compassionate and wise. And Georges is younger than he looks, bald pate and thick girth notwithstanding. He has a young man's lust for life and an eye for female beauty. He and Berthe could conceivably find themselves suited to each other.'

'How serious are Georges's intentions toward her?' Paul asked.

'To be a good friend. I believe that she reciprocates. The rest lies in the lap of the gods.'

AUTHOR'S NOTE

The Parlement of Paris was one of thirteen royal high courts in France, and by far the most important. It consisted of several hundred magistrates, plus a small army of lawyers, clerks, and other functionaries. It was situated on the Isle de la Cité, the principal island in the heart of Paris. The magistrates were nobles of the robe, a wealthy, privileged class. Their positions could be bought and sold and transmitted to heirs. The Parlement heard cases on appeal from lower courts. It also automatically reviewed all cases involving capital punishment.

One of its functions was to examine royal decrees to determine if they were consistent with previous legislation. If they found a discrepancy, they were to notify the king. He could either alter the decree or he could state that he intended to change the previous legislation. Out of that essentially clerical function, the Parlement of Paris in the eighteenth century drew a virtual veto power over the exercise of the king's authority. The Parlement insisted that it was the guardian of the kingdom's basic unwritten law and custom. Numerous battles were fought between king and Parlement over the former's claim to unchecked authority over taxation. In the summer of 1788 the conflict came to a head. Demonstrations in support of Parlement broke out across the country. The king yielded and convoked a meeting of the Estates-General for the following spring. Royal autocracy was doomed.

Prostitution had been a crime and a significant concern to the modern Paris police ever since its founding under Louis XIV at the end of the seventeenth century. For reasons of public health as well as morality, attempts were made to suppress the practice. The women were supposed to be registered and brothels licensed. For the most part prostitution flourished beyond the pale of the law. Annually, as many as 900 female prostitutes, but none of their clients, were summarily condemned to prison.

Grinding, pervasive rural and urban poverty, exacerbated by failed harvests, crushing taxes, and other pressures on the common people, contributed to making prostitution a major social problem in Paris on the eve of the Revolution. There were between 15,000 and 30,000 full- and part-time prostitutes among the 300,000 women living in Paris. The Palais-Royal was one of the most notorious centers of the problem.

My treatment of this issue is based on Erica-Marie Benabou's *La prostitution et la police des moeurs au XVIIIe siècle* (Paris, 1987), a sympathetic as well as thorough and authoritative study of the policing of prostitution in eighteenth-century France.

The Marquis de Sade and the Libertines were a notable phenomenon on the fringes of upper-class French society. About Sade there is a large literature. See Laurence L. Bongie, *Sade: A Biographical Essay* (Chicago, 1998), for a readable, critical assessment of the man. Pertinent to the themes of *Cruel Choices* is his view of prostitutes as a subhuman species. Killing such persons, he claimed, is like pruning a tree of unhealthy branches. Sade also rejected any law that restricted his sexual or other natural impulses. In 1772 the Parlement of Aix-en-Provence condemned him to death for poisoning several prostitutes, two of whom became critically ill. His well-connected family saved him from punishment, as on many similar occasions.

The Salpêtrière, a major unit of the Paris General Hospital, was (and still is) located on the Left Bank near the botanical gardens. A vast complex of buildings, the hospital was constructed in the late seventeenth and early eighteenth century, mostly by the Sun King, Louis XIV, primarily for women.

Its immense size and outward grandeur reminds the visitor of the Invalides, the hospice for old soldiers, built in the same period. On both of them, King Louis XIV left his mark – his personal taste for magnificence, his bold vision of a unified French state under his own unchecked authority.

Like the Invalides, the Salpêtrière is centred on a great chapel surmounted by a tall dome. Eight arms radiate out from the middle, each serving a different section of the hospital's population. In the late eighteenth century the hospital housed several thousand of the city's most unfortunate citizens: the indigent sick and elderly as well as prostitutes, petty criminals, sociopaths, and the insane. Conditions in the hospital, which suffered from chronic lack of funds and overcrowding, appalled enlightened observers, such as the British prison reformer John Howard, as well as high government officials, notably the Baron de Breteuil. Subsequently, the Salpêtrière has developed into a renowned institution for medical care and research.

Philippe Pinel (1745-1826), a real historical character who has been called 'the father of psychiatry', was placed in charge of the Salpêtrière in 1794. He removed shackles from the insane and carried out other humane reforms in the spirit of the Enlightenment. See Bernard Mackler's *Philippe Pinel: Unchainer of the Insane* (New York 1968), for a brief, readable account of his life.